"Tuffet!" Daisy called in vain.

They had come quite a distance from the village, and Daisy was afraid the dog might not find her way home. Around the next corner, a thatched lean-to slumped against the cottage's back wall. Perhaps Tuffet had found a way into it.

As she went to investigate, Daisy glanced up. Above, in the gable of the end wall, she saw the window of an upstairs room. It was boarded up. The boards should have been grey, weathered, splitting. Instead, they were the color of newly-sawed wood. Bright nail heads gleamed.

Daisy's heart began to thump. She backed away, turned, and hurried around the corner to the front. "Tuffet, come! Come here, you naughty dog. Time to go home."

The door swung open, smoothly, noiselessly, on well-oiled hinges. A large man in braces and a collarless shirt stood on the threshold, his baleful glare adorned with the fading remnant of a black eye.

"Just walking the dog!" Daisy squeaked. "Have you seen her?"

"Nah."

An impatient voice behind him snapped, "We gotta stop 'er."

By then, Daisy was halfway to the gorse bush marking the path. Feet pounded after her. At that moment Tuffet appeared from nowhere, frisking about her ankles. Daisy tripped, staggered a few steps trying to regain her balance, and fell.

Hands like iron bands gripped her arms.

"Gotcha!"

Daisy Dalrymple Mysteries by Carola Dunn

DEATH AT WENTWATER COURT
THE WINTER GARDEN MYSTERY
REQUIEM FOR A MEZZO
MURDER ON THE FLYING SCOTSMAN
DAMSEL IN DISTRESS
DEAD IN THE WATER
(coming soon)

Published by Kensington Publishing Corporation

DAMSEL IN DISTRESS

A DAISY DALRYMPLE MYSTERY

CAROLA DUNN

KENSINGTON BOOKS
Kensington Publishing Corp.
http://www.kensingtonbooks.com

KENSINGTON BOOKS are published by

Kensington Publishing Corp.
850 Third Avenue
New York, NY 10022

All Kensington Titles, Imprints, and Distributed Lines are
available at special quantity discounts for bulk purchases
for sales promotions, premiums, fund-raising, and educa-
tional or institutional use. Special book excerpts or customized printings can also be created to fit specific needs. For
details, write or phone the office of the Kensington special
sales manager: Kensington Publishing Corp., 850 Third
Avenue, New York, NY 10022, attn: Special Sales Depart-
ment, Phone: 1-800-221-2647.

First Printing: March 2002
10 9 8 7 6 5 4 3 2

Printed in the United States of America

*In memory of Margaret C. Brauer (1917–1996)—
always encouraging, always sure my latest work was
the best thing I'd ever written. Thanks, Mum.*

1

Phillip strained his ears. Yes, there it was, that sinister knocking noise again.

The aging engine of his Swift two-seater made a deuce of a racket going up the steepish hill, and odd squeaks and rattles from chassis and body were inevitable. He worked the old bus pretty hard. For every joint oiled, for every bolt tightened, another loosened. But the knocking was new, different, and bally sinister.

Safely over the crest of the Surrey Downs, he pulled off the "B" road into a convenient gateway. A cow looked at him over the five-barred gate and mooed.

"I'll be gone long before milking time," he assured her, jumping out.

Taking off his blazer, he dropped it on the seat and rolled up his sleeves before he opened up the bonnet. As he peered into the oily depths, the hum of a well-tuned engine approached along the road. He glanced round to see a scarlet Aston Martin zip past, stop, reverse, and come to a halt beside him.

"Say, are you stuck?" enquired the girl behind the wheel, putting back her dust-veil to reveal a pretty face surrounded by blond curls. "Can I give you a ride?"

"Thanks awfully, but I'm not exactly stuck."

"Oh." The American girl—Phillip was sure she must be

American—looked enquiringly at the Swift. "You have the hood up."

"The hood?" He glanced at the hood, folded down on this mild, dry spring day. Ah, but she was American, she probably called it the roof. "You mean the bonnet? Something's knocking in the engine," he explained, "but if a few minutes' tinkering with my own tools won't solve it, I'll drive on to the next garage and borrow their tools."

"You fix your own automobile? Gee, that's real smart."

"Nothing much to boast about," Phillip said modestly. On a closer inspection those curls were gold, not mere blond, and her face was the prettiest he'd seen in years, not smothered in powder and paint, either, like most these days. "I like messing about with motor-cars," he confessed, glad that he hadn't yet got around to crawling underneath and getting oil on his face. "Just wish I could spend more time at it."

"I've always wanted to take a whack at it." She was a girl in a million! "But Poppa won't let me. He says it's not ladylike. Real set on me acting ladylike, Poppa is. Why, it took me years to talk him into letting me drive. Now I test automobiles for him, just motoring around to check out how they feel to an amateur driver."

"Is that what you're doing with this beauty? Don't see many of them on the roads."

"It runs swell. Poppa's thinking of investing a few bucks so they can raise production. That's what we're doing in England, looking for up-and-coming auto manufacturers for Poppa to invest in. I guess you can tell I'm not English?" she asked wistfully.

"I think your accent's absolutely ripping."

"Honest Injun? And there I was wanting to learn to talk like a proper English lady. I just love England, the quaint little villages and the history and flowers everywhere."

She waved her hand at the verge and hedge-bank. Phillip

suddenly noticed the April profusion of primroses, violets, celandines, and stitchwort, hitherto unobserved.

"But gee," the girl continued, sounding quite regretful, "I mustn't keep you from your tinkering. The truth is, I'm kinda lost. The signposts all point to places I don't want to go. Can you direct me to the main London road?"

Phillip opened his mouth to say, "Second to the right and straight on till morning," or whatever the directions were, when he was struck by a brain-wave. At least, he rather thought it might be a brain-wave. The Honourable Phillip Petrie was not sufficiently acquainted with the bally things to be quite sure at first sight. In fact, he was all too accustomed to being regarded by family and friends alike as a bit of a chump.

Still, it did look awfully like a brain-wave. "It's rather complicated," he lied, "from here to the London road. If you're not in a frightful hurry, if you wouldn't mind waiting a few minutes, you could follow me."

The girl's dazzling smile made him blink. "What a swell idea," she exclaimed.

Much heartened, Phillip produced the second part of his inspiration. "I don't know about you," he said recklessly, "but I'm getting jolly peckish. It's nearly tea-time and there's a frightfully good little tea-shop in Purley. Would you . . . Do you think you might consider joining me for tea?"

"Golly gee, I'd love to," said the wonderful girl. "We don't have anything like the English afternoon tea, but when I get home I'm surely going to keep it up. I'm Gloria Arbuckle, by the way." She held out her hand.

"Phillip Petrie." Shaking hands, he frowned. "You shouldn't accept invitations from strangers, you know, Miss Arbuckle. Come to that, your father shouldn't let you drive around the countryside alone. What if you broke down?"

"I'm supposed to take Poppa's assistant with me," she admitted, "but he was busy, and on the first fine day in ages, I wanted to get out of that smoky city. As for the invitation, it's not like you asked me to go drinking and dancing in some speakeasy. You don't even have speakeasies over here."

"No," said Phillip, rocked by another brain-wave, "but we have jolly good dance floors, perfectly respectable, and I'd be most frightfully bucked if, one of these days, you'd go dancing with me?"

"We'll see," she said, but she smiled.

"What-ho, old thing."

At this unceremonious greeting, Daisy looked up in annoyance from her second-hand Underwood. She had assumed the footsteps in the hall were someone calling on Lucy, who shared the "bijou" residence with her.

"Oh, it's you, Phillip. What do you want? I told Mrs. Potter I can't see anyone. I'm busy."

"She said you were just writing," Phillip said defensively, dropping his grey Homburg hat on the desk.

"Just writing! I'll have to have a word with her."

"Well, perhaps I put the 'just' in. No need to rag the poor old dear."

"For heaven's sake, Phillip, writing is how I make my living and I've two articles due. I keep forgetting to allow for how long the post takes to New York. The American magazine pays jolly well and I don't want to risk losing the work by being late. So unless you've got something urgent to say . . ."

"Not exactly urgent, but it won't take a minute, honestly." With a diffident gesture, Phillip smoothed his sleek, fair hair. His conventionally good-looking face bore such an appealing look that Daisy gave in.

"All right," she sighed. "Let's hear it."

Perching his loose-limbed frame on the corner of her desk, he swung a long leg clad in pin-stripe trousering and contemplated the well-polished tip of his shoe. She swivelled her chair to face him.

"Well," he said, a faint flush creeping up his cheeks, "it's like this. Er . . ."

"Phillip, get a move on!"

"Yes, well, dash it, this is a bit difficult, old bean."

"Is it *necessary?*"

"I should ruddy well think so. A proper cad I'd look if I didn't. . . . You see, the thing is. . . . I say, Daisy, you know I've proposed to you once or twice?"

"At least half a dozen times."

"That many?" he said, rather aghast.

"And I've turned you down just as many. I know you only ask because you feel Gervaise would expect you to take care of me." Daisy's brother, killed in the Great War, had been Phillip's best pal since childhood, growing up on a neighboring estate. "Which is rubbish, so out with it. You've found someone else, haven't you? Someone you really want to marry?"

"By Jove, how did you guess?" Phillip's patent relief almost made Daisy laugh.

She managed to control herself. "Who is it? Someone I know? One of the latest crop of debs?"

"As a matter of fact, she's American. You like Americans, don't you?" he asked anxiously.

"I've met some charming Americans. The one who especially springs to mind is Mr. Thorwald, my editor." Daisy looked longingly at the half-typed sheet of paper in the typewriter. "Tell me about her," she said, resigned.

"Her name's Gloria—Gloria Arbuckle. She's a poppet."

Daisy had expected a "stunner," an "angel," or a "jolly good sport." The old-fashioned word Phillip chose to describe his beloved impressed her even more than the glow in his blue eyes. Unlike others she could name, he wasn't given to falling for pretty girls, so perhaps he really had found his true love. She hoped so.

"Miss Arbuckle is here with her family?" she asked.

"Her father. Her mother died a couple of years ago, and she's an only child. Mr. Arbuckle's a millionaire. I know what people will think, Daisy," he said earnestly, "but you don't believe I care about the shekels, do you?"

"Of course not, old dear, not when I haven't a bean and you've been proposing to me regularly once a month for ever. I take it Miss Arbuckle's convinced of your unmercenary nature, but what about her father?"

"He's a good sort and he seems to rather like me. In fact, Gloria says he's taken to me in a big way, but he doesn't know yet that I want to marry her."

"Does he know your father's a lord?" Daisy asked. Republicans though they were, quite a lot of Americans seemed to consider a title for their daughters well worth the price of purchase.

"Yes, but I don't think he has a frightfully high opinion of the peerage. Besides, I've explained it all, that I'm a younger son with no chance of inheriting the title, and I'll never be more than an 'Hon.' or have more than a small allowance." He grimaced. "My people haven't met them yet."

"Aha! You're expecting a ragging from . . . What is it, Mrs. Potter?"

Breathing heavily, the stout charwoman beamed as she set a tray of tea-things on the desk. "The kettle were just on the boil, miss, so I thought I'd bring up a nice cuppa for you and the gentleman. No biscuits," she added regretfully. "We finished 'em up for elevenses, miss, remember?"

"Yes," Daisy said guiltily. Though no slimming diet could possibly make her rounded figure fashionably boyish, she really ought to make an effort. At least, Lucy said so. Frequently. "Thank you, Mrs. Potter."

"I'll pour," Phillip offered, leaving his perch and pulling the other chair up to the desk. "The typewriter's in your way."

"This is *not* turning into a tea-party! One cup, and off you go. Happy as I am to hear your news, I've work to do."

"You'll be free this weekend, won't you?" he asked hopefully, passing her a steaming cup. "I want you to meet Gloria and Arbuckle, and . . . well, actually, I hoped you'd go with me when I take them to meet my people. Lend your support, and all that."

"You're going to brace up and bite the bullet? I could spare a couple of hours, if you really think my presence would help. Are Lord and Lady Petrie coming up to town specially to meet them?"

"Lord no! The Arbuckles are staying in Great Malvern, at the Abbey Hotel. Gloria wanted to get out of town—she adores the English countryside—so I persuaded Arbuckle that Malvern's convenient for his business doings in Oxford and Coventry and Birmingham."

"Hardly! And apart from the Malvern Hills, the countryside isn't anything special."

"It's easy to drive to both the Cotswolds and the Welsh mountains," Phillip argued, "and none of those cities is more than fifty miles away. Not to mention the concerts and tennis and golf. . . ."

"You needn't go on," said Daisy, laughing. "I've read the adverts. 'Healthiest of health resorts, lowest death rate in the kingdom, purest water in the world.' "

"I threw all that guff at him, but the clincher was the Morgan Motor Company being in the town. Arbuckle's looking to invest in British motor manufacturers to diversify his holdings. He made his packet by selling out his railway stocks—railroad, they call it—and going into automobiles, in America, at just the right moment."

"Stocks and shares, just your line."

Shaking his head, Phillip pulled a face. "I can't stand the perishing City much longer. I'm an absolute duffer at it. If Gloria will marry me, I hope her father will find me a job in the technical end of the motor-car business, but I'm going to tell the pater I'm getting out anyway."

"You've always hated it," Daisy sympathized. "Like me and stenography."

"I'd rather be a common-or-garden hired motor mechanic, greasy overalls and all, and what's more, I'd make more money at it. I'd even rather sell second-hand cars. If that don't suit the pater's notions of consequence, he can jolly well cough up the ready to set up my own business. I know a fellow who's dying to go into partnership, and . . ."

"Not now, Phillip. I can't make it to Malvern this weekend, but if you can wait till next, I'll come along to hold your hand."

"Will you? You're a real brick, Daisy!"

"I owe Mother a visit. She's feeling neglected, as she never hesitates to let me know."

"I'll pop in and see her. I'm buzzing down on Saturday anyway—I've been home every weekend since Gloria left town. There's a chappie staying at the hotel," he added darkly, "who's been making a dead set at her. I get down as much as I can."

"Your parents must be a bit surprised by the sudden excess of filial devotion, and the Arbuckles that you haven't yet introduced them. You've only just plucked up the nerve?"

Phillip was indignant. "Not at all. It's only last week I began to think I had a real chance with Gloria, and then I had to talk to you first. The mater . . . All right," he said hastily, standing up as she thrust his hat at him, "I've talked. I'm going. You'll like her, Daisy. She's got golden curls and the bluest eyes you ever saw, and . . ."

"Toodle-oo, Phillip," said Daisy, cutting short the rhapsody.

"Oh, right-ho, pip-pip. And you honestly don't mind?"

"I honestly don't mind a bit."

Phillip went off at last with an air of enormous relief.

Her fingers resting on the typewriter keys, Daisy pondered a moment before taking up her interrupted train of thought. So Gloria had golden curls and blue eyes, did she? And no doubt a million-dollar wardrobe. Well, her own eyes were blue, but her shingled hair was an intermediate brown and her wardrobe mostly last year's, if not older, and bought at Selfridge's Bargain Basement.

Not that she was jealous. Phillip was an honorary brother. He had never even pretended to be in love with her. She was just afraid the dear old ass might have fallen for a pretty face without considering what was behind it.

But he had described Gloria as a poppet, not a stunner. Daisy could only hope she was going to like the American girl.

Occasional gateways in the hedges revealed Bredon Hill on the horizon to the right; the Malvern Hills loomed ahead. From a cloudless sky the sun shone down on drought-parched fields and orchards, rotten luck for the farmers but perfect for a fellow in love.

" 'It's three o'clock in the morning,' " Phillip warbled merrily, if inaccurately and off-key, as he tootled along the narrow, winding lane across the Severn plain. " 'We've danced the whole night through.' "

Nearly home. He'd have a quick wash and brush-up, change his clothes, and then drive into Great Malvern, stopping at Violet's for a box of chocs. After tea with the Arbuckles at the Abbey Hotel, he and Gloria would stroll by the swan pool in Priory Park. Later they might go to the pictures, if there was anything decent showing, or dance at the Winter Gardens ballroom to the music of Billy Gammon's All-Star Players.

Dancing, he hoped. If there was any bliss greater than

doing the Charleston, tango, or fox-trot with Gloria, it was waltzing with Gloria.

Lost in a dream, he zipped round a bend—and jammed on his brakes. A large motor-car, though pulled into a gateway, blocked half the lane.

"By Jove!" Phillip muttered. "It's a good job I overhauled the brakes the other day. What the deuce . . . Oh!" His irritation with the idiot who'd stopped in such a spot vanished as he recognized Arbuckle's vast blue Studebaker touring car.

Arbuckle, sitting in the back seat, turned and waved. And there was Gloria, perched on the top bar of the gate, slim, silk-clad ankles very much in evidence, golden hair outshining the stubble of the hayfield behind her.

"Phil . . . Mr. Petrie," she cried, "aren't you just an angel? A regular White Knight rushing to the rescue!" She started to climb down.

Phillip leapt from the Swift, squeezed between Studebaker and hedge, and arrived just in time to catch her as she jumped the last two bars.

"Careful," he said breathlessly, his arms about her waist. She gazed up at him, eyes blue as the sky, rosy lips parted. Overhead a lark poured out a burst of melody, and the air was full of the fragrance of wild roses.

Mr. Arbuckle coughed. Phillip and Gloria sprang apart.

"Waal now," said her father, a short, spare man with a long face lengthened by a receding hairline, "if this isn't quite a coincidence."

"You've broken down, sir?" Phillip asked, at last noticing the Studebaker's bonnet open on both sides. "I'll have a look, shall I?"

"It's mighty kind of you to offer, young fella, but I guess it's not something that can be fixed on the spot. Me, I'm the financial wizard, don't pretend to understand the mechanical stuff, but Crawford, my technical man, was driving us. Say, you've met him."

"Yes, you introduced us." He hadn't pursued the acquaintance, not having taken to the American engineer, despite his enviably extensive knowledge of motor-cars' design and manufacture.

"Crawford knows autos if anyone does. He went off with some broken part or other to hike to the nearest garage."

"I might as well have a dekko." Phillip already had his aged tweed jacket off. He tossed it into the Studebaker and rolled up his sleeves. He wasn't about to pass up a good excuse to examine an unfamiliar engine.

Gloria came and stood beside him. "Mr. Crawford said something about the radiator," she said uncertainly. "Didn't he, Poppa?"

"Beats me, honey."

"That's it." Phillip pointed. "Look, the hose is gone. It must have split. I think I have a spare in my tool-box which just might fit. Let's give it a try."

"Atta-boy!" said Mr. Arbuckle with a nod of approval. "That's what I like to hear. Be Prepared. It's a wunnerful motto, yes sirree, and not just for Boy Scouts."

"Yes, sir." Phillip grinned at him. He was growing quite fond of the old bird.

He fetched a couple of lengths of different-sized hose, a knife, spanner, and screwdriver from the tool-kit attached to the Swift's running board. As he bent over the Studebaker, a brown Ford motor-van with FARRIS, BUTCHERS painted on the side panel came along the lane and stopped.

A burly man, shabbily dressed, stepped down. Touching his cap to Arbuckle and Gloria, he addressed Phillip, "Wotcher, cock. Need an 'and?"

"No, thanks. It's just a matter of getting a new radiator hose clamped in."

The man leaned with meaty hands on the Studebaker's nose. "Yer'll need water to fill 'er up, gov'nor," he pointed out.

"True," Phillip agreed. "I'll buzz over to the nearest farm

in my bus." Gesturing with the screwdriver towards the Swift, he turned his head slightly. From the corner of his eye he caught a sudden motion.

Arbuckle cried out. Phillip swung round. Heavy boots thudded on the dry, packed earth of the lane as four men masked with handkerchiefs rushed around the front of the van.

Two dived over the side of the Studebaker reaching for Arbuckle. One grabbed Gloria. The fourth swung a crowbar at Phillip.

He ducked the blow.

"Gloria!" he shouted, and went for her attacker with the screwdriver.

The van's driver caught him from behind and wrenched the screwdriver from his grasp. A second swing of the crowbar caught him on the side of the head.

Exploding stars blinded him. His ears rang. Distantly aware of a heavy, sweetish odour, he sank into darkness.

2

Chloroform! The word came to Phillip in the instant of rousing. Then the explosive roar of the big guns inside his head claimed all his attention.

After a while, he grew almost used to the internal shelling. He was lying curled up on his side, he realized. His wrists were tied behind his back and his shoulders ached dully. The dark red inside his eyelids suggested a dim light. Cautiously he opened his eyes.

A narrow sunbeam streaked, flickering, across dusty, uneven floorboards, then zigzagged upwards, climbing, gleaming on beige silk stockings . . . Gloria! Ye gods, how could he have forgotten? The devils had bagged her too!

"Miss Arbuckle?" he whispered. "Gloria?"

She did not move. Praying her stillness was just the effect of the chloroform he had smelled, that they hadn't hurt her, Phillip raised his head. The pain sent him spiraling back down into the dark.

He roused again—five minutes, half an hour, half a day later, he had no way of knowing—to feel a drop land on his cheek. The detonations inside his skull had diminished to mere hammer-strokes. Some seemed to come from a distance, *tock-tock-tock,* like a woodpecker. And that angry chattering scold sound like a squirrel. Was he in a wood?

The air he breathed had a damp feel, a woodsy, mildewy smell, but the surface he lay on was too hard for leaf-mould and there was a faint odour of paraffin. He remembered floorboards, warped and split, with cracks between. And Gloria!

Opening his eyes as another drop plopped onto his cheek, he turned his head and looked up into Gloria's face. There was just enough light left to see her heavenly blue eyes red and swollen with tears.

"Don't cry, Glow-worm. We'll get out of this somehow."

"Oh, Ph-Phillip, I was afraid you were d-dead," she sobbed, positively raining on him.

"Well, I'm not. So be a good girl and dry your eyes and blow your nose and let's put our heads together."

"I c-can't reach my handkerchief. I couldn't even wipe the blood off your poor head."

Her hands were tied in front of her. Phillip seethed at the sight of the cord cutting into her slender wrists. He gritted his teeth—an outburst would help neither of them.

"Perhaps you can reach mine," he said calmly, "if you think you can use it when you've got it. In my shirt pocket." His jacket, he supposed, must still be in the Studebaker where he had dropped it . . . how long ago?

While Gloria, kneeling beside him, fumbled for his handkerchief, Phillip studied what he could see of their surroundings. The low ceiling, sloping downward on two sides, was rough, discoloured plaster, speckled with mildew, between ancient, sagging beams. In one corner, a dark brown stain looked like the result of a leak in the roof above.

The stain ran down the wall. On the floor at the bottom lay a few chunks and a small heap of crumbled plaster.

A hole? Phillip silently cursed the confounded bonds about his wrists. Not that a way into the attic seemed frightfully useful, always supposing he could have reached it, but it irked him that he couldn't even investigate properly.

"I have it!" With two fingers Gloria triumphantly fished the handkerchief out and shook it open.

"Well done."

She promptly dropped it on the floor. "Darn. Now it's

too dirty to use to clean your head." Groping, she picked it up between finger and thumb. This time when she shook it, a cloud of dust flew.

Phillip held his breath till the dust settled. The way he felt, a sneeze might take off the top of his head. "You'd have had to use spit, anyway, Glow-worm. I expect I look a frightful mess, but on the whole I'd rather you didn't touch it."

"Poor honey, it must be real sore. Does your head ache badly?"

In spite of their situation, Phillip revelled in her solicitude. "Not as bad as it was," he assured her, awkwardly rolling over and sitting up. The bursting shells promptly returned full force and his sight blurred. For a ghastly moment he thought he was going to be sick. Then the pain diminished again to a dull throb. "But it does still ache rather, and I don't want to find out how tender it is where I got whacked. How do you feel?"

"I was sure woozy when I woke up, but I'm okay now. Do you know what it was they used?"

"Chloroform, by the smell. I was put out with it once when I broke my arm and had to have it set. I wish they'd used that on me instead of a crowbar!"

"Oh, Phillip, why did they hit you and drug me and bring us here? What are they going to do with us? What do they want?" She bit her lip, but a sob escaped. "What have they done with Poppa?"

She sat beside him, nestled against his side. Had Phillip possessed a fortune, he would have given every penny to be able to put his arms around her now. But Arbuckle was the one with the fortune.

"Ransom!" he said. "They won't hurt your father because he'll have to be free to cough up the dollars."

"Do you think so?"

"I bet that's what it's all about. They're always doing it

in America, aren't they? Speakeasies and gangsters and kidnappings, you read about them all the time."

"You make it sound terrible, and it's not. Most places aren't like that at all. Ordinary people don't have a thing to do with gangsters."

"But you're not ordinary, Glow-worm," Phillip pointed out gently. "Apart from being the sweetest, prettiest . . . Yes, well, I won't go into all that now. But apart from that, it's no secret your poppa's simply rolling in the stuff. He's practically a walking target for hoodlums."

"But we aren't in the States. And the guy who drove the butcher's van sure sounded English to me. He was one of them, wasn't he? I figure the rest were hiding in the back of the van."

"Probably. Yes, he was definitely English, a Cockney actually, though the number plate was local. They must have stolen it, or the van."

"Cockneys are from London? You all sound just plain British to me."

"And all Americans sound American to me. I didn't hear the other men speak, did you? They could have been Yanks."

For once Gloria didn't tick him off for his use of the slang term for her countrymen and threaten playfully to call him a Limey. As an effort to distract her, the scheme was a dismal failure.

"I hope they're not," she said with a shiver. "Some of those gangsters don't think twice about spraying bullets around."

"They won't do that. Your father will want proof of your safety before he'll hand over a farthing. A dime."

"Oh Phillip, I'm glad you're here. I'm scared, but I'd be even more scared without you."

She needed him, not like Daisy, who tended to regard his efforts to protect her as an irritating intrusion. But what was a fellow to do, when all he wanted was to shield his sweetheart against the world and he couldn't even hold her little hand to comfort her?

He bent his head and kissed her forehead. It wasn't quite the circumstances he had imagined for their first kiss.

It didn't help morale that the light was fading fast. The small, square window, in the centre of one wall of the small, square room, was barricaded with heavy boards, nailed in place. The streak of sunshine which had earlier squeezed between the planks was long gone. Outside, the long summer evening might linger. Inside, it would very soon be dark.

Time was a-wasting. He didn't think more than a few minutes had passed since he came to, but what an absolute ass he was, sitting here chatting!

"Glow-worm, you've tried the door?"

"Yes. There's no keyhole but it won't budge. I guess it's barred on the other side."

"Oh well, not much chance they'd forget it. Before the light goes you'd better see if you can untie my hands."

"I tried before, when you were unconscious. The knots are too tight. But I guess I could try to cut the rope with a bit of broken glass. There's some over there under the window." She struggled to her feet, crossed to the window, and crouched down. "I didn't dare try as long as you might wake up and move any moment. I was afraid of cutting a vein and killing you."

Phillip joined her. Among the scraps and splinters of the broken window-panes were three or four largish shards. "Can you pick up a piece without cutting yourself?"

"Yes, but I can't get a real good grip on it. I won't be able to see too well, either. Gee, I wish I really was a glow-worm."

"I'll turn around, so you have all the light there is. Hack away, and don't mind my groans when you stab me."

Stab him she did, and nick him, and slice him. After an "Oh, Phillip, I'm sorry," at the first sign of blood, she sawed away in silence and he managed neither to groan nor to twitch. It might have been worse if his hands had not been pretty well numbed by cut-off circulation.

In the quiet, Phillip heard voices. They seemed to come from below, through gaps between the shrunken floorboards.

"Hear that?" Phillip whispered. "Hold on a jiffy, I want to see if I can hear what they're saying." He lay down and pressed his ear to one of the wider cracks. The smell of paraffin grew stronger.

". . . still out?" someone asked.

"Out to the wide, last time we 'ad a butcher's." Butcher's hook—look; it was Cockney rhyming slang. Not a Yankee, nor a local man, but another Londoner. "That chloroform's powerful stuff."

"You *sure* you didn't clobber the bloke too 'ard, Jimmy?" The third voice, also Cockney, held the anxious note of an oft-repeated query.

"Not bloody likely. D'ya fink I wants to dangle? Pity I didn't 'ave me sandbag 'andy but we wasn't supposed to need anyfing else, just the chloro. Anyways, I got it down to a fine art, 'asn't I, so not to worry, cock."

"Better start worryin'." That was the first voice again, the van driver's, Phillip was almost sure. "The Yank's mad as fire 'bout you bringing the young cove along too."

"Us! 'Oo was it said 'e talked like a nob, and 'oo found 'is card-case in the two-seater? 'E's a Hon, you says, and what that means is, 'is pa's a lord."

"Did I tell ya to grab 'im for ransom along wiv the girl?" the driver demanded aggrievedly. "Did I? Like bloody 'ell, I did! The Yank's right, most nobs's dough's tied up in land and big 'ouses and art and such. They ain't got the ready, not quick, any'ow, not like Mr. Moneybags. Yer want ter 'ang around a few weeks while 'is bloody lordship sells a few of 'is fancy pitchers?"

"Weeks? Gorblimey, no."

"Right, then."

"So whatta we do?" asked the anxious voice. "We can't just let 'im go. "E'll 'op it to the rozzers straight orf."

"We'll 'ave to keep 'im till the ransom's paid and we let the girl go."

" 'E's no use," the driver said carelessly. "Just get in the way. The Yank says, you're ter get rid of 'im—for keeps. Rub 'im out, pronto."

A long silence followed this announcement.

Phillip shuddered. Nothing in four years of appalling trench warfare had affected him quite like that apparently casual order to murder him in cold blood. Shells and shrapnel, poison gas, machine-gun bullets, even a sniper's fire, were impersonal. One didn't know the name of the man one bayonetted face to face, and anyway it was a case of kill or be killed. But Phillip was no threat to these men, no mortal threat at least, though he'd gladly see them rot in gaol for the rest of their lives for what they were doing to Gloria.

"I dunno . . ." said one, hesitantly.

"Not me," the crowbar-wielder affirmed. "I don't swing for nobody."

"Yer'll all be assessories anyways," the driver advised them. " 'E don't care who does it, but summun's gonna 'ave ter or the deal's orf. 'E reckons no one won't miss 'im for a while, the way 'e's always 'opping about, 'ere today and gone termorra. If ya wants yer share o' the goods, don't cross the Yank. Ya'd better pick cards or summat."

"Us? What abaht you?"

"Me, I'm orf back to the Smoke. The old man saw my face, it ain't safe for me round these parts. Done my bit, I 'ave, all I were brung in for, and bin paid my bit f'rit. Them as wants ter scoop the pool 'as to work 'arder. Enjoy yerselves among the clod'oppers, mates. Bright lights, 'ere I come!"

His blithe voice grew fainter as he spoke, and a moment later, Phillip heard a door slam shut. He sat up.

"Have they gone?" Gloria asked softly. "What did they say?"

He thanked heaven she had not listened. "One of them has left. The rest are still here, or only stepped out for a moment. They're after ransom, as we guessed. They were talking about letting you go when it's paid."

"Poppa will pay, just soon as ever he can."

"Of course." Not soon enough for Phillip, however. He wasn't going to go without a fight, though. "Gloria, are you almost through the rope?" he asked urgently.

"It's awful slow work, honey," she apologized. "There's one strand about ready to part, but I can't see properly any longer and . . . and it's hard to hold the glass steady now it's slippery."

"Slippery" Have I bled all over it? Try another piece."

"I . . . It won't help for more than a minute. I . . . I'm bleeding, too." She held out her hands. The last light was just enough to show the blood welling in slow drops from her fingertips.

"Oh, Glow-worm!"

She came to him, looping her bound wrists over his head and pressing herself to him as her soft lips brushed his.

"I'm okay as long as you're with me. Oh, here they come." At the sound of boots clomping upstairs, she removed her arms from around his neck, but she stayed close. "We'll ask them to untie us. Why shouldn't they? We can't get out of here."

"You might as well ask." Phillip was desperately trying to formulate a plan.

There were four men, he thought, if they all came, but the doorway was too narrow for more than one to enter at a time. Still, it was the only way out, and if he got past the first, the rest would be waiting.

It looked hopeless, yet he could not just let them lead

him away like a lamb to the slaughter, or, worse, do away with him right there in front of Gloria. Now was the time to discover whether tennis and squash had kept him as fit as he hoped, not the moment to remember that a gentleman does not brawl in the presence of a lady.

Even without the use of his hands, surely he might at least give them something to remember him by.

With a creak and a thud, the bar was withdrawn. The door swung open. On the threshold stood a brawny figure silhouetted against the flickering light of a paraffin lamp.

Phillip's head took the brute in the stomach. He went over backwards, cannoning into the man behind. Together they tumbled down the stairs.

Struggling to regain his balance, Phillip caught just a glimpse of shadowy shapes closing in on either side of him on the tiny landing. He kicked out desperately as they grabbed his arms, as the sweet, sickly smell of chloroform wafted to his nostrils.

A damp pad clamped across his face. He couldn't breathe. His head hurt like hell. He didn't care.

He drifted dizzily into nothingness.

3

What was that place Roman Catholics went to after death if they weren't bad enough for Hell nor good enough to go straight to Heaven? Pur-something, Phillip thought dizzily. By Jove, they were right. He was damp and chilly, his head and his shoulders ached, his hands managed to be both sore and numb at the same time, altogether deucedly uncomfortable. Definitely not Paradise, but not the burning, fiery furnace, either.

Somewhere a cuckoo called. The air smelled of wild roses, like a promise of Paradise to come.

Something warm and wet slithered across his face. Startled, Phillip opened his eyes, and looked up into the grinning muzzle of a liver-spotted spaniel.

"Pepper, heel!"

The dog gave a short, sharp, self-satisfied bark and bent its head to lick Phillip's cheek again.

Ye gods, was he alive?

He lay in long, dew-soaked grass under a hawthorn hedge wreathed with pink roses. Above his head, a spider's web spangled with dewdrops sparkled in the slanting rays of the early morning sun. An insect crawled invisibly up his neck, a maddening tickle. He couldn't brush it off. His hands were still tied.

He was alive!

"Pepper? What have you found there?" called the fussy, schoolmasterish voice.

"Help!" croaked Phillip.

The dog wagged its stumpy tail approvingly and uttered another bark.

Boots swished through the grass. A stocky man in his midforties, wearing tweed knickbockers, a deerstalker, and pince-nez, stood over Phillip. He looked vaguely familiar.

"A tramp," he said, displeased, tapping his cane on his hand in a thoroughly schoolmasterly fashion.

"Help," Phillip croaked again.

"My good man, if you're hungry you may go up to the kitchen and tell them I said to give you bread and cheese. Then be on your way. Our local magistrates are hard on vagrants."

By the time he finished, Phillip had both cleared his throat and recognized him. "I say, Lord Dalrymple," he said, "I must look like the most frightful vagabond, but I'm Phillip Petrie. I'm afraid I'm in a bit of a spot."

Daisy's cousin—second or third, and once or twice removed—hitched the pince-nez lower on his nose and stared down at Phillip over the top.

" 'Pon my soul! Petrie? So you are. My dear fellow, give me your hand and let me help you up. No, wait a moment." Leaning down, he pushed his eye-glasses back up and peered through them. "That is, if I am not mistaken, the larva of *Calothysanis amata* on your neck. The Blood Vein moth's caterpillar, you know."

"Would you mind removing it?" Phillip asked with what patience he could muster. "I've lost enough blood lately, as a matter of fact."

"Dear me no, it feeds on dock leaves, not blood. None of our native moths and butterflies is a blood-sucker— though some do, admittedly, feed on the juices of decaying meat—and I rather doubt whether even any tropical . . ."

"Please," begged Phillip, who felt not unlike a piece of decaying meat himself. He was also suddenly aware of his own juices, long pent up, suddenly demanding egress.

"Yes, yes, let me rid you of it. There. Not a rare species, alas. But you don't want a lecture on the *Lepidoptera*. Your hand, my dear fellow."

"I can't. My hands are tied behind my back."

"Good gracious! Well, happily I always carry a pocket-knife, to collect the leaves fed upon by any larva I wish to try to hatch. If you will roll over, I shall see what I can do."

Clucking in horror over the dried blood on Phillip's head and hands, Lord Dalrymple efficiently severed the cords. Phillip's hands stung like blazes as the circulation was restored, but his bladder insisted on more immediate attention. He clambered shakily to his feet and, with a word of apology, pissed long and satisfyingly into the hedge.

During this exercise, Lord Dalrymple politely turned his back, moved away a few paces, and hummed a verse of the Eton Boating Song. Phillip, amused, recalled Daisy telling him her cousin had taught at a very minor prep school before unexpectedly inheriting Fairacres and the viscountcy from her father.

Fairacres, presumably, was where Phillip now found himself. He had been dumped not ten miles from the site of the kidnapping, considerably less from his own home, and alive. At least half alive, he amended, as he struggled with smarting, tingling fingertips to button his fly.

He took a few steps towards Dalrymple and found himself staggering. The bright morning blurred before his eyes, poppies, ox-eye daisies, and purple knapweed swirling in a vast kaleidoscope with the blue sky and green hedges. He sat down and buried his head between his knees.

"I'm awfully sorry," he gasped, "but I seem to be a bit wonky. I'll be all right in a minute."

"You *have* been in the wars." A comforting hand patted Phillip's shoulder. "You just sit here, old chap. I'll pop down to my gamekeeper's cottage and between the two of us we'll carry you up to the house."

"Gad no," said Phillip, revolted, "I'll be able to walk in a minute." He raised his head. The blood red poppies, as always, reminded him of Flanders, but at least they kept still now.

"Sure? Then I shall send him along to lend you a hand while I go ahead to warn Geraldine to expect a guest."

"I don't want to impose on Lady Dalrymple."

"Nonsense! Fate has put me in Gervaise's place, and the least I can do is welcome his friends as if he were still with us. Carlin will be with you in a trice. I'll leave Pepper to keep you company."

The spaniel, having drawn his master's notice to his find, had gone off after rabbits, but he rushed back when called. Told to stay, he sighed and lay down with his head on Phillip's ankle.

Phillip watched Dalrymple tramp off, noting that what he had taken for a cane was actually a butterfly net. He blessed the man's apparent lack of curiosity. Before he told anyone at all about the kidnapping, he had to try to get in touch with Gloria's father. The poor fellow must be quite frantic.

How Gloria was feeling, Phillip didn't want to think.

The few minutes before Carlin arrived did much to restore his strength. As the stalwart, grizzled gamekeeper approached, Phillip stood up with only a touch of giddiness. With a growl, his stomach reminded him he had not eaten since lunch yesterday, and then no more than a slice of cold pork pie in a pub on the drive down from London.

He had been saving every shilling to buy Gloria chocolates and take her dancing. The hollow in his stomach was nothing to the hollow in his heart.

"Well now, Master Phillip," Carlin greeted him, "what have 'e bin up to now?"

He spoke in just the tone of patient reproach he had used when Phillip and Gervaise got stuck up trees, or fell out of them or into streams, in early youth. Later he had taught the boys to shoot—and dug the shot out of Phillip's retriever pup when she rushed ahead and Gervaise accidentally peppered her.

"Does Lord Dalrymple shoot?" Phillip asked with curiosity as they set off.

"Nay, sir, not he. Nor hunt, leastways nowt but butterflies. He don't properly understand country life, if 'e'll excuse my boldness. He don't have much need for the likes of I, but he knows better than to turn off them as've served the Dalrymples time out o' mind."

"I'm glad you're still here." If Phillip had to be ignominiously helped up to the house, he'd as soon it was by Carlin as anyone.

All the same, he was pleased to find he needed little help. The combined effects of the blow to the head and the chloroform were wearing off, and his hunger would soon be satisfied, he trusted. Climbing a stile was an effort; he accepted Carlin's hand to steady him. Otherwise he walked slowly but under his own steam, across a hayfield, already cut, through a plum orchard (scene of many a raid in the old days), and into the park.

The rear façade of the house rose above gardens and a balustraded terrace. Fairacres, though too large to be called a manor, was no vast ducal mansion. The formality of its classical symmetry was offset by the patchwork appearance found in many local buildings. Pinkish sandstone, amber Cotswold limestone, pale grey stone from who knew where, placed at random blended into an attractive whole.

It was once Phillip's home from home. The War had kept him away for four years. Since the death of Daisy and Gervaise's father four years ago, in the great 'flu epidemic of '19, he had called only two or three times, for politeness' sake. He still thought of Edgar Dalrymple, ex-schoolmaster, and his wife Geraldine as intruders.

He could not blame Daisy or her mother for not accepting their offer of a home.

Dash it all, he had promised Daisy to drop in and see the Dowager Lady Dalrymple at the Dower House. Not a chance, not for the foreseeable future, not while Gloria suffered in the hands of those vile brutes.

The swine had added insult to injury by pinching his wallet and all his change, as he discovered when he felt for a shilling for Carlin. Thank heaven they had not dumped him in the middle of nowhere!

"I must make a telephone call," he said to the butler, new since Daisy's time, who met him in the marble-floored front hall with its twin semi-circular staircases. "At once."

"Certainly, sir." The butler, no doubt forewarned by Lord Dalrymple, was not visibly perturbed by the arrival of a guest in his shirtsleeves, filthy and encrusted with dried blood. "If you will be so good as to . . ."

But Lady Dalrymple came hurrying down the stairs, followed by her husband.

An angular woman, an inch or two taller than his lordship, she looked Phillip up and down po-faced, but she said civilly enough, "Mr. Petrie, I am so sorry to hear you have had an accident. Edgar was not certain whether we ought to send for the doctor?"

"No, thank you, Lady Dalrymple. I'm much better already."

"At least you must have some sort of dressing on your head."

"And hands, dear," said Lord Dalrymple.

"And hands. Let me see them."

Reduced to a schoolboy, Phillip obediently held out his hands, himself examining them for the first time. They looked far worse than they felt. "I'm afraid I'm rather a mess," he apologized.

Lady Dalrymple was too polite to agree, but she said, "I shall see to the dressings when you have bathed. Lowecroft, have Mr. Petrie shown to the Blue Bedroom, and a bath drawn immediately." She glanced doubtfully from Phillip to her considerably shorter husband. "I suppose you have a change of clothes at Malvern Grange, or in your motor, if it was not too badly damaged to retrieve your luggage?"

So she assumed he had pranged his car. Wondering for a moment what had become of the dearly loved Swift, Phillip seized his chance. "At home, yes, but I don't want to worry the mater by sending for clothes. Any old thing will do for the present. But if you don't mind, before I take a bath I'll make a 'phone call."

"Yes, of course. Your parents will be worrying. Lowecroft, show Mr. Petrie to the telephone."

Phillip didn't explain that his parents, far from requiring notice of his visits, expected him when they saw him. His eldest brother, with wife and children, and his youngest sister all lived at Malvern Grange. One more in the house was neither here nor there. He had no intention of ringing them up.

The butler ushered him into Lord Dalrymple's den. The deep leather chairs and red Turkey carpet were unchanged since the old days. Phillip had a vague, uncomfortable sense of being in a museum, though any major changes might have disturbed him equally.

"The instrument, sir." Lowecroft crossed to the knee-hole desk, where the telephone still stood. Gravely he took a handkerchief from his pocket and spread it over the chair. "No offence, sir, but her ladyship is particular. Will that be all?"

"Yes, thank you, and I *would* like a bath as soon as I'm finished."

Phillip knew the Abbey Hotel's telephone number by heart. He had spent enough 'phoning there in the past few weeks to condemn him to lunch daily at the A.B.C. instead of the Piccadilly Grill. Lifting the earpiece, he waited impatiently for the operator to answer.

The hotel's number was engaged. "Will you ring back later?" the girl asked him.

"No, I'll hold on. Please put me through as soon as you can. It's urgent."

"If it's an emergency, sir, I can ask the other party to get off the line."

"N-no . . ."

He was tempted, but the instinct which had stopped him blabbing the whole story to the Dalrymples took over. Claim an emergency and people would require explanations. It was up to Arbuckle and the police to decide whether the kidnapping should be broadcast or kept quiet.

Which raised another question: Should he notify the police while he waited to get hold of Arbuckle? And if so, who?

He didn't have much faith in the local bobby's ability to do much more than move on a tramp or catch boys scrumping cherries. Call in the county force and his father would have the news within the hour, whereas if Arbuckle notified them, Phillip might manage to keep his own name out of things.

The best man for the job would be Daisy's friend, Detective Chief Inspector Alec Fletcher of Scotland Yard. Not that Phillip approved of the friendship. Daisy had a genius for picking the wrong sort. Just look at that conchie she'd been engaged to! Agreed, the Friends' Ambulances' work was not to be sneezed at, and the fellow had the grace to get himself blown up by a mine, just like any soldier, but it was the principle of the thing.

And now Daisy had taken up with a middle-class copper, a widower with a child at that. Still, he was no conscientious objector—he'd been an officer in the Royal Flying Corps—and there was no denying the man knew his stuff. Clever was the word; he'd even gone to one of those new provincial universities where they only took swots. He wasn't a bad chap, either, when he wasn't fixing one with an eye like an eagle's, sharp as a bayonet, enough to convince a fellow of his own guilt.

But Phillip had a feeling there were all sorts of obstacles to bringing in Scotland Yard. Was it worth a try?

"Hullo, caller, I'm connecting you now."

The hotel receptionist was not at all keen to fetch Mr. Arbuckle to the telephone. "It's only just after eight," she said crisply. "We don't disturb our guests so early unless they request a call the night before."

Phillip glanced at the brass clock on the mantlepiece. Five past eight it was. He was dashed lucky Dalrymple was an early riser or he might still be lying under that hedge.

But nothing was more certain than that, if Arbuckle had slept at all with his daughter in peril, he would want to be roused for news of her. That was assuming he was actually there. Phillip had assured Gloria her father must be safe. It had seemed logical at the time, but kidnappers might not be logical.

There was only one way to find out. "I promise you," Phillip asserted, "Mr. Arbuckle won't kick up a dust if you wake him, but he'll very likely have you shot out on your ear if you don't."

"I'll take a message and give it to him when he comes down."

"No soap. Just tell him my name and he'll come running."

The woman put up a fight but eventually was persuaded to send a page-boy for the American.

"Petrie?" The tense, slightly breathless voice came over the wire so soon, either Arbuckle had run downstairs in his dressing-gown or he had been already dressed. "Is she okay? Where in all tarnation are you?" He sounded worried, but not as frantic as Phillip had expected.

"She *was* all right when I last saw her. At least, not hurt. Sir, I'd have given anything to . . ."

"Not on the telephone. There's no knowing who's got an ear to the wire. She's not with you?"

"No." Phillip swallowed the lump in his throat. "I don't know where she is."

"Then just tell me where *you* are."

"At Fairacres. Lord Dalrymple's place. I expect his chauffeur would run me into Great Malvern."

"This here lord, what have you told him?"

"Nothing. He didn't ask any questions, though, believe me, a few would have been justified."

"Can he be trusted?"

"Of course!" The idea of the kindly but stuffy exschoolmaster getting mixed up in any shady business, let alone kidnapping, boggled Phillip's imagination.

"You know the guy? He won't spill the beans?" Arbuckle persisted.

"Oh, that!" Discretion must go with schoolmastering, he thought vaguely. Not upsetting the parents and all that. And he hadn't mentioned Phillip's bonds to his wife. "No, I should think he's pretty good at keeping mum."

"Then I'll come to you. How do I get to this place?"

Phillip gave directions. "I'll tell them to expect you."

"Don't tell 'em why," Arbuckle said sharply. "Okay, I'll be right over."

A click as the line disconnected left Phillip with his mouth open, about to ask what he should say. He had to give his host—and still more his hostess—some explanation for the imminent arrival of an American businessman at an ungodly hour of the morning. Hanging up, he cudgelled his brains for some story to satisfy the Dalrymples without saying more than Arbuckle would like.

Come to think of it, all this secrecy twaddle was dashed queer. Shouldn't they be rousing the countryside to hunt for Gloria? Yet he himself had instinctively held his tongue when he could already have had search parties sent out.

His head was too muzzy still to work out his own reasons. Heaving himself to his feet, he returned to the front hall, where a youthful footman awaited him.

"Lor," gasped the stripling, all agog at the sight of the battered gentleman. "Your motor must be smashed all to bits." Recollecting himself, he straightened into rigidity. "If you'll please to come this way, sir, your bath'll be ready by now."

"Look here," Phillip said, following him up the stairs, "an American gentleman by the name of Arbuckle is going to be popping in to see me in about half an hour. We don't want to disturb anyone, so just park him somewhere out of the way and drop me the word, will you?"

The footman glanced back, a conspiratorial gleam in his eye. "You can count on me, sir," he whispered. "I'll tip you the wink."

What the deuce did he think was going on? Phillip wondered.

Wallowing in the bath was bliss but, regretfully, he made it a quick wallow. He didn't want Arbuckle to arrive and be left fuming and fretting. When he got out, he hurried, wrapped in a borrowed dressing-gown of startling buttercup hue, to the assigned bedroom. Clean clothes awaited him there, laid out on the bed and emitting a pungent odour of mothballs.

The grey flannel bags and white shirt could have belonged to anyone, but he recognized the lightweight blue and grey herring-bone tweed jacket. It was Gervaise's, no doubt resurrected from a trunk in boxroom or attic. Phillip's soul revolted against donning his dead friend's clothes.

He forced himself to be practical. He was no good to Gloria lounging about in a bright yellow dressing-gown. His nose revolting against the stink of naphtha, he dressed.

Adjusting the navy, grey-striped tie in the looking glass, he regarded his reflection and winced. The clothes hung loose, exposing wrists and a good deal of sock. Gervaise, though taller than the present Lord Dalrymple, had been somewhat shorter and broader than Phillip. Phillip liked to consider himself a natty dresser, except when delving into motor-engines, of course. At present he looked, and smelt, like an overgrown orphan clothed by the Salvation Army.

A shock of damp blond hair usually confined by pomade didn't improve the picture. Nor did the trickle of blood seeping from his head wound. The hot water of the bath must have started it up again. Luckily someone had thought to provide a large white handkerchief. Clamping it to his head with one hand, the other holding a hairbrush, Phillip endeavoured to subdue his rebellious locks.

The young footman, Ernest, brought his cleaned shoes. "Brilliantine, that's what you wants," he observed sagely.

"Can you get me some?"

"Yes, sir, but her ladyship's waiting to bandage you up. Looks like you need that worser nor hair stuff," he added, kneeling to tie the shoelaces so that Phillip didn't have to let go the red-stained handkerchief. "She's in her sitting room, an' not to worry, the Yankee gent didn't turn up yet."

Phillip wasn't sure whether he was glad or sorry that Arbuckle hadn't yet arrived. On the one hand, he was impatient to set about rescuing Gloria. On the other, he was beginning to think he must be an absolute duffer not to have rescued her while he was actually with her. A cleverer chap would surely have found a way. How was he to explain his failure to her father?

4

Lady Dalrymple liberally bedaubed Phillip's wounds with boracic ointment, as she had very likely done in her time for hundreds of scrubby schoolboys. Though she accepted with reluctance his refusal to have sticking plaster on any but the worst cuts on his hands, she insisted on bandaging his head. By the time she finished, not much hair was visible to be pomaded.

"Oh dear," she said, looking him up and down, "I'm afraid you will have to miss Church."

"I'm afraid so," Phillip said without regret. "I say, a fellow, an American chappie, is going to drop by here this morning to have a word with me. It's fearful cheek, I know. I hope you don't mind awfully."

Obviously a bit put out, she muttered something about "rackety young people nowadays."

Aloud, however, she said with conscious graciousness, "Not at all. You must consider Fairacres your home from home until you feel well enough to return to the Grange."

"Thanks awfully," said Phillip, deciding instantly that he was feeling pretty rocky. He wasn't going home to face his parents' interrogation.

"This American was responsible for your accident, I take it? Disgraceful! Foreigners should not be allowed to drive in this country. I understand many of them are accustomed to motoring on the wrong side of the road."

Phillip murmured a vague agreement.

"I hope he means to make proper amends." She stood up. "Have you breakfasted, Mr. Petrie?"

"As a matter of fact, I'm most frightfully hungry." Weak with hunger, he thought, as he rose with a huge effort to his feet.

Once again she eyed him askance, from bandaged crown to exposed ankles, sniffed with wrinkled nose, and blenched. "Fortunately our only guests this weekend are my brother and his family. But perhaps you are too shaken up to come down?"

"I do feel a bit grim." This time Phillip's agreement was wholehearted. He was only too delighted to cater to her sense of decorum by breakfasting in his room. "Could you possibly have Mr. Arbuckle shown up when he arrives?" he requested.

"Certainly. Perhaps seeing your condition will persuade him he ought not to drive in England. And I shall send up your breakfast immediately."

Phillip thanked her and returned to the bedroom. The bed looked immensely inviting. Turning his back on temptation, he sank into an easy chair by the window.

The glorious morning sun, shining on the formal gardens below and the park with its oaks and chestnuts, only reminded him of the tiny gloomy room where his beloved was imprisoned. How terrified she must be, all alone. He wished he were still there to comfort her, and, given enough time, to work out how to escape.

He had botched it, he thought wretchedly, and the worst of it was, Gloria was the one to suffer for his bungling.

Before he could worry himself into a decline, Ernest brought up his breakfast. "Cook says she hopes as how you still likes your eggs done four minutes," he announced, setting his tray on a small folding table, "and coffee to drink."

"Tell her, yes." The eggs in their eggcups nestled under knitted cosies beside a full toast-rack, butter and marmalade dishes, and a small plate. Phillip peeked under the silver cover over the large plate. "Bacon, sausages, kidneys, absolutely ripping! Mr. Arbuckle's still not here?" He slathered butter on a piece of toast.

"No, sir. I won't have to tip you the wink on the quiet, like," the footman added regretfully. "Her ladyship said to bring the gentleman straight up here when he arrives."

"Yes, do, please," said Phillip, topping the first egg. "Perfect! My compliments to Cook. When Mr. Arbuckle gets here, you might ask him if he's eaten this morning."

"Righty-oh. I mean, very good, sir. Will there be anything else, sir?"

Phillip mumbled his thanks through a mouthful of egg. The very taste of it made him feel better.

Surely the kidnappers would feed Gloria? It was in no way to their advantage to let her go hungry. The thought took the edge off his appetite; nonetheless, when Ernest ushered in Arbuckle a few minutes later, both eggs, most of the toast, and half the plateful had vanished.

Pushing back his chair, Phillip jumped up. If he had thought the American sounded too little concerned, the sight of him was enough to confound that impression. The man's long face was pale and hollow-cheeked, with dark pouches under his bloodshot eyes. He looked as if he hadn't slept a wink, and had aged ten years overnight.

Phillip's bandaged head gave him a shock. "Jeez, they sure. . . ." He stopped, glancing at the footman who was fetching a second chair. He held up the jacket folded over his arm. "Here's your coat."

"Thanks." Phillip slung it over the back of his chair and held out his hand.

Arbuckle shook hands without appearing to notice the sticking plasters. In a low voice he asked, "You haven't told anyone?"

"Not a soul. Come and sit down, sir. You don't mind if I finish my breakfast?" he went on, as Arbuckle slumped onto the chair the footman moved to the table. "Will you join me?"

"Coffee, thanks. I'm not hungry, son."

Behind him, Ernest shook his head slightly: the American gent had not breakfasted.

"You must eat, sir, to keep up your strength." Phillip nodded to the young footman, who winked and slipped out.

The moment the latch clicked behind him, Arbuckle leant forward, saying eagerly, "Okay give me the low-down. You said she's all right? She's not hurt?"

"Only her hands." Phillip displayed his own. "She's a real sport. You see, her hands were tied in front and mine behind me. I couldn't do much of anything but Miss Arbuckle found some broken glass and had a go at the cords around mine. It was getting dark, and we both got a bit sliced up."

"Getting dark? This was last night?" He frowned as Phillip nodded. "She freed your hands and you escaped?"

"By Jove, no!" cried Phillip, outraged. "You can't imagine I'm the sort of blighter who'd toddle off and leave her there!"

"Pardon me." Arbuckle leant his elbows on the table and sank his head in his hands. "I'm half out of my mind with worry. How about you start at the beginning and just tell me what happened?"

"Right-ho. They knocked me out—you saw that?"

"Yep," the American said wearily. "That is, I saw you attacked with a crowbar. I figure they only had enough chloroform prepared for me and Gloria. I ought to ask, how's your head?"

Gingerly, Phillip pressed the tender spot. "Sore, but it seems to have stopped aching. I woke up with a heck of a headache. We were shut up in. . . ." He stopped as Ernest entered with another trayful.

"Fresh coffee, sir," the footman said cheerfully, unloading, "and another cup an' saucer. More toast. An' I took the liberty of bringing a spot of breakfast for the gentleman." He set down a plate in front of Arbuckle and whisked away the cover.

"Good man!" Phillip approved.

"Thanks," said Arbuckle with more politeness than enthusiasm. He grimaced but picked up knife and fork. "Okay, I guess you're right, I better eat."

Ernest reluctantly departed, looking about to burst with curiosity. Phillip took up his story.

"We woke up in a small room with the door and window barred. With my hands tied there wasn't a damn thing I could do. Actually, I don't know that I could have done much anyway, but if Miss Arbuckle had managed to free my hands, I'd have had more of a chance when they came for me."

"Came for you?"

"Four of 'em. I got past the first two," Phillip said with pardonable pride. "You see, I overheard them talking. They'd been told to . . . er . . . rub me out. I can't understand it." He shook his head, puzzled anew at his continued existence.

"That you're still alive? Don't question it, son, just thank the good Lord." Having cut up his bacon, Arbuckle put down his knife and shifted his fork to his right hand. "But who told them to bump you off? They didn't mention a name?"

"Not exactly. They all sounded English, and they just called him 'the Yank.' "

Arbuckle groaned. "I knew it. This business never smelled to me like a homegrown Limey plot. Much more the kinda thing they do back home."

"You have enemies in America?"

"Enemies! Who needs enemies? All it takes is a few bucks in your pocket and half the world feels entitled to a share."

"They referred to you as 'Mr. Moneybags.' It was because the Yank didn't think my father could come up with much cash on short notice that he told them to get rid of me. And that's why I went for them when they came for me."

"Nothing to lose." Arbuckle nodded. "Still, you've got guts, one against four and your hands tied."

"Well, by my reckoning I wouldn't be any use to Gloria—Miss Arbuckle—dead, so I might as well give it a try. But it was nearly dark and I didn't see the second pair of men till too late. They bagged me with chloroform. I couldn't believe it when I woke up this morning under a hedge. And what luck to find myself here at Fairacres!"

"So this Lord Dalrymple took you in?"

"I must say it was jolly decent of him. I was a frightful mess."

"How well do you know him?"

"Not well. He's my father's neighbour, of course, but he's only a distant cousin of the people who used to live here when I was growing up." Phillip started to attempt to tackle the intricacies of entails, primogeniture, and inheritance through the male line.

Arbuckle was not interested. "Never mind all that baloney. You told me on the 'phone he wouldn't spill the beans, but if you don't know him that well. . . . I hoped I could maybe ask his advice as well as yours."

"*My* advice?" Phillip was staggered. No one ever asked his advice.

"Sure thing. I'm a stranger in England. I've learnt a bit about the way business works over here, but I don't pretend to unnerstand the rest. And with my girl in trouble, I don't pretend to be able to think straight."

"I don't expect I can, either. I . . . I'm dashed keen on Miss Arbuckle, you know. The police are the people to advise you."

"No!" Arbuckle dropped his fork, his shoulders sagging. "If I contact the police, they'll kill Gloria."

Phillip opened his mouth, and closed it again. The silence lengthened.

"K-kill her?" he stammered at last. "What makes you think so?"

"When I came round from the chloroform, there was a note saying so beside me in the auto."

"They left you in the car?" He clung to irrelevant details to avoid the enormity of the threat to the girl he loved. "There in the lane?"

"No, not there, or Crawford would have found me pretty quick. I guess they fixed the radiator with your bit of hose. They drove it back to the hotel and parked it with the top up in an out-of-the-way corner, under that big old tree out front."

"The cedar? Yes, no one would go near it there. But Crawford must have returned to Great Malvern when he found the Studebaker gone?"

"That poor guy! I feel real badly about him. He walked miles to a garage, and when he got there he found he'd left his note-case behind."

"They pinched mine," Phillip said, still aggrieved. Arbuckle stuck his hand into his pocket. "Here, you'd better take this." He brought out a fistful of notes.

"I wasn't angling for money!"

"No, no, but you'll need a few bucks—quids—and you don't want to have to ask your folks. You can pay me back later. Now where was I?"

"Crawford left his wallet behind."

"That's so, and I guess it took him a while to talk the garage man into driving him back to the Studebaker."

"And it wasn't there when they got there."

"Crawford thought he must have mistaken the spot. All these lanes of yours look pretty much alike."

"It's quite easy for a stranger to get lost," Phillip agreed, refilling their coffee cups.

"They motored around awhile, till the mechanic figured

he'd been had for a sucker. To cut a long story short, Crawford ended up hoofing it darn near all the way back to Great Malvern, except for a short ride on a hay-wagon. He was beat and he was kinda mad, though in general he's a real cool customer."

"He must have thought you had abandoned him, having somehow replaced the hose."

"You'd think a guy oughta know after ten years that's not how I treat my employees," said Arbuckle, rather querulous. "Waal, he spotted the Studebaker there under the tree, but what with one thing and another he just went on up to his room to nurse his blisters and his grievances."

"Leaving you to wake up in your own time." The subject of the threat to Gloria could no longer be postponed. "What exactly did the note say?"

"That they have my daughter. I'm to wait for further instructions on how to pay to get her back, and how much, and if I contact the cops, I'll never see her again alive."

"They talked about killing me, but they didn't," Phillip pointed out hopefully. "None of them wanted to get mixed up in murder."

"Your crooks just don't have itchy trigger-fingers like ours do, and the boss, the man they call the Yank, wasn't there, was he? He'll rub out my girl himself if I don't do what he says."

"I don't see why. He'd have nothing to gain by it."

"As a warning. Next time he pulled the same trick, someone would remember Gloria dying and pay up. It works. It happens all the time in the States, and the result is I'm not going to the police."

"Our police are pretty good on the whole," Phillip contended. "At least, Scotland Yard is."

"I've the greatest respect for your Scotland Yard, son. A swell bunch of guys, I hear, not dumb stiffs or on the take like half ours at home. But I'm not prepared to risk Gloria's life." Arbuckle's gaze at once pleaded and demanded. "Are you?"

"No," said Phillip unhappily. By no means convinced that the proper authorities were not the best people to deal with the situation, he was all too aware of his inability to present persuasive arguments. "Of course not. Only. . . ."

"Swear you won't go to the police."

"You have my word as a gentleman."

"I guess that'll do. Now, maybe you can advise me what to say when people ask where Gloria is. We've gotten kinda buddy-buddy with some of the folks at the Abbey Hotel, see. They're sure to ask. The last thing I want is for anyone to think there's something fishy going on, or next thing we know some busybody will be starting rumours that'll get to the ears of the police."

"Oh . . . er. . . ." Phillip looked for inspiration to one of the plaster cupids on the ceiling. He was racked by a sudden vision of Arbuckle disenchanted with him and turning for advice to that bounder at the hotel, Major Purvis, who had his eye on Gloria.

"The best I can come up with is to say she wasn't feeling too good so I sent her to Lunnon to see one of those classy Harley Street doctors. Only no one would believe I let her go alone."

"I should rather think not! Besides the Harley Street johnnies aren't on call at the weekend like one's local medico. Can't you just tell people she's gone to stay with friends for a few days?"

"But they'll want to know who, and where, and why I haven't gone too. Wise me up. Give me some plausible answers, something that won't make 'em raise their eyebrows. Your English swells have a way of raising their eyebrows, and I never can be sure what's going to get 'em going."

"By Jove, sir, if anyone asks such infernally impertinent

questions, you jolly well raise your eyebrows at *them*. Not at all the thing."

Arbuckle was surprised into a snort of laughter. "Attaboy," he said, standing up. "I figured you'd come through with the goods. Waal, I'd better be getting back to the hotel."

"Would you like me to come with you?"

"I don't say I wouldn't appreciate your company, son, but that surely would raise eyebrows, you calling on me when Gloria's gone off visiting." His knowing look made Phillip blush. "No, you'll have to steer clear of the hotel. Better not come into town, either, because I'll be damned if Gloria would have accepted an invitation from anyone but royalty knowing you'd be in this part of the country. I'll be able to get hold of you here?"

"For the present." Phillip was suddenly overwhelmed by a wave of fatigue. He really was too rocky to face his family's inevitable questions if he went home. No earthly use raising his eyebrows at *them!* "I'll ring you up before I leave. You will keep me in the picture, let me know at once if there's anything I can do? Anything at all!"

"Sure thing. Just be careful what you say on the 'phone." Arbuckle wrote down the Dalrymples' telephone number. Shaking Phillip's hand, he said, "I reckon my girl's found her a mighty fine guy, yes sirree. Now don't you go tearing your hair. I'll pay whatever they ask. Gloria's going to be okay."

If so, Phillip thought miserably, escorting his visitor down to the hall, why was her father so haggard?

For want of anything more helpful to do, he trudged back up to the bedroom. How he wished he were the clever sort of chap who always knew the answers, who had a plan at his fingertips to meet any situation! Someone like Bulldog Drummond, who not only knew just what to do but had the devil's own luck. Perhaps if he sat down, closed his eyes, and concentrated. . . .

Or lay down. His bones ached and the bed looked awfully inviting. One could think just as well prone as sitting up, he assured himself, as he hung his jacket on the back of a chair, kicked off his shoes, and stretched out on top of the bedspread.

Sleep hit too fast to be resisted.

When Phillip woke up, he knew precisely what to do. The notion buzzing around in his brain was an absolute corker, he decided, examining it from every angle.

What did Bulldog Drummond do when his back was to the wall? He called in his friends. Phillip would consult Daisy.

Daisy not only had brains, she was quick-witted. She was forever getting mixed up in shady business and finding her way out in one piece, even helping the police, he gathered. He didn't approve. He had done his best to dissuade her from letting herself be drawn into murder investigations, so he'd look an absolute ass calling her in now, but this was different.

This was Gloria in danger. Besides, if it came to taking any risks, he would keep Daisy well out of the way. Even Gervaise could not have faulted him for asking her advice.

Nor could Arbuckle object. Phillip would make Daisy swear not to contact the police, and he trusted her if he trusted anyone in the world.

Sitting up, he swung his legs off the bed and reached for his shoes. He must wire her at once, begging her to hop on a train this very afternoon. Surely she didn't slave over her blasted articles on Sunday afternoons?

As he tied his shoes, Ernest arrived. "Oh, you're awake at last, sir," he said. "Her ladyship wants to know—wishes to enquire, that is—will you be coming down to dinner?"

"To dinner! What time is it?"

"Half past six, sir. The dressing-bell will ring in half an hour."

"Ye gods, I've slept the whole day away!" said Phillip, shocked.

"Yes, sir."

"I must send a telegram immediately."

"Yes, sir. Dinner, sir?" the footman ventured to enquire as Phillip sped past him.

"I'm abso-bally-lutely ravenous," Phillip called back over his shoulder, well on his way to the stairs. Dash it, he thought, bounding down, how could he have wasted so much time? Daisy might not be able to come till tomorrow now.

If only she had a telephone, he'd be able to persuade her of the urgency of his plea without blowing the gaff to any inquisitive operator. A wire was going to take some thought.

5

Alec opened the passenger door of the Austin Chummy. Daisy stepped out onto the pavement. A whiff of petrol fumes ceded to the lingering smell of his aromatic pipe tobacco and the fragrance of the roses in the front garden.

"It's been a lovely evening," she said, not wanting it to end. "Will you come in for a nightcap? Only South African sherry, I'm afraid, unless Lucy's splurged on Spanish 'cognac.' "

"I'd better not."

"Binkie might have left some whisky, or there's always coffee, or cocoa."

Alec laughed. "Fear of South African sherry couldn't stop me, though I'd hesitate to drink Lord Gerald's Scotch. Unfortunately, crooks don't cease operations over the week-end. It's early to rise for me tomorrow. If anything is certain in this life it's that the stack of paper on my desk will have grown since I last scowled upon it."

"My stacks of paper are all ready to be posted," Daisy said with satisfaction as he escorted her up the short path to the front door. She stopped on the step, fumbling in her evening bag for the key by the light from the street lamp.

"Well done. The best I can say is that there are a couple of cases I can close and send down to Files."

Key in hand, Daisy paused. "Alec, I don't suppose you could get away next weekend for a day or two?" Was she being frightfully presumptuous? She had ragged Phillip about being slow to introduce Miss Arbuckle to his parents, and she had known Alec much longer. These days a girl didn't have to wait for a man to make all the running, she reminded herself. "I'm going down to Fairacres, to Mother at the Dower House, and I'd like awfully for you to meet her."

Without warning, she found herself enveloped in an ardent embrace. The key clinked on the step as she put her arms around his neck and kissed him back with great enthusiasm.

"Gosh!" she said shakily when at last forced to come up for air, "can all coppers kiss like that?"

"I hope you have no intention of trying to find out." He let her go and stepped back, running a hand through his thick, dark hair. "Daisy, that was shockingly ungentlemanly of me," he said ruefully.

"What rot! You can't say that without implying that I was unladylike."

"In that case, I withdraw the apology." He smiled. "Do you mean you won't withdraw the invitation?"

"Of course not, idiot," Daisy said lovingly. "Can you accept?"

"I have a few days' leave due. I can't . . ."

". . . promise—I know. A second Jack the Ripper might be on the prowl at this very moment." Her involuntary shiver led Alec to put his arm around her shoulders. She looked up at him. "But you'll try?"

"That I can promise. You'd better give me the name of the nearest hotel so that I can ring up and book a room."

"There are lots of hotels in Great Malvern, but the inn in the village is nearer, and I'm told it's quite comfortable. The Wedge and Beetle at Morton Green."

"The Wedge and Beetle it shall be. I'll try to get away for lunch one day this week, too." He bent his head.

This time Daisy was prepared to be kissed. To her frustration, a motor-car promptly pulled up behind the Austin and she heard Lucy's penetrating soprano.

Alec's lips brushed hers. "I really must be off," he said regretfully. "Lunch on Tuesday, if I can make it?"

"Spiffing. Wire me if you can't."

She watched him walk down the path, a broad-shouldered figure in the lamplight, with a spring in his step despite the lateness of the hour. He paused at the gate to exchange good-nights with Lucy and Binkie, turned to wave to Daisy, then was eclipsed as the other two approached.

"What-ho, Daisy," said Lord Gerald Bincombe, a large, taciturn ex-rugger Blue.

"Solved any mysteries tonight, darling?" Lucy asked sardonically.

"No, darling, but you can help me solve one. I've dropped my dratted key."

"Aha!" Lucy sounded amused. "I wonder what made you do that?"

Feeling herself blush, an outdated affliction she was mortifyingly prone to, Daisy stooped to search. She said crossly, "Give us a hand, do."

"Hullo, here it is." Binkie bent down, retrieved the key from the path, and presented it to Daisy with a slight bow.

"Thanks." She opened the door and flipped the electric light switch. A yellow envelope lay on the mat inside. "Oh, there's a telegram. For me," she added, picking it up and dropping it on the hall table while she took off her hat and gloves.

They all went down to the semi-basement kitchen for cocoa. Sitting at the kitchen table, Daisy opened the telegram.

"Who's it from?" Lucy asked, pouring milk into a saucepan with the utmost care to avoid splashes on the hip-waisted yellow silk georgette clinging to her slender figure.

"Phillip. How odd! 'Urgent emergency,' " Daisy read. " 'Come pronto Fairacres not Dower House need you now

please.' With his name, it's one word over the twelve—the
'please' was an afterthought."

"Urgent, emergency, pronto, now; he's certainly keen to
get you there in a hurry."

"But why? I suppose it's too late to telephone from a
box to find out."

Binkie consulted his wrist-watch. "Nearly midnight."

"Too late, and you don't know where he is," said Lucy.

A horrid possibility crossed Daisy's mind. "Oh Lucy,
you don't suppose Mother's fallen seriously ill? Why should
he say to go to Fairacres not the Dower House? He hardly
knows Edgar and Geraldine."

"Surely not, darling. You would have heard from your
cousin, or maybe a doctor, not Phillip. You know what an
ass he is. No one would leave it to him to contact you.
Mysteriouser and mysteriouser—just your line—but I
shouldn't worry about the dowager."

"No, I expect you're right." Could it be that the Arbuck-
les had met his family by chance with disastrous results?
Daisy debated whether to tell Lucy and Binkie about Gloria.
Not her tale to tell, she decided.

"Drive you down tonight, if you want," Binkie offered
gruffly. "Back in time to toddle to the office."

"You're an angel, but Phillip can't possibly expect me
to leave at this time of night, not to mention what Edgar
and Geraldine would say if I turned up on their doorstep
at dawn. I'll take the first train in the morning. Where's the
Bradshaw's, Lucy?"

"You used it last. Oh drat! The milk's boiling over."

Binkie coped manfully with the emergency, and Lucy
made cocoa with what was left of the milk. Daisy took her
three-quarters of a cupful up to her den to look for the
railway timetable, more to give the other two a spot of pri-
vacy than because she was in a hurry to find the best train.

On her way upstairs, she wondered what on earth had
put the wind up Phillip. He was by nature on the phlegmatic

side, not easily excited to more than a bit of minor bluster or a temperate enthusiasm.

Why had he not been more explicit, if not to avoid worrying her? Lucy was right, of course, about Phillip being the last person anyone would ask to get in touch with her if her mother was ill. All the same, Daisy could not help being anxious. She could not imagine why he should tell her to go to Fairacres rather than the Dower House, or even Malvern Grange, if the Dowager Lady Dalrymple were not involved.

Unless he didn't want her ladyship to *get* involved—which suggested a row with his family over Gloria. The question then became, did Daisy want to get involved? To be present at their meeting, to help smooth the way and prevent a row was one thing. Landing in the middle when he was already hock deep in the soup was quite another.

Sitting down at her desk, she reread the telegram. "Urgent emergency" sounded positively desperate. She had better go, but she'd really give it him in the neck if all he wanted was his hand held!

The train service to Malvern was excellent, the Victorian spa enjoying a renaissance since the Armistice. Reading, Oxford, the long, slow pull up into the Cotswolds and the rush down the steep slope into the Vale of Evesham, with Bredon Hill dominating the plain to the south. A brief stop in Worcester, then over the Severn and Daisy was in her home country.

At the ripe old age of twenty-five, one ought to be blasé, but she still felt some of the excitement of the end-of-term return from school.

The rich, red soil, orchards, hop-fields, and market gardens, streams and pastures, woods crowning the low rises, and always the Malvern Hills to the west—this was home. She had climbed the hills, walked and ridden through the woods and fields, cycled along the twisting lanes, through the villages of brick and stone and half-timbered cottages.

Puffing and sighing, the train drew into Great Malvern station. The porter who opened the compartment door for Daisy greeted her by name.

"Morning, Miss Dalrymple. Mind the wet paint."

The pillars and elaborate brackets holding up the roof over the platform had just been repainted red and blue; their fanciful wreaths of ironwork leaves and flowers were glossy green, yellow, and white; men were scrubbing the patina of soot from the walls of the long building, patterned with vari-coloured stone. Daisy stepped down to the platform with an involuntary sense of civic pride in the uniquely decorative station.

"What-ho, Daisy!" Phillip loped along the platform towards her. "I hoped you'd be on this train, old dear."

"I had to get up frightfully early to. . . . Gosh, Phil, what have you done to your head?" she exclaimed as he took off his tweed cap, revealing an encircling bandage.

Hastily he clapped the cap back on his head. "You should have seen me yesterday. I looked like a ruddy native in a turban."

"What happened? What's going on? I hope you have a jolly good reason for dragging me all this way!"

"I can't tell you here." He glanced furtively over his shoulder, then turned to her porter. "Is this all your luggage?"

"Yes, I don't expect to stay long and anyway I have a few things at the Dower House. Phillip, Mother's not ill, is she?"

"Ill? Lady Dalrymple? By Jove, no. At least, not that I know of. Why?"

"For pity's sake," Daisy said, exasperated, as she handed in her ticket, "because your telegram was so urgent and so obscure I didn't know what else to think. Unless it's something to do with Miss Arbuckle?"

"Sshhh!" he hissed in an agony of apprehension, casting another rapid glance over his shoulder. "I'll explain when we get there."

Daisy sighed. They emerged onto the station forecourt and she looked around. "Where's your car?"

"I don't know," Phillip said gloomily. "Please, Daisy, don't ask questions, just wait till we get to Fairacres."

A green Vauxhall pulled up in front of them. Daisy recognized the chauffeur. Bill Truscott had worked for her father before the War, returned when demobbed, married a parlourmaid, and stayed on with the new viscount. He grinned at her, jumping out and tipping his peaked cap.

"Hello, Bill. How's Mrs. Truscott?"

"Morning, Miss Daisy." He opened the car's back door for her. "The wife's doing fine, still helping up at the house now and then. Three nippers we've got now, and his lordship's moved us into the lodge."

"Good for you. The flat over the garages wasn't designed for a family. Edgar seems to be doing quite well," she added to Phillip, stepping up onto the running board as the chauffeur went to open the boot for her bag.

"Considering he wasn't brought up to it, and his head is full of moths and butterflies."

Laughing, Daisy conceded, "He still has Father's bailiff, who knows what he's about. I doubt Edgar has to do much but approve his plans."

"Lady Dalrymple acts as if she's still married to a housemaster," Phillip grumbled, "and the rest of the world is made up of small boys."

Daisy laughed again. "I know what you mean. She's never actually ordered me to wash off my powder and lipstick, but she looks as if she'd like to. Only Scarlet Women paint."

"She forbade me to drive this morning because of my head." Phillip joined Daisy in the back seat after tipping the porter. "It's perfectly all right now."

Bill took his place behind the steering wheel and pressed the self-starter. The Vauxhall proceeded in stately fashion out onto Avenue Road and turned down the hill away from the town.

The back of the chauffeur's head before her, Daisy managed to subdue her rampant curiosity but for one low-voiced question. "Does Geraldine . . . do she and Edgar know why you called me down here?"

"Actually," Phillip said sheepishly, "as a matter of fact, you see I spent last night there and I'm afraid I rather left them with the impression that I was going home. I didn't actually say so, mind."

"They aren't expecting me? And they think they've rid themselves of you? Phil, you hopeless ass, I can't just march in as if I still lived there. We'd better go to the Dower House if you don't want to go home yet."

"No, I can't stay at your mater's. You'll think up a story to tell your cousins, old bean. I know you can if you'll just put your mind to it. After all, isn't that what writers do for a living?"

Reluctantly flattered by his confidence, Daisy bit back a vigorous protest and a reminder that she wrote factual articles, not fiction. She put her mind to it.

The final details fell into place as they rolled past the Dower House, a charming red-brick Georgian residence set in its own gardens at the edge of the park.

"You promised to call on Mother," she said.

"I haven't had half a chance!"

"No, that's the basis for our story. You asked Bill to stop while you popped in to say hullo and . . ."

"He knows I did nothing of the sort."

"No one is at all likely to ask him, and if they do, he won't mind telling such a little fib for me. I'll ask him." She leaned forward. "Bill, you remember stopping at the Dower House on your way to the station, to let Mr. Petrie call on my mother?"

"If you say so, miss." He flashed a grin over his shoulder. "Won't be the first taradiddle I've told for you or poor Mr. Gervaise. Quite like the old days."

Coming to the lodge, they turned in through the open gates and proceeded up the elm avenue, while Daisy rapidly explained the rest to Phillip.

"Mother asked you to pick me up at the station, because her car wouldn't start."

"*She* won't fib for you."

"She hardly speaks to Edgar and Geraldine. She still resents their getting Fairacres. Listen, we're nearly there. When we got back to the Dower House, you were deadbeat. . . ."

"Oh, I say, a feeble sort of chap that makes me out!"

"Do you or do you not want to go on staying at Fairacres?" Daisy snapped, thoroughly peeved. "If you want me to make up a farrago of lies for you, just let me get on with it. You were feeling pretty rotten because of your head so I insisted on you coming back here, Mother being what she is. Like it or lump it, it's too late to change," she added, as the Vauxhall drew up before the front door.

Coming back to Fairacres now it was no longer home was too painful for her to have much sympathy with Phillip's chagrin. Memories, which might have been exorcised had she gone on living there, haunted every nook and cranny.

She had no time to dwell on the spectres. Geraldine, looking disconcerted and somehow dowdy despite her smart tailored costume, was coming down the steps beneath the pillared portico.

"Hello, Daisy," she said. "I didn't know you were down here. I'm always happy to see you, naturally, but if you have come to call, I'm afraid I'm on my way out. I have an appointment in Worcester and I've just been waiting for Truscott to return with the motor." She frowned at the chauffeur as he opened the door for Daisy.

"You mustn't blame him for taking longer than intended." Daisy stepped down and brushed cheeks with her cousin's wife. Glancing back, she saw Phillip leaning heavily against the Vauxhall, with one hand pressed rather theatrically to his bandaged head. He was going along with her story. She just hoped he wouldn't overdo it and groan.

Geraldine greeted the tale with annoyance visibly repressed. "Of course you must stay, Mr. Petrie." She spoke to the butler who stood on the threshold, then turned back to Daisy. "You'll have to excuse me, though, and Edgar is out after butterflies. Will you do the honours? Make yourself at home. You know Edgar and I wish you would look upon Fairacres as a second home."

"Thanks, Geraldine. I'll try to make Phillip comfortable," Daisy said diplomatically. "I expect a spot of brandy will buck him up."

"Spirits? I hardly think . . ." The arrival of a footman to help Phillip into the house mercifully cut her short. "Well, dear, I'll have to leave it to you. Worcester, Truscott."

Daisy and Phillip settled in the formal drawing-room since Daisy was reluctant to make herself sufficiently at home to use the family sitting room. The drawing-room's furnishings, an eclectic mix of the best of the past two centuries, hadn't changed a bit. It gave Daisy an eerie feeling, as if her father or Gervaise might walk in at any moment.

Phillip refused with loathing to put his legs up on an elegant Regency sofa but condescended to raise his feet onto the footstool solicitously provided by the footman. Luckily his face was tanned enough from sporting weekends to conceal the absence of invalidish pallor.

"Coffee, miss?" inquired the butler, who had followed them in.

"Yes, please."

"Ernest, coffee."

"Right away, Mr. Lowecroft." Passing Daisy, he whispered, "I'll bring the brandy, too, miss."

"Thank you, Ernest," said Daisy, noting for future need his willingness to brave her ladyship's disapproval, though she did not intend to let Phillip drink a drop. She wanted a straight explanation from him, unclouded by a spirituous haze.

He would not say a word until the young footman had departed, returned with brandy, coffee, and strawberry tartlets, and left again. Then he kicked away the footstool.

"Right-ho," he said, accepting the cup of coffee Daisy handed him and absently helping himself to two tarts. "Here we go."

6

Before Phillip's story had progressed far, Daisy whipped a notebook and pencil from her handbag. In her own peculiar brand of Pitman's shorthand, indecipherable to anyone else, she made notes as he spoke. It allowed her to listen to the terrifying tale without interrupting.

"So that's it," he said at last. "Arbuckle's gone up to town to see about getting hold of the ransom money. He insists Gloria's in no danger as long as he pays up and doesn't involve the police, but he's not acting as if he believes it. He's like a cat on hot bricks."

"Having met—if that's the right word—the villains, do you believe it?"

"Well, they kindly didn't do me in, but then there's the Yank. . . ."

"One does read awful stories about American kidnappers taking the ransom and leaving a body," Daisy admitted.

"Don't!" Phillip shuddered, his face pale in spite of the tan. "In any case, Gloria's alone and frightened and in their power. I *can't* sit back and do nothing. That's why I wired for you."

"I can't see what you expect me to do, old dear. The police are the ones to tackle it—not the locals, Scotland Yard. I should think a foreigner being involved would be a good enough excuse for them to butt in. You can trust Alec to investigate without letting the world know." She put down her coffee cup and rose. "I'll ring him up right away."

"No!" He jumped up and grabbed her arm. "I gave Arbuckle my word not to contact the coppers. He won't like it that I've brought you in."

"Are you afraid he won't let his daughter marry you? He may not *have* a daughter if she's not found."

"It's too big a risk, Daisy. He showed me the letter. The slightest whiff of the police and the Yank will kill her."

Sighing, Daisy sat down and took another strawberry tartlet. Breakfast had been a cup of tea and a slice of toast, snatched on the run.

"All right, let's see what, if anything, we can do without them. I have half a hundred questions." Ruminatively munching, she studied her notebook. "But first, I'd say the cottage they took you to must be quite nearby, within a few miles."

"Why?"

"Simply because they dropped you off here after snatching you not far away. It would make less than no sense to bring you back to the same area from a distance. Was the van plain, or did it have a tradesman's name on it?"

"It had a butcher's name painted on the side."

"What name? Was it a local firm? We might be able to trace it?"

"No address. The name began with P, I think. Potter, Parslow, Paget . . . Ah, I have it: Ferris, or maybe Farris."

"Never heard of him," Daisy said, disappointed. "Not local, then, though the police might be able to trace it."

"No! Besides, they could easily paint over the words."

"I suppose so. It was a long shot at best. You said the van driver sounded Cockney."

"Yes, definitely, and so were the others."

Daisy perked up. He hadn't mentioned the accents of the other men before. "All of them?" she asked eagerly.

"All those I heard talking." Phillip was puzzled. "What difference does it make?"

"For a start, Londoners don't understand the countryside.

Imagine being used to the East End, all the back-to-back buildings, people swarming everywhere. A few streets away you're in a completely different district where no one will recognize you."

"By Jove, so they may have thought they'd taken me a long way!"

"Quite possibly. Besides, this must seem like a desert to them. I shouldn't be surprised if they left you under that hedge half expecting you'd never be found. They may have regarded it as a compromise between disobeying the Yank and actually doing you in."

"They didn't sound at all keen on actually doing me in. The one who hit me boasted of his skill at knocking people out without killing them."

"It's the Yank we really have to worry about, but the others may lead us to him, or to Gloria. Even if they've laid in supplies, you can bet they'll be popping into the nearest village for cigarettes or a pint. With Cockney accents they'll stand out like a sore thumb."

"Won't they realize that?" Phillip suggested dubiously.

"I doubt it. We had lots of Cockneys in the military hospitals in Malvern during the War. If they paid any attention at all to how people spoke, they tended to think they were normal and everyone else talked 'funny.' Whereas country people notice like a shot when they hear an accent that's not local."

Phillip grinned. "Anyone from more than ten miles off is a furriner."

"Exactly. Of course, the Yank might warn the men."

"He may not even have noticed their accents. Gloria said we all sound plain British to her."

"That's a point! I suppose their boss really is an American, by the way? It could be just a nickname, we have no way of knowing."

"He wants the ransom half in pounds, half in dollars. Arbuckle showed me the note."

Frowning, she refilled their cups and helped herself to yet another tart. "He's probably American, then, unless he's an Englishman planning to do a flit. It's more of an American sort of crime. I wonder if it's just for money, or does Mr. Arbuckle have enemies?"

"He said not. Daisy, what's the point of all these questions? I want to *do* something, not sit here chatting and scoffing pastries."

"If I've learnt anything from Alec," Daisy said severely, "it's the importance of seemingly unimportant details. I've already dragged a whole lot of helpful stuff out of you that you didn't bother to mention. There could be more."

"Oh, right-ho," he said, abashed. "If it's helping you decide what to do, fire away."

"I still think the best thing to do is to tell Alec everything, but don't worry, I won't without Mr. Arbuckle's permission. I must say I'm rather surprised you didn't telephone the police as soon as you reached the house, even before you spoke to him. You didn't know about the threat in the first note until he arrived."

"I didn't want to bring the local force in unnecessarily. The Chief Constable's a pal of the pater's."

"Aha," said Daisy understandingly.

"As a matter of fact, I thought of trying to get hold of Fletcher, but then I got through to Arbuckle and he told me not to breathe a word to a soul."

"You haven't told anyone at all but me?" She raised her eyebrows as he shook his head. "Not even Edgar and Geraldine, I gather. You must have said something to them, after turning up under a hedge trussed like a chicken!"

"Dalrymple didn't seem interested in the least in how I got there."

"As you said, his head is full of butterflies. Anyway, I expect it's a relief not to have to know what everyone is up to all the time as he did with his schoolboys. Geraldine's another kettle of fish."

"She didn't see me trussed up, and all Dalrymple told her was that I'd had an accident. She assumed I'd cracked up the old bus, and that Arbuckle had caused the crash and came to set things right. Her brother and his family were here for the weekend, but luckily they left last night. I didn't even see them."

"I wonder what happened to your car. If the police find it abandoned, they're going to want an explanation."

"Oh lord!"

"Well, we'll cross that bridge when we come to it. So you and I and Arbuckle are the only people who know about the kidnapping, besides the villains?"

"He told his assistant. The poor fellow was driving them and ended up tramping all over the countryside when the Studebaker disappeared. But he didn't tell him I'm involved, in case word might get back to the kidnappers."

"They know you're involved," Daisy pointed out.

"They don't know I survived, nor that I'm going to pull out all the stops to find Gloria."

Ernest stuck his head around the door. "Telephone call for you, sir."

"Mr. Arbuckle?"

"No, sir, a lady as won't give her name."

"Fenella," Phillip groaned, and hurried out.

"More coffee, miss?"

"No, thanks."

He came in and started to clear up the coffee-things. "Cook wants to know, miss, will you and Mr. Petrie be here for luncheon?"

"Yes," Daisy said absently, her thoughts on the sudden introduction of Phillip's young sister into the affair. Fenella knew he was at Fairacres, if no more.

"Very good, miss."

Daisy suddenly woke up to the fact that she was no longer at home at Fairacres. "Here" for lunch, the footman had said, not "in." "Oh, Ernest!" she said as the door closed. He reappeared. "We haven't exactly been invited to lunch."

He gave her a friendly if unfootmanly grin. "Not to worry, miss. Her ladyship's lunching out and there's no knowing when his lordship'll turn up. 'Sides, you're family, miss. Luncheon for two it is."

She smiled at him. "Thanks!"

Abandoning for the moment the puzzle of Fenella, Daisy turned over in her mind all she had learnt from Phillip and tried to decide how to approach the problem of Gloria's whereabouts.

They could go from village to village enquiring in shops and pubs as to whether any Cockneys had been sighted— heard, rather. If only one or two villages were so distinguished, that would narrow down the search area. Two would be better, in fact, since one could presume the kidnappers were hiding somewhere in between.

It would be much easier, however, if they could narrow the search before they set out. If only Phillip had some sort of clue as to where they had taken him. She gathered he'd been completely unconscious both coming and going, but she'd better make sure.

What else had she not asked him? Alec would probably come up with dozens more questions. How she wished he was here!

Phillip came back, looking disgruntled. "Sisters!" he said bitterly.

"How much does she know?"

"Only that I'm here and don't want the parents to know. I had to get hold of some clothes from home somehow. She cycled over with a bag yesterday evening."

"Jolly decent of her. And now she's let the cat out of the bag?"

"What? Oh! No, but she's been thinking and she's decided I must be in trouble, so she wants to help. I managed to put her off, but I bet she'll go on pestering. Dash it, girls shouldn't be allowed to think!"

Torn between umbrage and amusement, Daisy plumped for the latter. Laughing, she observed, "And there I was believing you brought me all the way from London to think for you!"

"I did. I say, old thing, don't fool about," he pleaded, adding humbly, "I know I'm not much brainier than Fenella. You are. I need you. Gloria needs you."

"I know, old dear, I know. I was teasing. If Fenella 'phones again, we'll think of a way to put her off. Phil, you have absolutely no idea where you were taken, where Gloria is?"

"Not the foggiest."

"You didn't see or hear anything at all, coming or going, even something you don't believe is significant?"

"I was out for the count both ways. It could have been any wood in the county, or outside it."

"Wood? For pity's sake, you know you were in a wood?"

"It was only an impression," Phillip said defensively. "I heard what sounded like a woodpecker, and then a squirrel. You know how they sort of chatter when they get annoyed? They might have both been in the only tree around." He knit his brows in thought. "There was something else, though, which gave me the same impression. What was it?"

"Imagine yourself back there," Daisy suggested.

He closed his eyes. "It makes my head ache. I've got it! The sunbeam flickered as if it was shining through fluttering leaves—that still could be just one tree, close to the cottage, though, couldn't it?"

"Yes. Nothing else?"

"The air seemed to be sort of damp," he said doubtfully. "Sort of mouldy—not rotten, just the way woods are. Sort of *green*. I might have imagined it."

"I know what you mean. It's not a smell you get from one tree. If it seemed damp after weeks of drought, you're probably right about the woods. Anyway, it gives us somewhere to start."

"I don't see how. There are dozens of woods and copses and spinneys within a few miles."

"Not many with an isolated, dilapidated, deserted cottage in the middle. Good, we don't have to search all the fields and commons and riverbanks—you didn't hear running water?"

"No."

"It cuts down the area enormously, and both of us know the local countryside like the backs of our hands. All the same, as you say, there are dozens of woods. It would take us centuries to explore them all."

Phillip slumped. "We're only guessing they're not more than a few miles off, anyway. It's hopeless, isn't it?"

Daisy had never seen him so downhearted. His usually equable temperament took the rough with the smooth, occasionally a bit ruffled but without a stumble. Even the dreadful years in the trenches of Flanders had left little apparent mark on Phillip, unlike so many more sensitive spirits who still suffered years later.

It must be true love. She remembered how her heart had hurt when Michael's ambulance unit left for the front, knowing his noncombatant status was no protection against stray bullets, poison gas, or landmines. Then there had been the awful time when Alec was in danger, and later his little girl. Daisy had been able to help both Alec and Belinda, though. Half the pain was the helplessness of wanting desperately to do something when there was nothing to be done.

Phillip must be given something to do, however useless. And you never could tell, it might prove useful after all.

"Buck up, old thing," she said. "We're not going to give up so easily."

"What can we do?"

"The first thing is to go round the villages making enquiries about Cockneys, or other conspicuous strangers. Or Americans, come to think of it, though I doubt he'd risk letting anyone hear an American accent near the hiding place. Still, with luck we'll be able to pinpoint a smallish area to search. I suppose it's no good asking Fenella to help?"

"The mater would want to know where she kept disappearing to. What's more, she'd tell. She's not much more than a child, in spite of that broken engagement."

"My mother's going to be a problem, too," Daisy reflected. "She's bound to find out I'm here and she'll want to know why I don't stay at the Dower House, and if I do *she'll* want to know where *I* keep disappearing to. Nor can you stay there without a risk of her catching the wrong sow by the ear."

For once Phillip was quick on the uptake. "You mean she'd think we were engaged?" he cried, aghast.

"Or on the brink." She continued the dispiriting list: "You can't go home without all sorts of explanations. Neither of us can stay at Fairacres without. . . . Phillip, I've got an absolutely spiffing idea!"

"What? What is it? Tell me!"

"Not yet. Just be quiet and let me work it all out. There may be an insuperable flaw I haven't seen yet. Hush."

7

Edgar arrived in the dining room after the green pea soup, just as Daisy and Phillip started on lamb cutlets with parsleyed new potatoes and salad. He apologized for his lateness.

"Very bad form when we have guests," he said with a severity directed at himself.

"Soup, my lord?" enquired the butler.

"Yes, Lowecroft, if it's still hot." Gazing at Daisy and Phillip with a puzzled air, he went on, "Please, carry on, don't wait for me. Odd, Geraldine's not here to entertain you?"

"She's lunching with a friend in Worcester, I believe, Cousin Edgar."

"I rather thought I should be lunching alone. She must have omitted to tell me you were expected, Daisy. And your mother . . . ? Ah!" He rubbed his hands together as Ernest set a bowl before him. "There's nothing like a soup made with new peas from one's own gardens. It pains me to admit that school food, though of course nutritious, was not always toothsome."

Daisy had decided to tackle Edgar first. Geraldine would find it difficult to express her inevitable disapproval openly if her husband had already succumbed. Now he had given her a perfect opening.

"There are so many things I miss about living in the country," she said, trying to sound wistful. "The fruit and vegetables are one, of course. By the time they've been carted up to Covent Garden and sold to greengrocers and carted off again to the shops, they're always a bit battered."

"My dear, I can very easily send you up a hamper of whatever's in season now and then. I wish you had mentioned the matter sooner," Edgar reproached her.

"How frightfully kind of you, Cousin Edgar," said Daisy, filled with guilt. "Lucy and I would enjoy fresh stuff no end. That's another thing I miss," she ploughed on gamely for Phillip's sake. "Lucy often invites me for country weekends at her parents', and I hate not being able to reciprocate. I'm afraid Mother's not really in a position to entertain a crowd of young people."

Edgar blenched, but equally game—perhaps also equally guilt-ridden, as a usurper, however legal—he squared his shoulders. "You know, Daisy, Geraldine and I have frequently begged you to regard Fairacres as your home still. Naturally that must apply to inviting your friends to stay. A crowd?" he added with misgiving.

"Just in a manner of speaking," she hastened to assure him. "Half a dozen or so. I wouldn't dream of trying to arrange formal dances or anything like that. Tennis and golf and bicycling and hiking. . . ."

"Hiking?"

"Oh, it's a rather slangy term for tramping, going for long country walks. Gosh, Cousin Edgar, do you really mean I may invite a few people down?"

It was only fair to allow him a chance to back out. For a moment it was touch and go and Phillip's face took on a painfully anxious expression. Daisy had forbidden him to put his oar in, for fear of mucking things up. To her relief Edgar turned up trumps—to use another slang term and mix the odd metaphor.

"Certainly," he said bravely. "Er, which weekend were you thinking of? We shall have to consult Geraldine, I'm afraid . . . that is, of course."

"No time like the present. I don't want to disrupt Cousin Geraldine's plans for weekend guests, or put her out in any way. I'll make all the arrangements and sort out menus with Cook and so on. Tomorrow?"

Edgar's jaw dropped. "T-tomorrow? Oh well, I suppose it's best to get it over with. I mean, yes, by all means, why not tomorrow? As far as I know Geraldine has no particular plans for the next few days. Though she doesn't always let me know in advance. . . ."

"Oh, if she's giving a luncheon or dinner party or anything, we'll clear out of the way with a picnic, won't we, Phillip?"

"By Jove, yes! Don't want to get in the way, dash it all. Awfully good of you, Lord Dalrymple, and all that."

Daisy gave her cousin's hand a consoling pat. "Now, don't you worry about a thing. I shall see to everything. I dare say you'll hardly notice we're here."

The utter disbelief in Edgar's eyes almost made her giggle, but she meant what she said. His unwanted guests were going to be invited solely to spend every minute of daylight scouring the countryside.

A gooseberry fool followed the cutlets. In spite of her persuasive exertions, Daisy thoroughly enjoyed the meal. At home she and Lucy subsisted largely on eggs, cheese, and sardines, for lack of both money and cooking skills. Her father had been fond of good food, and the prospect of several days of his cook's creations was almost enough in itself to reconcile her to the ignoble wiles she had used on Edgar.

Phillip's patent relief removed the last qualms.

Magnanimous in victory, she listened with every appearance of interest to Edgar's lepidopteran blather. As pleased as any big game hunter, he had captured several caterpillars of *Pyronia tithonus,* the Gatekeeper butterfly. This afternoon he would prepare and finish a tank in which to keep and study them until they pupated and hatched, when he intended to release them.

"I'm glad you don't spend your time massacring inoffensive creatures for the sake of displaying their remains," Daisy told him.

"It is their life-cycles that interest me," he said a trifle pompously, then added with a disarming honesty, "Besides, I have never had the good fortune to come across a rare butterfly. The most casual collector can easily procure a specimen of the Gatekeeper."

Daisy pondered the irony of his snaring Gatekeepers on the very day he had proved himself so inadequate a gatekeeper. She had stormed the gates of Fairacres without firing a shot.

She had to remind herself not to triumph too soon. Geraldine was a harder nut to crack than her defenseless husband, who was accustomed to facing the simpler stratagems of small boys. Daisy's interview with her mother was bound to be difficult, too. To fortify herself for the battles ahead, she gratefully accepted a second helping of gooseberry fool.

"When will Lady Dalrymple be back?" Daisy asked the butler as they left the dining room.

"Her ladyship expected to return for tea, miss, at half past four."

"Not till tea-time?" exclaimed Phillip, agitated.

Daisy gave him a warning glance. He was a pretty hopeless conspirator, especially as he was the one who insisted on secrecy.

"It *is* awkward, Cousin Geraldine not knowing yet that Cousin Edgar has invited us to stay," she said. "Lowecroft, I expect you heard Lord Dalrymple ask me to invite a few people to come to Fairacres tomorrow for a few days? I'll let you know the exact numbers as soon as I can, but perhaps you would like to begin preparations."

"Very good, miss." The butler's stolid face gave no hint of whether he had noticed and appreciated her brilliant wangling. "I shall speak to the housekeeper."

"Thanks. Mrs. Warden is still here, isn't she? I'll have a word with her later."

Conveniently, Edgar had asked them to excuse him if he took his postprandial coffee in his conservatory-insectarium. Daisy and Phillip went out to the terrace for theirs.

"We can't wait till tea-time," Phillip fretted as soon as they were alone. "Tom Pearson and Binkie will have to arrange with their offices to be gone for a few days."

Tommy Pearson was a solicitor in his family's firm. Binkie did something obscure (to Daisy) with stocks and shares in the City, like Phillip but with somewhat more success. All three, having gone straight from school into the Army, were in junior positions.

"Did you telephone your office?" Daisy asked.

"I rang up first thing this morning and said I couldn't come in this week. They can give me the sack if they want, I don't care. But Tom and Binkie won't want to risk their jobs."

"Lucy will have to notify clients, too," Daisy pointed out dryly, "and you're jolly lucky I'm free at the moment. You're right, though, we must notify them right away. We can't wait for Geraldine's say-so. Anyway, however livid she is with Edgar, she's far too proper to rescind his invitation." *I hope,* she added to herself.

Phillip's resolve wavered, his highly developed sense of social fitness momentarily coming to the fore. "It's not at all the thing, inveigling an unwilling hostess into putting us up."

"It's for Gloria," she reminded him. "Come on, let's decide how much we can safely say to the others to persuade them to come. Then you can wire Lucy and telephone the others while I go and deal with Mother."

"Right-ho."

"And you'd better ring up Fenella. Tell her it's a house-party and we're having a treasure-hunt. That will explain us haring about the countryside."

"She'll want to join in," Phillip objected.

"Say she wouldn't enjoy it; everyone's older than she is."

"Oh, right-ho."

Half an hour later, Daisy wended her way across the park along the footpath leading directly to the Dower House. The afternoon sun was hot enough to make her regret that parasols, and even broad-brimmed straw hats, were out of fashion. She could practically feel the freckles appearing on her nose as she walked.

In the green patches beneath the clumps of trees, pale amber Jersey cows clustered in the shade, their tails swishing against the flies. Elsewhere the grass was parched to a golden brown. The only moisture it had received for weeks must be dew at dawn, evaporating before it soaked in except where protected from the sun. Even the air smelled dry. Most years the park stayed lushly green all summer; Daisy could not recall ever seeing it dried up so early.

Her footsteps kicked up puffs of dust. The sight lent weight to the scanty evidence that Phillip had really been confined in the midst of woodland.

Which still left a lot of ground to be covered. Even if enquiries pinpointed a general area, Daisy had little hope of finding Gloria Arbuckle before her father paid the ransom. The crooks surely wouldn't want to hang around for longer than necessary. But the searchers just might strike it lucky, and the quest would be worth the effort just to stop Phillip sinking into despair.

It might even be quite amusing, rather like the treasure-hunts so popular among young people at house-parties.

She came to the gate in the high, neatly-trimmed beech hedge around the Dower House. The garden inside was equally neat and flourishing. One thing the Dowager Lady

Dalrymple hadn't grumbled about for some time was the young Welsh gardener Daisy had foisted on her. Owen Morgan was a hard worker who knew his stuff.

Seeing him up a ladder picking cherries, she begged a handful and asked after his family before going on into the house.

Her mother was in the sitting room, seated at the satinwood Sheraton bureau, writing a letter. Daisy regarded her oblivious back with fondness mingled with anticipated exasperation.

A short, plumpish woman in her mid-fifties, the dowager viscountess was never happy without something to moan about. In her eyes, the charming and very comfortable Dower House was utterly inadequate. Its mere five bedrooms—not counting servants' quarters—made guests other than family out of the question. Even her elder daughter Violet's family could only be squeezed in with the greatest difficulty. It would be unbearably cramped if her younger daughter came to live with her, yet she strongly objected to Daisy's working to support herself in London.

Both daughters neglected her terribly, their rare visits always much too short. What she would say when she discovered Daisy was in Worcestershire but staying with the enemy up at the big house remained to be seen.

"Hello, Mother."

Lady Dalrymple started and swung round. "Good gracious, Daisy, what a horrid shock you gave me! I suppose it's too much to expect you to give me a few hours' notice if you mean to come down."

Daisy kissed her. "I hoped it would be a nice surprise."

"Of course I'm always glad to see you, dear, but I have the Waddells and Miss Reid coming to dinner and bridge tonight."

"I shan't upset your numbers, or put you out in any way. Edgar and Geraldine have invited me and several friends to stay for a few days."

"Indeed! So now the encroaching parvenus are attempting to alienate my children from me? How *could* you accept?"

"It was very kind of them. One can't refuse all their olive branches, Mother. I'll be able to pop in to see you now and then without upsetting your bridge evenings or your other engagements."

"If only you would learn to play bridge, Daisy. It's very awkward not being able to call on you to make up a table."

Having sedulously avoided learning the game, Daisy had no intention of starting now. "I'd never meet your high standards," she said. "I think my mind works the wrong way."

"You take after your father. He never did play well." This, by an inevitable progression, called to mind another of the late viscount's faults. "It's a great pity he didn't leave you better provided for, so that you would have no excuse to work."

Though she knew it was pointless, in defense of her father Daisy trotted out the old arguments. "You know he always assumed Gervaise would inherit Fairacres and give me a home and an allowance. And he was too shattered after Gervaise . . . afterwards to get around to making a new will at once. He was still comparatively young and healthy. He thought he had plenty of time."

"I can't think why he went and succumbed to the 'flu," the dowager fretted, as if her husband had deliberately died to inconvenience her. "If you only had the sense to get married, like Violet. . . ."

"As a matter of fact," Daisy said cautiously, "there's a man I want you to meet."

Her mother brightened. "Who is he?" she asked eagerly. "He'll be at your house-party, at Fairacres?"

"No, actually. . . ."

"I knew it. He's unsuitable!" she lamented. "Since you will insist on working, you're bound to mingle with *hoi polloi*. What is he? Some scruffy, penniless intellectual?

A wealthy upstart with pretensions? Oh, Daisy, not a *foreigner?*"

In comparison, a middle-class police detective just might come as a pleasant surprise, Daisy hoped. Let Mother worry for a few days. "You'll find out when you meet him," she said. "I was going to write and ask if this coming weekend would be convenient."

"Let me look in my diary. For you, yes, but I really cannot have a stranger staying in the house, especially if he's not one of us. Besides, it's quite impossible to entertain properly with only three indoor servants."

"He's booking at the Wedge and Beetle."

"Well, at least he has the decency not to thrust himself in where he's not wanted."

"Mother! I don't expect miracles of cordiality, but unless you promise to be polite, I shan't bring him. We'll get married quietly in a Registry Office and . . ."

"My daughter marry in a Registry Office? Over my dead body!"

"You wouldn't know about it until afterwards," Daisy pointed out. "Do be reasonable, Mother."

"Naturally I shall be polite," the dowager sniffed. "I trust I am never otherwise. I can only hope seeing the bounder among well-bred people of your own class will make you see sense."

Daisy bit her tongue to hold back a futile retort. "Yes, well, I'd better be getting back," she said. "I'll drop by again tomorrow. Oh, by the way, Phillip Petrie sends his best regards."

"Phillip? Is he at Fairacres? You'd do well to marry Phillip," her mother lamented. "The Petries are an excellent family.

"Phillip may be neither scruffy nor an intellectual but he hasn't a bean, and anyway, he's in love with someone else. Cheerio, Mother. See you tomorrow."

Phillip was in love, Daisy reflected as she made her way

back across the park, and he believed his beloved was in danger. Daisy could not help wondering whether he had unwittingly exaggerated Miss Arbuckle's peril, or altogether misunderstood the situation. On this peaceful June day, the notion of a band of murderous thugs marauding about the countryside was awfully hard to credit.

Still, he was afraid for his Gloria, and for some reason he had chosen Daisy to come to the rescue. She, in turn, wanted nothing more than to lay the burden on Alec's broad and admirably competent shoulders. That expedient being ruled out, she'd have to do her best without him.

She had set things in motion. With any luck, reinforcements would arrive tomorrow. In the meantime, she needed to prepare a plan of campaign.

"Maps," she said aloud. Her father had kept two inch to the mile Ordnance Survey maps of the county in the desk in his den. To judge by the lack of change in the parts of the house she had seen, they were very likely still in the same drawer. Ferreting them out would keep poor old Phillip occupied for a while.

Half-way back to the house, she saw him coming to meet her, very long-faced.

"Tom can't get away till noon tomorrow," he reported. "Some beastly court case. And Binkie was out seeing a client when I rang up. I sent him a wire."

"That will give us time to make plans," Daisy consoled him. "We need maps, and bicycles, and as I said, there may be places easier to explore on horseback. You told them all to bring riding togs, as well as asking Lucy to bring me some more clothes?"

"Yes, and I said to motor down, not take the train, so we'll have their cars, too."

"Good. But I've no idea what, if anything, Edgar has in the stables, so you'll have to check, and if there's nothing suitable, arrange to hire a couple of hacks when and if we need them. Or you could beg, borrow, or steal them from your people. Now that we're a duly constituted house-party, it won't matter if they know you're here. Is Geraldine back yet?"

"I saw the Vauxhall drive up. That's why I ducked out the back way to meet you," Phillip admitted sheepishly. "At least I don't have to worry about the mater. She's taking Fenella up to town for a few days."

Daisy laughed. "Ready to face any dragon for your damsel in distress," she said, "but not Cousin Geraldine or your mother? Tut, tut!"

8

As predicted, Cousin Geraldine was outraged to discover, on her return from a pleasant jaunt to Worcester, that her husband had committed her to a house-party. Daisy had made Phillip stay with her to share the brunt of her ladyship's displeasure. However, Geraldine was scrupulously, if stiffly, polite to them.

Later, Daisy squirmed when she overheard Geraldine berating Edgar for inviting a horde of rackety modern young people. Her guilt faded when she realized Edgar was not humbly excusing himself but burbling rhapsodically and with magnificent irrelevance about the hatching of a Dingy Skipper.

Erynnis tages, she gathered as she moved out of earshot, though not actually rare was usually found on chalky soils. She must remember to congratulate him at a suitable moment.

She managed to keep Phillip busy enough that evening to stop him brooding. Binkie rang up to say he and Lucy would arrive at Fairacres by tea-time the next day. Daisy was glad the reticent young man had 'phoned—not Lucy, who would have demanded explanations.

Shortly before they went to bed, Mr. Arbuckle telephoned to speak to Phillip. His arrangements for the ransom money were under way, Phillip reported in a whisper in the hallway outside Daisy's bedroom. Though he would not have the cash till the end of the week, he'd leave his secretary, who had stayed in London all along, to deal with that end of things. He himself hoped to be back in Malvern by Wednesday evening to receive any further messages from the kidnappers.

"The end of the week!" Phillip repeated in anguish. "Suppose the brutes demand the money sooner? They might think he wasn't going to pay up and take it out on Gloria."

"Bosh," Daisy said in a heartening voice, thinking fast and furiously. "They'll allow more time. Once she's dead, their chance of striking it rich is gone. They wouldn't be so stupid."

"They might hurt her."

For the first time a shiver of real apprehension ran down Daisy's spine. A glimpse of what it might be like to be utterly in the power of evil men flashed through her mind.

"The Yank's not stupid," she argued. "He guessed your father wouldn't be able to produce a large amount of cash on demand. He must realize it takes time to convert even securities into cash, especially as the certificates or what-not are in America, I presume."

"Oh yes, I hadn't thought of that."

"Besides, since they threatened dire revenge if he contacts the police, they must be watching him. They know he's doing what he can."

"Of course," Phillip said gratefully.

Bidding him good-night, Daisy could only hope she was right.

Tuesday! The thought brought a surge of drowsy happiness as warm as the sunbeam on Daisy's face. Tuesday lunch, Alec had said. If he could get away, to be sure, but it was no use anticipating bad luck.

Unlike many people, she had always enjoyed being awakened by the morning sun. Vi and Gervaise had been more than glad to let her have this east-facing bedroom. She had arranged the bed specially to catch the rays as often as possible, and it had not been moved.

Moved? she thought, sleepily confused.

Oh yes, years had passed and this room was no longer her own.

This room had nothing to do with Alec, in place or time. He was in London and she was back at Fairacres, where nothing had changed. She opened her eyes to see the sun pouring in at the open window between the pulled-back blue chintz curtains printed with meadow flowers, buttercups, ox-eye daisies, poppies, faded now. More faded than she remembered, but otherwise unchanged.

Perhaps Edgar and Geraldine could not afford to change things. She hadn't considered the possibility before, though these days everyone complained about death duties.

Edgar and Geraldine: still half dozing, she wondered what she was doing in their house, in her old bedroom, when she was supposed to be going out to lunch in town with Alec?

Suddenly remembering, Daisy sat bolt upright. Phillip's girl was being held by kidnappers. She shook her head in disbelief. Surely a dream . . . but it couldn't be, or she wouldn't be at Fairacres when she badly wanted to be in London.

She'd have to 'phone Alec. The trouble was, if she rang him at home, she would interrupt the bustle of his preparations for work and Belinda's for school. Resenting the disturbance, his mother would see it as further proof of Daisy's unsuitability for her son. Mrs. Fletcher no more approved mixing the classes than did the Dowager Lady Dalrymple.

Yet Daisy hated to telephone Alec at Scotland Yard. He was a busy man. She didn't want to disrupt his work or try his patience—or embarrass him before his colleagues and subordinates.

While she wondered which was the lesser of two evils,

a maid brought her early morning tea. Sipping it, she decided to ring up Alec's home. If he did not answer the 'phone himself, she wouldn't ask for him, just leave a brief message.

In the event, Belinda answered. "Sorry, Miss Dalrymple, Daddy's already left," she reported.

"Oh bother! He hasn't been called out of town, has he?"

"No. He said he had lots of work to do and he wanted to get an early start because of meeting you for lunch. So its no use me taking a message, is it? Because you'll see him first."

"I can't make it. I'll try to get hold of him at work, but just in case, will you tell him I'll 'phone this evening to explain?"

"All right." Her voice faded momentarily: "Coming, Gran. I've got to go, Miss Dalrymple. 'Bye."

" 'Bye, darling. See you soon."

Daisy held down the earpiece hook for a moment, realized Alec was probably en route from St. John's Wood to Whitehall, and reluctantly hung up. She went to join the others for breakfast.

Her telephone call to Scotland Yard later was equally fruitless. Alec and his sergeant, Tom Tring, had both been called out, though not, she was glad to hear, to the farthest ends of the kingdom. The police operator didn't know how long they would be gone. Would she like to speak to another officer?

"No, thanks," Daisy said hastily.

Very likely Alec was going to have to call off lunch anyway, a not unusual occurrence. He wouldn't arrive in Chelsea to find her missing.

All the same, she wished she had at least heard his voice. Though she had promised not to mention the kidnapping, she felt the very sound might give her confidence and encouragement in the task she had taken on.

The maps she and Phillip consulted last night had pointed out the magnitude of that task. Where was Gloria Arbuckle?

"She's not here? Where is she?" Alec demanded of Daisy's cool, faintly antagonistic house-mate. Though the tall, elegant Miss Fotheringay had softened towards him a trifle recently, she could not be described as approving. "Will she be back soon? We were to go out to lunch."

"She won't be back for lunch." Nothing so homely as a frown marred the smooth, expertly made-up face, framed by a sleek, dark bob, yet the amber eyes held a shade of anxiety. She appeared to come to a decision. "Actually, she's at Fairacres. Perhaps you'd better come in for a minute, Mr. Fletcher." With a languid gesture she waved him past her into the narrow hall, made narrower by a pair of large suitcases.

"At Fairacres? With her mother?"

"No, not at the Dower House, at Fairacres itself. Her old home. Here, read this." Miss Fotheringay picked up a yellow telegram from the hall table and handed it to him. "See what you make of it."

" 'Urgent emergency,' " Alec read with alarm. " 'Come Fairacres house-party pronto Binkie too bring riding togs and Daisy's clothes.' Signed 'Daisy,' but that's an odd way to word it if she wrote it. Why not *my* clothes'?"

"The combination of an urgent emergency with a house-party isn't exactly normal either, would you say?" drawled Miss Fotheringay. "I'll be damned if I can make head or tail of the business."

Alec tried not to wince too obviously at her language. He was all for women working if they chose to, but he was old-fashioned enough not to care for their swearing. "An urgent house-party does seem to be something of a contradiction in terms," he agreed dryly.

"The first two words echo the wire Phillip Petrie sent her, which took her haring down there in the first place, so I suspect he wrote or dictated it."

"Petrie? She went because he sent for her?" Alec firmly squashed a pang of jealousy. Daisy had often enough described the young man as an amiable ass. Socially he was of her class; intellectually a definite also-ran. "Judging by the baggage, you too are obeying the summons. You haven't telephoned for an explanation?"

"Binkie rang up last night to say we'd go. He spoke to Daisy, but the old dear's the strong, silent type. He didn't ask any questions. I tried 'phoning this morning, but the butler said both Daisy and Phillip were out and he didn't know when they'd be back. I've been too busy to keep buzzing down to the telephone box. I haven't the foggiest what clothes Daisy wants so I've just guessed." She waved at the bags. "Too, too maddening!"

"You don't know anything about this emergency, I take it?" He ran his hand through his hair as she shook her head with a rueful moue. "At least it appears to be Petrie's problem, not Daisy's."

"To start with, anyway. Knowing Daisy, whatever it is, she's taken it to heart. But where Binkie and I come in, I simply can't imagine. Of course, it may be some sort of lark, in which case I'll kill both of them. I've had to put off half a dozen clients."

"You're leaving now?" Alec took in her motoring dustcoat, fashionable as well as practical, and the veiled hat sitting on the hall table.

"As soon as Binkie arrives with the Alvis. His wire asked him to drive, not go down by train. Curiouser and curiouser, is it not?"

"It is. Dash it, I wish I could go with you, but I can't get away for at least a couple of days, quite possibly not till the weekend. Will you tell Daisy I'll telephone this evening? Lateish. I'll be working late."

"Right-o, Chief Inspector. Heaven knows what it's all about, but to tell the truth I'm quite glad to know you're hovering in the background."

"Even coppers have their uses," Alec said mildly, recalling past battles. "Don't let Daisy get into too much trouble if you can help it. I shan't hold you responsible, though. I know only too well how impossible it is to stop her once she has the bit between her teeth!"

"Riding togs," he brooded as he returned down the path to his little yellow Austin Seven. Of course all Daisy's set rode horses, practically from birth. Was it too late for him to learn?

Daisy might like to teach him, and Belinda.

What had she got herself into this time? What on earth sort of trouble could Phillip Petrie have landed himself in which would require not only her help but that of their mutual friends to extricate him?

And why disguise it as a house-party?

As the hour of the house-party's assembly approached, Geraldine asserted her right as nominal hostess and waited in the drawing-room to greet her guests. Daisy and Phillip couldn't very well hang about in the front hall to waylay them.

"They're bound to demand explanations right away," Daisy said in a low voice.

"Don't I know it! I'd have had a hard time with Tom yesterday if he hadn't been called away from the 'phone just in the nick. Lady Dalrymple's going to wonder what the deuce is going on."

"We'll just have to stand behind her and shake our heads madly. Lowecroft will think we're potty, but it's just too bad."

"He already does," Phillip averred.

Geraldine called for their attention. "Since I find myself

giving a house-party," she said a trifle acidly, "suppose you tell me something about my guests? Who are the Pearsons?"

"Madge was Lady Margaret Allinston," Daisy informed her. "She doesn't use her title because Tommy doesn't have one. She was at school with Lucy and me, but a year older, so we didn't know her awfully well. Then quite by chance she VAD'ed in the same military hospital in Malvern where I worked in the office, so I saw a lot of her."

"You worked in a hospital office? Mrs. Pearson was with a Voluntary Aid Detachment?" Geraldine seemed surprised, as if she had not realized many of today's bright young things had actually done their bit during the War.

"And Lucy was a Land Girl. She didn't mind the work so much, but she claims wearing that hideous uniform nearly killed her. She still has nightmares about finding herself on a dance floor in it."

"I was VAD."

"You can swap stories with Madge, then. She met Tommy in the hospital—he was pretty crocked up."

"Pearson was in our outfit," Phillip put in, "with Gervaise and me. He finished up a major."

"His family are Pearson, Pearson, Watts & Pearson, one of the top solicitors' firms in London, old-established and frightfully respectable." Daisy paused, suddenly wondering whether Tommy was too respectable and too legally-minded to be dragged into a scheme which involved concealing a crime from the police.

Geraldine interrupted her fruitless speculation. "I'm glad to learn you have friends in respectable professions," she said austerely. "You were at school with Miss Fotheringay, were you not? And now you share lodgings, in *Chelsea.*" Her tone of voice equated residence in that district with the worst excesses of Bohemia.

"Yes. She's a photographer. Her grandfather is the Earl of Haverhill." A good splodge of blue blood nicely balanced out the artistic profession, Daisy hoped. She was about to move on to Binkie's pedigree when voices and footsteps approached the drawing-room.

Lowecroft appeared on the threshold. "Mr. and Mrs. Pearson, my lady."

Geraldine rose and moved towards the door. Daisy and Phillip hung back behind her. They shook their heads vigorously and Daisy put a finger to her lips as Madge and Tommy entered the room.

Tommy, bespectacled, brown-haired, and stocky, looked startled and rather bewildered. Madge, whose froth of blond curls and effervescent manner often misled people into taking her for a bubble-head, was quicker on the uptake. She deftly steered her husband through conventional greetings.

"Explain later," Daisy hissed at the first opportunity.

She and Phillip went through the same pantomime when Lucy and Binkie arrived, a few minutes later. They both caught on at once.

Lowecroft's face simply grew stiffer and more wooden. "Tea, my lady?" he enquired.

"Yes, on the terrace, please, and inform Lord Dalrymple that our guests are here."

Edgar's presence at afternoon tea to some extent relieved the frustration of the delay in clarifying matters. He discoursed with his usual knowledgeable enthusiasm on the annual migration from Africa of *Vanessa cardui,* the Painted Lady butterfly. Since Geraldine kept casting sidelong, scandalized glances at Lucy's skillfully painted face, everyone but she and Edgar was in a state of barely repressed hilarity.

Even Phillip relaxed, once he realized what the joke was. Daisy was glad to see his lips twitch. His anxiety returned soon enough when Edgar and Geraldine went into the house. The four newcomers sat up and looked expectant.

"Right-o," said Lucy, "this Painted Lady is simply dying to hear what's up. Let's have it. Oh, before I forget, darling, your tame copper's going to 'phone this evening."

Phillip blenched. "Chief Inspector Fletcher? You haven't told him what's happened, have you?"

"I don't *know* what's happened. He popped round to take Daisy out to lunch and found her gone—frightfully bad form, darling," she added in a severe aside to Daisy.

"I tried to get hold of him."

"Well, I was on the point of leaving, too, and it seemed only decent to show him the wire. I think it rather put the wind up him. Anyway, he's going to ring up tonight to make sure everything's all right."

Turning to Daisy, Phillip said urgently, "You won't tell him?"

"I still think it would be best, but I promised."

"Gosh, this gets more and more mysterious." Madge's eyes sparkled with excitement. "Too, too divine. Do tell."

"First," said Daisy, "what we tell you must go no further. Absolute secrecy is essential."

Tommy frowned. "I don't like the sound of this," he said bluntly, taking off his horn-rimmed glasses and polishing them with his handkerchief. "I hope I know you both well enough to be sure you wouldn't do anything you believed morally wrong, but I have to consider the legal aspect, too, don't y'know. You must admit keeping secrets from the police sounds downright fishy."

"What piffle, darling!" Madge's merry laugh rang out. "It was just the other day you were grumbling like billy-o about some nosy policeman who wanted information you regarded as confidential. Don't be an old stick-in-the-mud."

"That was a matter of privileged communication between client and solicitor, my pet, not to be confused with aiding and abetting, let alone committing . . ."

"This is a matter of life and death!" burst forth from Phillip.

"It could be," Daisy confirmed with more caution. "At least I can promise you we're trying to foil a crime, not commit one. I can't say more unless I have your word to keep mum. If you don't feel able to give it, Tommy, then we must apologize for dragging you all the way here for nothing."

"Count me in," Binkie said tersely.

"I'm with you." Lucy covered a delicate yawn with a well-manicured hand. "As long as it isn't too frightfully fatiguing."

"I'll help as much as I can." Madge's rosy cheeks grew pinker. "I can't ride a horse, though, I'm afraid. You see, I'm preggy."

"Darling, how marvellous," cried Daisy, jumping up to kiss her.

"Congratulations, darling," Lucy said dryly, "or do you prefer condolences?"

"Actually, we're rather pleased," Madge admitted, "aren't we, pet?"

Daisy and Lucy both turned to look at Tommy. He was quite pink-faced himself, self-consciously proud.

"Time to bring another little solicitor into the world," he said half mockingly, then sighed. "Right-ho, I'll rally round. Can't let the side down, don't y'know. Unless your scheme is actually criminal, I'll lend a hand."

"Spiffing!" said Daisy, and got down to brass tacks.

Dinner was over and the long Summer Time evening waned. Swifts swooped over the gardens, wreaking devastation on the clouds of midges. All her plans laid and approved by the others, Daisy was glad to relax at last. In the twilight on the terrace, chaffing about indifferent subjects since her cousins were there, she could almost pretend nothing had changed since she was a girl.

Lowecroft came out of the house. "Telephone call for Miss Dalrymple. A Mr. Fletcher, miss."

"The Drinker!" cried Edgar. Before Daisy could object to his casting utterly unwarranted aspersions on Alec, he seized his butterfly net, never far from his side, and dashed down the steps to the lawn. The spaniel, Pepper, loped after him. *"Philudoria potatoria,"* came floating back.

Daisy hurried in to the telephone. "Alec?"

"Hello, Daisy." He sounded tired. "I hope I'm not interrupting anything."

"Oh no. We were just sitting out on the terrace. I'm glad you rang. I'm so sorry I didn't manage to let you know in time about lunch."

"You tried. I take it I wasn't abandoned for a common or garden house-party?"

"As though I would!"

"You're not in trouble, are you?"

"No, honestly."

"Petrie is?"

She hesitated. "Not exactly," she said. Strictly speaking it was the Arbuckles who were in the soup.

"Daisy, I know how far you'll go to help someone you've taken under your wing. Don't go and land yourself in a hole trying to pull him out."

"It's nothing like that."

"What is it? Why don't you tell me? Perhaps I can advise, if not help."

"I'd like to tell you, Alec, but I can't."

"Can't, or won't?"

"Mustn't. Don't worry, I shan't do anything stupid." Time to change the subject. "It feels frightfully peculiar staying at Fairacres as a guest." She went on to describe the eerie effect of the changed residents and the unchanged furnishings. "I'll show you around this weekend," she finished. "I'm sure Edgar won't mind. You can come, can't you?"

"You still want me to?"

"Of course! I just wish you were here now," Daisy said with fervour.

"I'll be there. The Super's promised to cope without me

even if a second Guy Fawkes blows up the Houses of Parliament. Belinda sends her love."

"Give her mine. Good-night, Alec."

"Good-night, love. Sweet dreams."

Daisy held the earpiece to her ear for several moments after the click of Alec hanging up came over the wire. He had called her 'love,' even though she could tell from his voice that he was hurt by her refusal to confide in him.

If Gloria was not free—rescued or ransomed—by the weekend, she would insist on telling him everything.

9

The first phase of Daisy's plan was for her and Phillip to enquire after strangers in the villages where they were known and could therefore expect people to talk to them. She had decided they would be less conspicuous—in case the kidnappers were on the watch—if they bicycled rather than motored. She and Binkie were to circle around Fairacres, Phillip and Lucy around Malvern Grange, where he was better known. All four were to meet for a picnic lunch in a copse on the boundary between the two.

Though Madge's doctor had banned only horseback riding, Tommy absolutely forbade her to bicycle. Daisy therefore sent them in their Lagonda to investigate some villages rather further out, beyond convenient cycling distance.

At that distance, she hoped, they were unlikely to be connected with the Fairacres party, should the villains be aware of Mr. Arbuckle's visit to Phillip. Strangers themselves, they would be regarded with some suspicion if they made direct enquiries, but they could ask whether many visitors came that way.

"Don't ask about deserted cottages, though," Daisy said. "It's a pity, but that's the sort of thing which might get back to the kidnappers."

Tommy nodded. " 'Someone's interested in that old place you're staying,' that sort of thing. We'll steer clear."

They all set off. As soon as the others were out of earshot, Daisy confided to Binkie, "I rather doubt this search is any use, but I can't think what else to do."

"Pretty hopeless," he confirmed tersely.

Having hoped for encouragement, Daisy consoled herself with a reminder of his generally pessimistic outlook on life.

"Still," she said, as much to herself as to him, "I can't really believe Miss Arbuckle is in danger of anything worse than a few days of discomfort."

"Regular brutes, these American gangsters," said Binkie. "Wouldn't put anything past 'em."

Daisy turned her head to glare at him. She wobbled as her bicycle wheel went over a stone, and thereafter concentrated on where she was going.

It was a beautiful morning for a ride. Garlands of pale pink roses and yellow honeysuckle in the hedges perfumed the air. Foxgloves, campion red and white, and yellow toad-flax flourished on banks and verges. A cock pheasant scurried down the road ahead of them for a few yards before diving beneath a gate. Small birds warbled, whistled, and twittered.

Impossible to envisage a girl locked up in a dingy room and in fear of her life!

Ahead of Daisy and Binkie a tower, stone horizontally striped with red brick, protruded above a knot of green trees. Like many local villages, Morton Green was dominated by its church, built on a slight rise. The village straggled around its namesake green. Cottages of brick with lichened tile roofs, whitewashed stucco with slate, red sandstone, yellow Cotswold stone, or half-timbering, mingled higgledy-piggledy.

The largest building was the Wedge and Beetle Inn, four-square, whitewashed, with scarlet geraniums in window-boxes. Daisy decided to tackle it first. The bar was not open yet, but she had an excuse for enquiries.

She and Binkie leant their bikes against the wall and

stepped through the open door out of the sunshine into the dimness of the lobby.

"Hullo, there!" Binkie called.

Mrs. Dennie, the landlord's wife, came bustling through from the back. "Why, if it's not Miss Dalrymple." She gave Binkie a curious look. "Come down for a visit, have you, miss? What can I do for you?"

"Good-morning, Mrs. Dennie. A friend of mine mentioned that he hoped to stay here. I just wondered whether you had room for him, whether he'd made a reservation."

"We've got a couple of fishermen—anglers they likes to be called, bless their hearts—and a young pair, honeymooners by our reckoning, the way they spoon, if you'll pardon the expression. The other room, well, there's casuals dropping in. The odd commercial, like, and the touring season's well under way already this year, what with the weather we've been having."

"Isn't it marvellous?"

"Not for the farmers, miss, but it don't hurt our business, I must say."

"People like to get out of town when it's hot. Do you have many Londoners?"

"Can't say we do, miss, not being a beauty spot like some. Mostly from Birmingham way. No, I don't believe as we've had a Londoner in the house, nor yet in the bar even."

"Nor many foreigners, I expect."

Mrs. Dennie laughed heartily at the notion of foreigners patronising her modest establishment. "This friend of yours, miss," she went on, "what's the name? I'll check and see if he's booked."

"Fletcher, for this weekend."

Alec had a room reserved for both Friday and Saturday nights. "Seeing he's a friend of yourn, miss," said Mrs. Dennie, "I'll move him to the back corner room. It's bigger and quieter, not being over the public bar."

Daisy thanked her, enquired after her family, and pre-
ceded Binkie back out into the sunshine. He hadn't said a
word after his halloo. An inarticulate companion was useful
in the circumstances, Daisy decided. Pessimist he might be,
but at least he didn't lengthen the already-chatty interrogation.

Mrs. Dennie's chatter was nothing to what Daisy met
with in the tiny, overflowing shop they called at next.

POST OFFICE, NEWSAGENT, TOBACCONIST, AND
SWEETS proclaimed the sign over the door. Miss Hibbert
had once sold pennyworths of dolly-mixture and bull's-eyes
to Daisy and Gervaise. Older and greyer now, she happened
to have seen one of Daisy's articles in *Town and Country,*
and she was dying to hear about her writing career. In exchange, she passed on a vast quantity of village gossip.

Interrupted by two or three customers, half an hour
passed before Daisy and Binkie escaped with the information they sought: neither Cockneys nor Americans had
bought tobacco or newspapers from Miss Hibbert, not recently. There had been a touring couple last year, or was it
the year before, who might have been American. Gentlemen
from London staying at Fairacres occasionally popped in
for cigarettes. And East Enders came down from London
for the hop-picking in August, of course, though not, Miss
Hibbert thought, in such swarms as went to Kent.

Dismayed, Daisy wondered if she had been too optimistic
in believing the kidnappers would not know the country.
She had forgotten the hop-pickers. It dawned on her, too,
that some of the Cockneys among the wounded soldiers in
the Malvern hospitals during and after the War might well
have roamed the countryside while convalescing.

"Blast!" she said, mounting her bicycle.

"You didn't expect anything so close to where Phillip
was dumped," Binkie reminded her.

She decided not to reveal her fresh qualms. "No, but
one always hopes," she said vaguely. "It would have been

so convenient. Do you think we ought to try the general store, too? They could have gone in for supplies."

"Might as well," grunted Binkie.

The general store, which purveyed flour and baking-pans, cheese and mousetraps with equal enthusiasm, provided as little information at almost as great a length. The day was already growing hot when Daisy and Binkie rode out of Morton Green. They were glad to plunge into the green shade of Bellman's Wood, just beyond the village.

"Don't we explore?" Binkie asked as they pedalled along the lane.

"No, not here. I know every inch of this wood. It belongs to one of the Fairacres farms, actually. There are plenty of squirrels and woodpeckers but no buildings, deserted or otherwise. At least, there could be something recently built, but what Phillip described sounded like an ancient cottage."

All too soon they left the shade of the trees. A motor-car passed them, raising clouds of dust. By the time they had pursued their fruitless enquiries in the next two villages, Daisy felt as if she had cycled across the Sahara, and the afternoon was yet to come.

Meeting the others for their picnic by the stream in Boundary Copse, she dismounted on leaden legs.

"I'm out of form," she confessed ruefully to a maddeningly cool-looking Lucy. "Maybe one never forgets how to ride a bicycle, having once learnt, but it must use different muscles from walking, and mine are telling me they're out of practice."

"We got here half an hour ago, darling, and I've had my feet in the water. Try it, it helps. No luck, I take it?"

"No. You?" Daisy asked, taking off her shoes.

"Not a bite. Phillip's frightfully pipped, the poor old fish."

Daisy glanced at Phillip, who was helping Binkie unpack the picnic from the bicycle bags. She sighed. Much as her thighs cried out for the afternoon off, she couldn't let him down. Sitting on the grassy bank with her feet dangling in the lukewarm stream, she dipped her hankie in the water and wiped her face.

Ginger-beer and sandwiches revived her somewhat, but better still was the thin layer of clouds which came up to cover the sky. It was still hot, but at least the sun would not blaze down on her head. A breeze rose as they left the shelter of the copse, cooling if not cool. With renewed vigour she and Binkie set off for the next village on their list.

The afternoon's circuit was wider flung than the morning's. There were more villages, and Daisy was less well known if recognized at all. This proved a mixed blessing.

Each interview was shorter, because less encumbered with gossip. On the other hand, it was more difficult to find an opening for her questions, and they had to purchase something at each stop as an excuse to ask. The saddlebags emptied of food were soon packed with cigarettes and pipe tobacco, fast-melting chocolate bars, and miscellaneous odds and ends.

Of useful information they collected none.

Daisy flagged before they finished the list. "It's tea-time," she pointed out to Binkie, "and very likely the shops in the next place will be closed before we get there anyway."

"You want to head back to Fairacres?"

"If we don't," she said frankly, "you may have to carry me home, and my bike too."

Binkie grinned. "Dashed if I don't think we've done our duty for the day. Wouldn't be surprised if Lucy's dragged Phil home by now."

They were the first back, but only by a few minutes. Geraldine had people to tea on the terrace. The weary searchers, four of them far too grimy to join the party, collapsed on the grass under a wide-spreading chestnut. Ernest, obviously bemused by the curious habits of the gentry who exhausted themselves for fun, brought them tea.

All reported equal lack of results. Five pairs of eyes turned to Daisy.

"It's hopeless, isn't it?" Phillip blurted out.

Daisy rallied herself. "Not at all, old dear. We've barely scratched the surface. Only I think tomorrow we'd better each go out on our own—is that grammatical? You know what I mean. We'll cover much more ground that way, and it'll be ground where Phil and I have no advantage. Tommy and Madge will go together, of course. You made it about half-way round your circle?"

"Just about," Tommy confirmed, "but Madge is finding it pretty tiring even by car don't y'know. I think she ought to stay behind tomorrow."

"Oh no," cried Madge, "I'll be perfectly all right after a night's sleep. You must admit, Tommy, people talk more to me than to you, and I want to do my bit."

"You can," Daisy said quickly, "without stirring a step. I've been thinking," she lied, "we ought to have someone here to sort of coordinate things. Each of us will ring up periodically, so if someone finds out something the others can all be told right away. We'll work out some kind of code."

"Good tactics," said Tommy with a grateful glance. "Definitely the best use of available troops."

"I hate to be a wet blanket," Lucy drawled, "but while people talk to Tommy, if less readily than to Madge, is anyone going to say a word to Binkie? Did you open your mouth to anyone but Daisy today, darling?"

"No," Binkie confessed, blushing.

Daisy hurried to rescue the embarrassed young man. "In any case, Lucy, you don't look at all the sort who'd be buzzing about on a bicycle without a man at your side. Binkie had better escort you. His moment will come when we find Miss Arbuckle and have to storm the castle, if we decide that's the best thing to do. Pass the cake, Madge, I'm starving."

Well fortified with Victoria sponge and Shrewsbury biscuits, Daisy spent the next couple of hours poring over maps and plotting new courses for the morrow. Knowing what had been covered today, she was dismayed to see how long it was going to take to survey even a ten-mile-radius circle. Before she went up to bathe and change, she cornered Phillip.

"You know, old thing," she said, "we'll find Gloria, but I'm dead certain the police could find her sooner. I do wish you'd let me consult Alec."

Phillip stubbornly shook his head. "They'd find out."

"With the local chaps, I expect so, but Alec will know how to keep things hushed up."

"Fletcher's a good chap," he said unexpectedly. "If I hadn't given Arbuckle my word, I'd consider putting it to him as a hyp . . . hypno . . . what's the dashed word I want?"

"Hypothetical case?"

"That's it. But I can't. You'd have to persuade Arbuckle. He should be in touch," Phillip added, his brow creased with worry. "You don't suppose he's having trouble collecting the money?"

"It just takes time," Daisy soothed him. "He'd have let you know if there was any difficulty."

Phillip accepted that, and Daisy went off to take her long-overdue bath.

After dinner she went over the next day's plans with the others. Then they joined her cousins in the drawing-room, the terrace being ruled out by Geraldine, who was sure it was about to rain. Somnolent after an excess of exercise, they were settling down to a quiet evening when Ernest appeared.

"Telephone, Mr. Petrie, sir."

Phillip dashed off, to return a few moments later and beckon urgently to Daisy.

Joining him, she asked in a low voice, "Mr. Arbuckle?"

"Yes. He's back in Malvern and he wants to come over. Is that all right? He's holding the line." Phillip started back to the telephone in the front hall and Daisy followed.

"Can't we go there?" she proposed.

"He doesn't want anyone to see me with him while Gloria's supposed to be away visiting friends."

"Oh yes, I forgot. He's right, people would talk. We must see him, and it's less conspicuous for him to come here."

"It's frightful cheek to invite him."

"I'll think of something to tell Geraldine."

"She thinks he ran me off the road."

"Right-o, how's this: You discovered he has pull with a publisher—a big investment or something—so you invited him to meet me. That will give us an excuse to talk to him privately, too. Warn him," she advised as Phillip picked up the telephone.

He spoke briefly to Arbuckle, then hung up. "He'll be here in half an hour."

"I'll ask Edgar if we can use his den. That will circumvent Geraldine nicely."

As they reached the drawing-room, Edgar was saying, "And then I spotted a Chinese character."

Startled, Daisy wondered if a Chinaman had somehow got mixed up in the kidnapping. Could "the Yank" be a deliberately misleading nickname? Didn't Chinese criminals favour the white slave trade rather than abductions for ransom?

"Cilix glaucata, you know," Edgar continued. "At rest, with its wings folded, the adult moth looks remarkably like a bird dropping."

"Really, Edgar!" exclaimed Geraldine.

Phillip chose that moment to announce, "I say, that was

Arbuckle on the 'phone. The American chappie, you remember, Lady Dalrymple?"

"Oh yes. Edgar, I wish you would not . . ."

"I discovered he's a publisher, or has influence in a publishing company, or something of the sort. Investments, what? So it seemed a good idea to introduce him to Daisy."

". . . discuss the revolting habits of your insects . . ."

"So I've asked him to pop over this evening. I hope you don't mind."

". . . in mixed company. By all means, Mr. Petrie. It's really most improper."

"There's nothing improper about it," Edgar argued. "It's a matter of scientific observation."

"Would you mind if we used your den, sir? Business matter, and all that."

Edgar waved permission. "Don't you see, dear, one must be able to describe the appearance accurately but in layman's language. And the Chinese Character looks like a bird dropping." He repeated the phrase with a defiant air. "Camouflage, you see."

"Spiffing," said Daisy, stifling a giggle as she caught Lucy's sardonic eye. "We'll wait for him there so as not to disturb you all when he arrives."

She hustled Phillip out before Geraldine's attention left the indecorous behaviour of moths and moved to the indecorous behaviour of a guest who invited a guest of his own.

They went to the den. Daisy, her legs still tired from bicycling, flopped into one of the vast leather-covered chairs. Phillip was too restless to relax. He went out again to pace the front hall.

Daisy's eyelids were drooping when he stuck his head back in a few minutes later to say, "I'm going to walk down the drive to meet him."

Shaking herself awake, Daisy set her mind to marshalling her arguments for calling in the police. Her thoughts on

Alec, she started wondering if her mother was going to treat him with the sort of icy politeness which was in effect a form of insult. That reminded her that she'd promised to pop in to see the dowager today and hadn't.

"Oh blast!" she said aloud.

"Pardon me?"

The American voice sounded infinitely weary. Daisy looked round. Arbuckle was not at all what she had expected of an American millionaire, that is large, overfed, and exuding a slightly false bonhomie.

About her own height, he was lean to the point of boniness. She guessed he had lost weight recently, for his charcoal suit, though of unmistakable Savile Row cut, hung on him as on a scarecrow. His long, gaunt face had a greyish cast to match his receding hair.

Mr. Arbuckle, she realized with a rush of sympathy, had no faith in his daughter's safety.

His desolate eyes brought home to her with a jolt that she and her friends were not engaged for fun in a treasure-hunt with which she was already rather bored. Their efforts might mean the difference between life and death.

10

"Well now," said Arbuckle, shaking Daisy's hand, "if this isn't mighty kind of you, ma'am. Petrie's explained to me what you're trying to do for my little girl. He tells me he has absolute faith in your discretion, yours and your friends'." The doubt expressed by his choice of words was echoed in his tone.

"We've all promised not to let the cat out of the bag, Mr. Arbuckle, and we're frightfully careful with our enquiries. I think you'd better meet the others—but later, if you feel up to it. Do sit down, won't you?"

A sigh escaped him as he sank gratefully into one of the big chairs.

Phillip leant against the mantelpiece, one hand in his trouser pocket. Despite the casual pose, Daisy saw he still had the jim-jams.

"We really are careful, sir," he said. "Daisy—Miss Dalrymple—has worked it all out."

"How do you mean?"

"I came up with ways to ask questions that sound like casual chit-chat. Local people aren't at all likely to gossip with Cockneys or Americans, anyway. They look on people from the other side of the Malvern Hills as practically foreigners."

"You folks can honestly tell the difference?"

"With Cockneys, certainly, if not with Hereforders."

"Waal, I guess a Middle Westerner like me knows a

Texan from a New Yorker, so why not? Say, Miss Dalrymple, you figure you guys have a real chance of finding Gloria?"

"A chance. The police would have a much better chance. Won't you let . . . ?"

"No dice," said Arbuckle with grim determination.

"I was going to say, at least let me consult a friend of mine who's a detective at Scotland Yard. Mr. Fletcher's discreet and absolutely trustworthy."

"Abso-bally-lutely," Phillip confirmed. "Besides, we could tell him it's a hypo . . . what was that word, Daisy?"

"Hypothetical."

"It's no go." Arbuckle was adamant. "You just don't unnerstand how things are back home. Kidnapping's by way of getting to be big business, see, like bootlegging, and Detroit where I come from's one of the places it's biggest. There's lots of lucre floating around on account of the automobile business."

He leant towards Daisy, hands on his knees, and asked her earnestly, "Now why do folks buy an automobile when they've always been contented with a horse and buggy? Because they see other people enjoy owning one. And why do folks do just exactly what kidnappers tell 'em? Because they see what happens to other people's loved ones if they don't. A kidnapper not doing what he's threatened to is like an auto not doing what the manufacturer's promised it will. Bad for business."

"Yes, I see that," Daisy said slowly. She had a feeling there was a flaw in the argument somewhere, but she couldn't quite pinpoint it. Alec would have seen it.

"So, they tell me 'no cops,' no cops it is. After Gloria's safe, now that's a whole different ball game. You can call in your Scotland Yard buddy then. What I want," Arbuckle snarled, "is I want to see the sons of bitches put away in the hoosegow for life."

"Oh, I say!" Phillip protested.

"If you'll pardon the expression, ma'am."

Daisy indicated that she considered a certain amount of heat was justified in the circumstances. "I hope you haven't had too much trouble coming up with the ransom money," she said.

"The bank will have gotten it for me by Friday. I'll have to go to Lunnon to pick it up."

"Don't want to leave anything to chance," Phillip put in.

"That's right, son. It's a heck of a lot of dough, though it won't bankrupt me by a long ways, no sirree. Not that I wouldn't bankrupt myself for my girl, Miss Dalrymple," he added earnestly. "But it makes me think they know what they're up to and aren't going to demand delivery before I've had time to round up the cash."

"That's a relief. We have at least a couple of days to go on searching for Gloria. Unless you want to call off the bloodhounds, Mr. Arbuckle?"

His brow wrinkled in thought. "No, I guess it sounds like you can't do any harm. If you came through with the goods, if you found where she's at, why then I'd sure have to think again about bringing in the troopers."

"We'll do our best," Daisy promised. "Would you like to come and meet the others now?"

"I surely would like to shake those folks by the hand."

"You'll have to be careful what you say," she warned. "My cousins, Lord and Lady Dalrymple, think we're just a house-party."

Arbuckle chuckled. "Petrie tells me I'm to pose as the guy who ran him off the road, come to make amends."

"I'm sorry, sir," said Phillip, flushing. "It seemed easiest since that's what Lady Dalrymple guessed."

"That's okay, son. I figure I owe you a new auto if yours isn't found in one piece."

Phillip's face darkened to crimson. He opened his mouth but nothing came out.

Daisy had never seen him at such a loss. "Gosh, that's

jolly generous of you, Mr. Arbuckle," she said for him. "Did Phillip explain that you're also posing as a partner in a firm of publishers dying to publish my work?"

"Sure thing." Arbuckle grinned at her. "Just tell me what magazine you want to write for, ma'am, and I'll buy it up."

She laughed. "How about the *Saturday Evening Post?*"

"Now that could be a mite difficult to purchase outright, but if shares are traded on Wall Street, I'll buy enough to have a say in the business."

"I didn't mean it!"

"I did. No one can say Caleb P. Arbuckle ever forgot a favour, and you couldn't do me a bigger one than trying to help my Gloria." His face sagged and his shoulders slumped. "My poor little girl," he said softly.

Daisy decided it was not the moment to argue about the *Saturday Evening Post* and wanting to sell one's work on its merits. "Let's go to the drawing-room and we'll introduce you to the others," she suggested.

His social savoir-faire once more in evidence, Phillip presented the American to Geraldine.

"How do you do, Mr. Arbuckle," she said with a stiff nod.

"Howdy-do, Lady Dalrymple. It's real kind of you to let me do my little bit of business with my young friend here in your beautiful house. I want to apologize for gate-crashing, ma'am, and me not even in my tuxedo."

Geraldine thawed slightly. "What quaint terms you Americans use. Gate-crashing is self-explanatory, I suppose. A tuxedo is a dinner jacket?"

"Sure is. I've been in Lunnon and I didn't have time this evening to change."

"Have you dined, Mr. Arbuckle?"

"Yes, I thank you, ma'am. I grabbed a bite on the train."

At Daisy's side, Lucy murmured, "Unorthodox vocabulary, darling, but acceptable manners."

"I rather like him."

"I was afraid he might turn out to be an absolute bounder. Too, too ghastly to discover we'd rescued some tawdry parvenu shopgirl."

"Not likely. Phillip's no more likely to excuse vulgarity than you are."

Lucy raised meticulously plucked eyebrows and turned an attentive gaze on Phillip, hovering anxiously nearby as Geraldine introduced Arbuckle to Edgar. "Aha," she said, "so that's how it is? Don't tell me Phillip has found his soul-mate!"

"Found," Daisy admitted, "and lost."

"That does add a certain piquancy to the situation."

"Let's just hope he finds her again. Don't tell anyone else, darling. His people don't know yet."

"My lips are sealed. By the way, that reminds me, Binkie says your tame 'tec is coming to stay in the village this weekend." Lucy's tone was languid but her eyebrows rose again in a shrewdly enquiring look.

Daisy's cheeks grew hot. "Yes, he's coming down." She tried to sound casual. "I'd promised to support Phil when he introduces the Arbuckles to his parents, and it seemed a good moment for Mother to meet Alec."

"Cupid's been busy, I see." Lucy sighed. "Perhaps it's about time I proposed to Binkie. The poor prune isn't likely to find the words to do the job. The best I can hope for is that your example will inspire him to utter, 'What about it, old girl?' "

"Alec hasn't proposed."

"He will. Isn't it going to be a bit awkward, his landing in the middle of all this? Our American friend won't be frightfully happy to see a full-blown Detective Chief Inspector on the doorstep."

"With any luck it will all be over by the weekend," Daisy said hopefully. "Mr. Arbuckle's fetching the ransom from town on Friday. If we haven't found Gloria by then, it'll be too late."

Phillip brought Arbuckle over to introduce him to Lucy. In a low voice, the American expressed his gratitude, sincere but not fulsome, for her assistance. Probably the sternest critic present, she appeared to continue to find his manners acceptable.

Daisy would have liked to regard it as a good omen for his reception by Phillip's parents. The Petries, however, were liable to be rather more exacting when informed that Caleb P. Arbuckle was to become a relation by marriage.

But that was jumping the gun. First catch your hare, as someone or other had said. Until Gloria was safe, there was no sense worrying about how Phillip's family would receive her and her father.

A few minutes later, after meeting the Pearsons and Binkie, Mr. Arbuckle sought Daisy out. "Say, Miss Dalrymple," he said, "could we have a quiet word?"

"Of course." Praying that he wasn't going to expect an optimistic estimate of their chances of finding Gloria, she led the way to a massive Victorian sofa relegated to an obscure corner of the room.

Sitting down beside her with an irresolute air, he hesitated a moment, then embarked upon a subject Daisy was sure was not on the top of his mind.

"Your cousin—Lord Dalrymple's your cousin, right?—he's a swell guy. I wasn't too sure at first. He kept talking about a red-necked footman, so I figured he was having trouble with a hayseed lackey. 'Red-neck' is what Southerners call farm labourers, see, and I've heard a lot about the servant problem since I've been over here, though it's usually the ladies complaining."

"Endlessly," Daisy agreed, "but I bet Edgar was talking about a moth, wasn't he?"

"Or a butterfly, I couldn't say for sure. Something that lays eggs that turn into caterpillars. He knew the Latin name right off. Me, I like a guy with a real good grasp of his subject, even if it's just bugs. That's one of the things I like about young Petrie."

"Really?" Daisy didn't want to queer Phillip's pitch, but if Arbuckle was labouring under the delusion that he was a stock market wizard, it might be better to disillusion him before it was too late. "Actually, I don't think he's frightfully keen on stocks and shares," she said with caution.

"Jeez no! I wouldn't trust him to buy me a hundred bucks worth of blue chips! That's *my* line. It's carburetors and radiators I'm talking about. Petrie has a real good practical know-how when it comes to the innards of an automobile—considering all his disadvantages."

"Disadvantages?" Daisy queried still more cautiously, wondering what a blue chip was.

"That swank family of his that thinks it's beneath a lord's son to meddle with mechanics," said Arbuckle with considerable heat. "Pardon me, ma'am, I guess I shouldn't talk that way to a lord's daughter."

"No, it's all right. My mother feels the same way about my writing, or working at all. As a matter of fact, Phillip told me just the other day that he wants to leave the City and have a go at something to do with motors. Anything to do with motors."

"Does he now? That's real interesting! I'm sure glad you told me that, Miss Dalrymple. Say, listen, I've been wanting to ask you something. I know you're a mighty good friend of young Phillip's and I hope you won't take offence if I've gotten hold of the wrong darned end of the stick."

"Ask away," said Daisy, dying of curiosity and throwing caution to the winds. "I shan't take offence and I'll answer if I can."

Arbuckle patted her hand. "It's like this, see. It seems to me Petrie's taken a shine to my girl. You don't mind?" he asked anxiously.

"Phillip and I are *friends*," she assured him, "practically since our cradles."

"Waal, that's a relief, I don't mind telling you. I wouldn't want Gloria pinching your boyfriend, specially now I've met you. Now, I've been a mite puzzled, not knowing just how things are done in your country, and not being able to ask the boy. Just let me ask you this: Him inviting Gloria and me to meet his folks this weekend, does that mean he's decided he wants to get hitched?"

"It does. You wouldn't mind your daughter marrying into a 'swank' family?"

"Miss Dalrymple," Arbuckle said passionately, "if I get my girl back safe and sound, she can marry the local ditch-digger if that's what she wants."

"Or the local motor mechanic?" Daisy asked. "Phillip said he'd mentioned he's not in line for the title or estate, and a very modest allowance is all he can expect from his family."

"Heck, if Honourable's good enough for Gloria, it's good enough for me, and even with the ransom paid, I've enough to support them in style. But it's my impression of the boy—correct me here if I'm wrong—that he'd rather earn his keep."

"He told me he hoped you'd find him a technical job, if Miss Arbuckle accepted him."

"If and when he marries Gloria, my notion is to make him my technical adviser."

"That would suit Phillip down to the ground!" Daisy knit her brows, struck by a sudden thought. "But what about the chap who advises you now? He'd be out of a job. Could he have foreseen it?"

"Don't you worry about him, Miss Dalrymple. I'd never fire a trusted longtime employee for no fault of his own. Crawford's been with me ten years, and I've him to thank for a good part of what I own today. It'll be easy enough to find him something else to do for the same salary."

Daisy pursued her thought. "What about people you've sacked for good cause? Phillip told me you haven't any enemies, but I should think you must have made one or two."

Arbuckle cast a shamefaced glance at Phillip, who was patiently submitting to one of Edgar's lectures on the far side of the room. A fortuitous lull in everyone else's conversations allowed his lordship's wistful words to float across. "The other evening I nearly captured a small elephant. Pink, you know, with some yellow, and really quite pretty."

Noticing Arbuckle's scandalized face, Daisy said, "It's all right, Edgar isn't a dipsomaniac. I'm sure it's another moth or butterfly."

"Oh, sure. By golly, he had me worried for a minute there. Though come to think of it, why shouldn't a lord be a lush same as any other guy? Well, like you were saying, ma'am, I haven't got where I am without making an enemy or two. I guess I didn't want Petrie to think Gloria's poppa was the kinda guy to go round treading on people's toes for kicks."

"Are you?" Daisy ventured to ask.

"I am not," he said emphatically. "But there's guys have it in for me because I fired 'em, like you guessed, or because I beat 'em to a bargain, or because I wouldn't invest and they went bust, or . . . heck, you get the picture."

She nodded. "I wondered why you were concerned about Miss Arbuckle's safety when you said American kidnappers know it's good business to keep their promises. No one would pay ransom if they killed their victims even when the families obey instructions to the letter. But if it's a matter of revenge . . ."

"If it's a matter of revenge," said Arbuckle in a hollow voice, "it's anyone's guess what they might do to my little girl."

11

"Be like a Turkish bath later," Binkie observed gloomily, as the searchers gathered in the stable-yard after breakfast.

The sky was still overcast, but Geraldine's prophesied rain had not materialized. The air was muggy, already warm, without a hint of a breeze.

"You like Turkish baths, darling," Lucy consoled Binkie. "Just think how shiny my nose is going to get. It's hardly worth bothering to take face-powder."

Truscott, wheeling out the last of the bicycles, hid a grin. "I've dusted 'em off, Miss Daisy," he said, "and checked the brakes and tyres. You're all set. And I topped up the oil in the Lagonda, sir," he added to Tommy. "The level was down a tad. You want to keep an eye on it."

Tommy thanked him, kissed Madge good-bye, and zoomed off down the avenue. The bicyclers set off at a more leisurely pace, Lucy and Binkie following the green Lagonda, Daisy and Phillip in opposite directions across the park.

Pedalling towards the Dower House, Daisy wondered whether she ought to have told the others what Arbuckle had said about the possibility of an enemy out for revenge. Their enthusiasm for the hunt had waned—except Phillip's, of course—at the prospect of another hot day's exertion on the offchance of sparing a girl they didn't know a day or two of discomfort.

If they understood Gloria's peril, they'd be keen as mustard to find her. The trouble was, Daisy was afraid if she told the rest, Phillip would find out, and the poor prune was already in a state. She didn't want to send him into a tail-spin.

Coming to the Dower House back gate, she wheeled her bicycle through. Owen Morgan peered at her from among runner-beans twice his height, aglow with scarlet blossoms buzzing with bees. Hoe in hand, he emerged and touched his cap.

"Morning, miss. How is the treasure-hunt going?"

"Not too well," she admitted with a grimace, amused that the cover story had spread as far as her mother's gardener.

She regarded the dark young Welshman appraisingly. He was on the skinny side, but wiry. Supposing they found Gloria and decided to rescue her, able-bodied men would be in short supply.

But for Daisy's intervention, Owen might have been tried for murder. She had arranged this job with her mother, too. A nice boy, he was eternally grateful. She might just temporarily shanghai him.

"Later on I might want to ask for your help, Owen," she said.

He beamed. "There's happy I'll be, look you, miss, to do aught I can for you."

She smiled, nodded, and went on towards the house. Bill Truscott was another who might join the troops, she reflected, and perhaps the footman, Ernest, who had for some reason taken a fancy to Phillip.

But it was no use enlisting volunteers until they knew where the enemy was bivouacked, if that was the proper military phraseology. Fuming at the waste of time, Daisy went into the house.

The Dowager Lady Dalrymple complained not only about her daughter's absence yesterday but the early hour of her presence today. Daisy apologized profusely and left as soon as she could, aware that the briefness of her visit was another cause for offence. She was not doing frightfully well at putting her mother in a good temper to meet Alec.

Perhaps it would be best to put him off this weekend, she thought as she rode on. Only he had such trouble getting away at all, she hated to postpone the introductions any longer. She had known him jolly nearly six months already. Who was she to rag Phillip for a few weeks' hesitancy before he plucked up the courage to present the Arbuckles to his family?

His devotion to Gloria was indubitable. Daisy was dying to find out what sort of girl inspired such feelings in her previously untouched friend.

She had plenty of time to consider the various charms which might appeal to Phillip, having decided to cycle straight to the farthest village on her list before the day grew any hotter. What was more, eyeing the sky, she suspected an afternoon thunderstorm was not out of the question. This way, when she was exhausted she would not face a long ride home with lightning flashing about her head.

The clouds darkened but still no rain fell as she worked her way back towards Fairacres. She telephoned two or three times to report her lack of success. Madge told her Tommy had learned of an American stopping to ask directions a week or two ago, but from the description of man and motor, it was Arbuckle himself. Phillip and the other two had had no better luck than Daisy.

A depressingly lonely picnic lunch, on top of a rise in the hope of catching any whisper of breeze, made Daisy wish she had not proposed solo searching. However, it also reminded her of how lonely Gloria must be feeling. She pedalled on, and approached the last village just when the prospect of the tea awaiting at Fairacres became unbearably enticing.

Little Baswell was one of the villages Daisy and Binkie had failed to reach the day before. The land roundabout belonged to an estate neighbouring Fairacres, well within reach of children on ponies or bicycles.

They had ridden that way quite often, the chief attraction being a favourite nursery-maid who had married the village blacksmith. Mrs. Barnard had always provided a slap-up tea for her former charges without expecting any notice. Surely she would provide Daisy with at least a cup of tea to cheer her on her way.

Freewheeling down a slight slope, Daisy noticed that the woodland on her right had gone to rack and ruin. Fallen trunks lay enmeshed in brambles and bracken; hazel and holly struggled with saplings for light and air under the tall oaks, ashes, sycamores, birches, and wild cherry trees. She remembered Cooper's Wood as a pheasant covert, well cared for at least to the eye of a passer-by. For some reason she had always gone around it, not cut across, still less explored, though it was an extensive wood, larger than most in the area.

Then she remembered why she had avoided it. Gervaise and Phillip had once taken her to spy on the aged crone, bent and wrinkled, who lived in the middle. They said she was a witch, who ate children for supper. She boiled them in her cauldron, picked the meat from the bones, and used the bones to tell fortunes and cast spells.

In fear and trembling, Daisy had told her sister. Vi, a year older than Gervaise, asked their nurse, who assured Daisy the woman was just a gamekeeper's widow, allowed to stay on in the cottage when her husband died. The boys retorted—not in Nurse's hearing—that the witch had used a spell to make the grown-ups believe she was an ordinary person. Though Violet was sceptical, she couldn't prove they were wrong. Daisy had swallowed the tale for long enough to make avoiding the wood a habit.

The old woman was probably long since dead. Judging by the condition of the wood, her cottage might well have been abandoned. Could it possibly be where Gloria was imprisoned?

Would the kidnappers have dumped Phillip so close to their hide-out?

Coasting to a halt as the lane levelled, one foot on the ground, Daisy tried to visualize the area as seen on the map. She intended to cycle home along a cart-track through the fields and then across the Fairacres park to the house. That way wasn't much more than a couple of miles. By road, with a motor-vehicle, from here to the spot where Edgar found Phillip must be more like six or seven miles. At least five, anyway.

Still not far, but she recalled what she had said to Phillip: To people used to the anonymity of the metropolis, a mile or two from home was another world. Five miles must be about the distance from fashionable Mayfair to the dockside slums of Limehouse, with the whole City of London, business heart of the Empire, in between.

The Yank might have a different view of the matter, but having disobeyed his order, they were not likely to tell him.

Daisy peered into the gloomy thickets of the wood. The urge to explore warred with the urge to hurry to Fairacres or Mrs. Barnard's for tea. What a triumph if she returned to announce she had found Gloria!

A russet-furred squirrel chattered at her angrily from a branch overhanging the lane. Somewhere in the depths of the greenery a woodpecker hammered, paused, and hammered again.

Just what Phillip had heard in his captivity! Of course it meant nothing; every copse and spinney had its squirrels and its woodpeckers. All the same, the sounds crystallized Daisy's intentions. She'd go and have a look at the witch's hut.

The tangle of brambles and bushes looked impenetrable just here. She pushed her bike on a bit until she found an opening, but it was little more than a rabbit path, still no good for cycling.

"Blast!" said Daisy. On a bicycle she might have pretended to be looking for a short-cut, but even Cockneys must realize no one would choose to walk for pleasure in this heat, under those threatening clouds. If they saw Daisy poking about, they'd be suspicious—always supposing they were there.

She didn't know her way through the wood, so she could not march right along like someone on an errand. What she needed was a dog. Dogs had to be exercised whatever the weather. No one could suspect a dog-walker.

The Barnards had had a dog, a lurcher called Kitchener. He must be long dead, but dog people seldom go without.

Daisy hopped onto her bicycle and set off again at a brisk pace. She'd pop into the village shop and the pub with her questions, then kill two birds with one stone: Get a cup of tea and borrow a dog.

The all too familiar negative answers to her queries rather dampened her zeal, but she rode on to the smithy. Amid showers of sparks and the clang of iron on iron, Ted Barnard was forging a shoe for a vast, patient carthorse. Daisy waved to him. His grin white in his blackened face, he waved back with his hammer.

She wheeled her bike around the smithy and leant it against the back wall, out of the way. The Barnards' whitewashed brick cottage was right next door, its tiny front garden ablaze with sweet williams, candytuft, tall blue delphiniums, and fragrant mignonette.

Mrs. Barnard, stout and grey now but as motherly as ever, was delighted to see Daisy. So was Tuffet, a tousled, dun-coloured bundle of energy with bright brown eyes behind her shaggy forelock, who danced around Daisy's feet, stumpy tail wagging madly.

"Go to your basket," Mrs. Barnard ordered. "She's got more bounce than I can cope with, Miss Daisy, and that's a fact. You just set yourself down for a nice cuppa, dear. The kettle's on the hob."

Over seed-cake and an amazing assortment of home-made biscuits, Daisy told Mrs. Barnard about her writing career. "And now I'm doing some articles on London museums for an American magazine," she finished.

"Well I never, fancy that! Such a naughty little moppet as you was, too, always running after your poor, dear brother and always a heap of pinnies to be ironed, so quick as you dirtied 'em."

Daisy laughed. "Unlike Vi, who was always clean and tidy, and still is." She looked down ruefully at her dusty blouse and skirt. "One of the advantages of writing is that no one sees you a lot of the time. Mrs. Barnard, do you remember Gervaise frightening me half to death with a tale of a witch living in Cooper's Wood?"

"That I do, dear, being as how it was me sat up with you through your nightmares for a week after."

"Is she still alive? Does anyone live in that cottage now?"

"Nay, the old 'oman died a few years sin'—ninety-four, she were! Mr. Feversham up at the big house being too old himself to care for shooting or much else nowadays, he's let the cottage moulder and the coverts grow wild."

"I thought I might go and have a look at the place. It would be a good setting for a story. Only I'd rather like company. Do you think Tuffet would like to go for a walk with me?"

At the magic word, the dog bounded from her basket and came to sit at Daisy's feet, peering up hopefully through her fringe.

"It's my belief," said Mrs. Barnard, laughing, "as she'd love to go with you. Nor you needn't be bringing her every step of the way back if it's out of your way. Tell her to go home and she'll be on the doorstep in no time flat, begging for her dinner."

Daisy stopped at the telephone booth by the pub, but it was out of order, so she rode on back to Cooper's Wood with Tuffet racing beside the bicycle, short legs at full stretch.

Finding the narrow path, Daisy lugged the bike a few paces in from the lane and hid it under a straggly laurel she was sure she'd recognize. The dog at her heels, she continued along the path until it forked.

Both branches led onward into the depths of the wood. Daisy hesitated but, nose to the ground, Tuffet forged ahead down the right-hand path, so she followed.

A jay screeched a general warning. The muted sounds of birdsong ceased abruptly. In the eerie quiet under the thick canopy of leaves a twig snapped like a pistol-shot beneath Daisy's sandal. She stopped, heart in mouth. Nothing came to her ears but the scuff of Tuffet's feet in the damp, crumbling leaf-mould.

The path gradually swung back on itself towards the lane. Loath to retrace her steps in the heavy stillness, Daisy kept an eye out for a side turning. Before she found one, a dense mass of holly barred the way.

Or rather, it barred Daisy's way. The dog scurried on, hot on the trail of a rabbit, squirrel, fox, or pheasant.

"Tuffet!" Daisy called reluctantly, in a low voice, to no effect. She tried to whistle, but her mouth was too dry.

So much for her camouflage. Presuming Tuffet would find her own way home, Daisy turned back. She soon came to another path leading the way she wanted to go—or did she? It led around the giant bole of a once-pollarded oak, wreathed with ivy, which had concealed it from the opposite direction.

She took it, telling herself firmly she had no reason for nerves as the chances that she had chosen to explore the right wood were practically nil. All the same, she walked carefully, avoiding stepping on dry twigs, like in the Red

Indian games Gervaise and Phillip had occasionally let her join.

The path twisted and turned, but as far as she could tell continued inward. She had to duck under low branches, climb over a fallen tree-trunk, unhitch her skirt from grasping brambles, and stop now and then to wipe the sweat from her brow.

She must be mad!

Birds were twittering again, having decided the intruder was harmless. Then came another jay's screech. A moment later, Daisy heard the patter of feet on the path behind her and Tuffet rejoined her with an ecstatic yip.

Heartened, Daisy pushed on. Around a last bend and they emerged into what must once have been a pleasant ride.

The abandoned bridleway had sprouted a forest of birch saplings, and blackthorn thickets, and masses of purple-pink rosebay willow-herb. Still, the going looked somewhat easier, and it seemed likely that the cottage would have been sited somewhere near the ride for accessibility. Tossing a mental coin, Daisy turned left.

She followed the path of least resistance. Within a few yards, her suspicions were aroused. The way was too wide and, though twisting around obstacles, too straight for fox or badger, or even deer. Though the ground was too dry and hard for footprints, here and there a plant appeared to have been crushed beneath a heavy boot. She spotted the odd broken branch, withered leaves brown against the green backdrop. In a blackthorn, among the swelling sloes, hung a scrap of blue cloth.

Daisy found she was holding her breath. She let it out silently and proceeded with stealthy tread.

Quickly tiring of this slow means of locomotion, Tuffet bounced ahead. To make use of the camouflage, Daisy ought to behave like a legitimate dog-walker, she realized, not skulk along like a poacher after pheasants. Besides, skulking was hard on tired legs. She tramped on at a more normal pace.

In any case, the way through the brush had probably been forced by someone genuinely walking a dog, she assured herself as Tuffet disappeared around a clump of gorse. Inhaling the coconutty fragrance of the yellow blooms, Daisy followed. Before her stood the witch's hut.

Beneath the branches of a towering sycamore, the cottage crouched like a cornered animal. Weeds sprouted from the sagging thatch roof. Whitewashed plaster had yellowed, peeled, and in places flaked away to show the wattle-and-daub walls beneath. The glass in the two small windows was broken. The door between was cracked and warped, its iron latch rusted.

Nothing could have looked more desolate, derelict, deserted. Daisy heaved a sigh, half disappointment, half relief. So much for her triumphant return with news of Gloria's whereabouts.

The dog had paused to snuffle at something in the small garden, where pink-flowered convolvulus smothered overgrown currant and gooseberry bushes. Now she sat down for a brief scratch, before trotting off around the end of the cottage.

"Tuffet!" Daisy called in vain.

They had come quite a distance from the village, and Daisy was afraid the dog might not find her way home. She followed. No sign of Tuffet. Around the next corner, a thatched lean-to slumped against the cottage's back wall. Perhaps Tuffet had found a way into it.

As she went to investigate, Daisy glanced up. Above, in the gable of the end wall, she saw the window of an upstairs room. At least, she assumed it was a window. It was boarded up.

The boards should have been grey, weathered, splitting. Instead, they were the color of newly sawed wood. Bright nail heads gleamed.

Daisy's heart began to thump. She backed away, turned, and hurried round the corner to the front, calling breathlessly for her camouflage. "Tuffet, come! Come here, you naughty dog. Time to go home."

The door swung open, smoothly, noiselessly, on well-oiled hinges. A large man in braces and a collarless shirt stood on the threshold, his baleful glare adorned with the fading remnant of a black eye.

"Just walking the dog!" Daisy squeaked. "Have you seen her?"

He blinked. "Nah."

"Get on wiv it," snapped an impatient voice behind him. The big man stepped out, uncertainly. "I dunno, she . . ."

"Too late, mate. She's seen yer now. We gotta stop 'er." By then Daisy was half-way to the gorse bush marking the path. Feet pounded after her.

Tuffet appeared from nowhere, frisking about her ankles, barking joyfully. Daisy tripped, staggered a few steps trying to regain her balance, and fell headlong into a bed of nettles.

Hands like iron bands gripped her arms.

"Gotcha!"

12

"Miss Arbuckle, I presume?" said Daisy gloomily as the bar thudded into place on the outside of the door behind her.

The grimy girl huddled on the lumpy mattress on the floor stared up at her wide-eyed. The room was too dark to make out the colour of her eyes, but her limp, unkempt hair was fair. No doubt gold and curly when shampooed, Daisy thought charitably.

Feeling rather limp herself, she stepped forward, saying, "Do you mind if I join you?"

"Gee, sure, please do." Miss Arbuckle moved over. "Excuse me, I wasn't expecting . . ." And she burst into tears.

The straw-filled palliasse crackled as Daisy flopped down beside her and put an arm around her shaking shoulders. With the other hand she absently rubbed a particularly painful patch of nettle-rash on her leg.

When the sobs showed signs of giving way to sniffs, she offered her handkerchief.

"Here, take this. My name's Daisy Dalrymple."

"I *am* Gloria Arbuckle. How did you know? Oh, I guess those guys downstairs told you."

"Actually," Daisy said in a low voice, "I was looking for you, and there can't be many girls locked up in tumbledown cottages in woods in this area. At least, I hope not!"

"Looking for me?" Gloria said in wonder, following

Daisy's example in speaking softly. "You? Wait a minute, though! Dalrymple? You must be Phillip's deceased friend's sister. Have they . . . have they found his body?"

As she started to dissolve in tears again, Daisy deduced that she was talking about Phillip's body, not Gervaise's. The last Gloria had seen of Phil, he was being dragged off to be murdered, Daisy recalled.

"He was so b-brave, trying to escape, and the one he hit was raising Cain, shouting about k-killing him."

"He's alive," Daisy said hastily. "He's perfectly all right."

The tears came anyway, but they were tears of relief. "And Poppa?" Gloria sniffled a few minutes later. "Phillip said they wouldn't harm him."

"I met Mr. Arbuckle last night. He's right as rain except for worrying about you, and being a bit tired from running round collecting ransom money. He'll have it by tomorrow."

"So they'll let me go soon, and you, too." Gloria heaved a shuddering sigh. "It's been horrible, but the worst was thinking Phillip was dead. Miss Dalrymple, I'm real sorry you've gotten mixed up in this."

"Daisy, please. Formality seems too, too idiotic in the circs. Phillip involved me in the first place, but it was my own fault I was caught. I'm never going to hear the last of it."

"Well, I can't help being glad you're here. You start imagining all sorts of dreadful things when you're alone."

"They haven't mistreated you?" Daisy asked. "I mean, apart from all this." She waved her hand at the squalid room, noting a covered chamberpot in one corner; noting also that it was already darker than when she arrived. The sun wouldn't set for hours yet, so the clouds must be growing thicker. "They haven't beaten you, or starved you, or anything like that?"

"No. They've even apologised for the food all being cold." Gloria managed a shaky laugh. "They don't dare light a fire because they're afraid the smoke would attract attention. What brought you here? Why did Phillip involve you?"

Already editing the story in her head to eliminate the upsetting parts, Daisy said, "I'll explain later. Right now, while there's still some light, I'm going to see what I can do about getting us out of here. I refuse to wait for them to let us go. A friend of mine's coming down from town tomorrow."

Stiffly, she hauled herself to her feet. The door she ignored, and a brief inspection eliminated the window as a means of egress. Even with a hammer, no fear of making a noise, and all the time in the world, she doubted she could have knocked out the sturdy boards.

That left the possible hole in the ceiling Phillip had mentioned. Unable to make use of it because of his tied hands, he had not examined it closely.

She crossed to the corner where the stain ran down the wall—the worst stain, rather; none of the walls was exactly pristine.

Actually, at that point the wall and the ceiling were interchangeable. The rear wall of the cottage ran up vertically for three or four feet. Then the incline of the roof forced an inward slope to a horizontal portion of ceiling running down the centre, which met the opposite roof slope at the front.

On tiptoe, Daisy could touch the flat part. She did not need to. The crumbled plaster on the floor came from an indentation just level with the top of her head.

She reached up to feel the hollow, and jumped back hurriedly in a cloud of dingy white powder as a large chunk came loose. Landing with a thump on the floor, it broke into little pieces. Daisy held her breath, swinging round towards Gloria with her fingers to her lips.

No outcry below, no footsteps rushing up: the men must be in the other downstairs room.

"Gee!" said Gloria.

Breathing again, shallowly because of the dust lingering

in the air, Daisy looked up to see a small patch of green. Leaves! Beautiful green sycamore leaves and a bunch of winged seeds . . .

"Oh blast!" said Daisy.

"What's the problem?"

"Is anyone likely to come up in the next few hours?"

"I guess they'll bring something to eat. Quite soon, because its going to get dark and they won't let me—us—have a lamp. Why?"

"They'll see the hole."

"Can't we stuff your handkerchief into it?"

"We'll try," Daisy said dubiously, studying the ragged edges of the opening, "though I'm afraid it may be rather too large."

"We could use my stockings, too. I gave up wearing them days ago."

"All right, that might work. I'd have preferred to make the hole still larger while we have some light, but that would never do. We'll just have to wait until dark."

They succeeded in fashioning a serviceable plug. It caught on the splintered spikes of broken, half-rotted laths and looked as if it would stay up for long enough.

"What good will a hole in the roof do us?" Gloria asked hesitantly.

"We'll work that out once we have one big enough to climb through," Daisy told her with an assumed confidence she was far from feeling.

She could not sit here tamely, hoping for release, wondering whether the Yank would murder one or both of them. She had to try to escape. Resolutely she turned her mind from the possibility of a fall from the roof leading to a broken leg or a broken neck.

As the Austin Chummy reached the end of the elm avenue and Alec saw the house before him, he let out a long, low whistle. Knowing Daisy's father was a viscount had failed to prepare him for anything quite as impressive as Fairacres.

The entrance portico boasted four Ionic columns, and behind it rose a cupola, white against the slate grey overcast. On either side stretched four tiers of windows: a semi-basement rustic below, attics above, and between them two rows with pilasters. The balustrade running along the top of the façade was interrupted at regular intervals by classical statues, with a smaller cupola at each end.

Both in the course of his duties and as a student of history, taking tours on open days, Alec had visited grander mansions. Wentwater Court, where he first met Daisy, was considerably larger and more impressive, for instance. It was the fact of Daisy's having grown up here that he found a bit intimidating.

More than a bit, he acknowledged ruefully, drawing up before the portico. He must be mad to imagine she might consider marrying a middle-class, widowed copper with a child, a resident mother, and a semi-detached in St. John's Wood.

Yet she had invited him to meet *her* mother.

Wearily stepping down from the car, he glanced up at the relief on the pediment above the pillars. Just distinguishable in the fast-fading evening light, a cornucopia poured forth fruits.

Somewhat heartened by the implied welcome, Alec trod up the steps and faced the choice of a knocker in the form of a pineapple, an old-fashioned bell-pull, or an electric button. He opted for modern convenience.

The youthful lackey who opened the door wore a maroon jacket with brass buttons. A footman, Alec diagnosed.

"May I see Miss Dalrymple?" he requested, and then wondered whether Daisy's cousin had daughters. "Miss Daisy Dalrymple," he amplified. "The name's Fletcher."

The youth regarded him with undisguised interest. "If you care to step in, sir, I'll see if Miss Dalrymple's in," he said in the sort of voice which indicated he had to check for form's sake though he knew the answer perfectly well. "Was miss expecting you?"

"Not exactly. That is, tomorrow, not today."

"Ah," remarked the footman profoundly. He glanced back as if to see if his superior, the butler, was creeping up on him across the polished marble floor. Reassured, he became confidential. "You'll likely know what it's all about, then, sir, this funny business?"

"Part of it," Alec said with caution, taking off his hat.

"That's all I knows meself," the lad admitted, discouraged. "Though I *did* think when I obliged Mr. Petrie right at the start that he'd let me in on it. Lor, what a sight for sore eyes he were!"

"Oh?"

The monosyllable failed to draw a description. "Then along come the American gentleman, as hadn't ate his breakfast yet, the which I asked him special. 'Ernest,' says Mr. Petrie, 'you ask him has he ate.' So I does, and I tips him the wink on the sly. Have you dined, sir?" he enquired solicitously.

Utterly bewildered, Alec was for a moment under the impression that the question had been addressed at some past time to an unknown American gentleman. Realizing it was meant for him, he confessed that no, he hadn't. "But I shouldn't dream of presuming on Lady Dalrymple's hospitality," he added.

"That's" all right, sir. Her ladyship's dining out, and a good job, too. Miss Dalrymple's guests kept putting dinner back, waiting for her to turn up, but . . ."

"Waiting for her ladyship?" Alec asked with a sinking feeling.

Ernest confirmed his suspicion. "For Miss Dalrymple. Her ladyship's dining out," he repeated patiently, "and so's his lordship, of course."

"And Miss Dalrymple was late for dinner?"

"Hasn't come back yet."

"Great Scott!" Alec exclaimed, biting back several more forceful imprecations. What the deuce was Daisy up to now, that even her fellow-conspirators were unaware of? What were they all up to? "I must speak to Petrie," he said determinedly.

"If you'll please to come this way, sir."

The footman ushered Alec into a formal dining room. On the white tablecloth six places were set, glasses sparkling, silver gleaming. Five soup-spoons halted between plate and mouth; five faces turned towards the door, premature relief giving way to disappointment, then worry.

And, in Petrie's case, to dismay. He started to rise.

"Mr. Fletcher here'd like a word, Mr. Petrie, sir," Ernest belatedly announced.

Petrie pushed back his chair, but Lucy Fotheringay intervened. "I think Mr. Fletcher had better have a word with all of us," she said with a crispness quite unlike her usual world-weary manner.

"We're all in this together," agreed a young man unknown to Alec, standing up. "I'm Pearson, Tom Pearson, and this is my wife."

The pretty, pixyish blonde beside him gave Alec a strained smile. "You're Daisy's friend, aren't you, Mr. Fletcher? We're awfully worried about her. We expected her back by tea-time."

"Do sit down, Mr. Fletcher," Miss Fotheringay invited, her drawl back in place. "Have you dined? You'd better take Daisy's place."

Alec did not protest his unwillingness to intrude, nor his lack of evening dress. The footman set a plate of soup before him and reluctantly left the room.

The moment the door closed behind the servant, Petrie said with forced optimism, "Daisy may have stopped at her mother's for the evening."

"There's a telephone at the Dower House," Miss Fotheringay pointed out, scarcely concealing her scorn. "You said yourself we mustn't ring to see if she's there in case she isn't."

"If she was, she'd have phoned you," Alec said. In a voice in which he tried to blend camaraderie with a certain official, no-nonsense tone, he went on, "All right, you'd better tell me what's going on. Why the urgent messages calling you down here? Where did Daisy go, what for, and why alone?"

He addressed the questions at large. The others deferred to Petrie.

"We're looking for some . . . something." He sleeked back his already sleek fair hair with a nervous hand. "It was Daisy's idea for some of us to go out alone, to cover more ground. She was the one who worked out where each of us would go, so none of us is too sure exactly where she was heading after her last telephone call." He glanced around the table and received confirming nods.

"I stayed here," Mrs. Pearson explained, "and the rest reported in now and then."

"You were expecting trouble, then?" Alec tried not to explode with anger, remembering his own inability to stem the tide of Daisy's determination.

"Lord no!" said Pearson, "or we'd never have let her go off on her own. We 'phoned in for news, don't y'know. We were just making enquiries."

"In village shops," Petrie elucidated.

"Making enquiries in village shops? What the dickens are you looking for?" Alec recalled Petrie's hastily covered pause. "Or should I say whom?"

Petrie's alarm told him he had struck gold. The young man pressed his lips together, aware too late that he was the last person capable of misleading an experienced detective.

"Miss Fotheringay?"

"We're sworn to silence," she said with uncharacteristic

uncertainty. "But Phillip, with Daisy missing. . . ." Her voice trailed away.

Alec turned a searching gaze on each in turn. Even Petrie's face expressed indecision.

"We can't!" he said, agonized.

"Mr. and Mrs. Pearson, I take it you know I'm a policeman?" They both nodded soberly. "So do the rest of you," Alec continued with a sternness he had no need to feign. "Quite apart from my . . . feelings for Daisy, I'm obliged to tell you that I can't simply overlook your determined efforts to keep from the authorities what is clearly a serious matter."

"I quite appreciate your position," said Pearson. "As a matter of fact, I'm a solicitor. I assure you, before I let myself or Madge become involved I ascertained that no crime has been committed by any of us. Nor is our intention to shield any other person who has committed a crime."

"Thank you, Mr. Pearson, that clarifies matters."

Taking a spoonful of cooling soup, Alec thought rapidly. He had often noticed that lawyers, though in general the cagiest of men, once they let themselves go frequently gave away far more than they intended.

That a crime had been committed seemed certain. The obvious deduction was that Phillip Petrie had called in Daisy to solve it, knowing her propensity for interfering in police matters. To be fair, Alec was forced to acknowledge that she had two or three times been almost as much a help as a hindrance.

But in this case, Petrie was the instigator of the interference. Why would that generally law-abiding young man choose to try to solve a crime himself, rather than reporting it to the police?

To protect a friend or relative was the most likely answer. Yet Pearson was convinced their purpose was not to shield a criminal, so probably the friend or relative was the victim—and blackmail the crime. If the blackmailer was using a village shop as a convenience address. . . .

No, they would know which shop, which they clearly did not since they had been scouring the countryside asking questions.

Only two other possible crimes sprang to mind where, for the victim's sake, the police might not be called in. One was a confidence trick, where the sucker—as the Americans so charmingly put it—was too embarrassed by his gullibility. Alec doubted that would have caused the deadly serious expressions in the five pairs of eyes fixed on his face, as he now observed.

He put down his spoon, having finished the soup without the slightest idea of what kind it had been.

"Am I correct," he said slowly, "in supposing your secret is a kidnapping?"

Four faces registered more relief than dismay. Petrie's was horrified, but Alec detected a hint of relief there, too. They both opened their mouths to speak. Alec, with a gesture, deferred to the younger man.

At this inauspicious moment, a butler appeared, his stiff back and impassive face somehow radiating disapproval, and announced, "Mr. Arbuckle has called."

Miss Fotheringay glanced around at the others, then, to Alec's surprise, she said in a resigned tone, "Show him in, please, Lowecroft, and you'd better serve the next course. Set another place for Mr. Arbuckle if he hasn't already dined."

"As you wish, miss." Lowecroft departed, stiffer than ever.

"It won't do Daisy any good if we starve," Miss Fotheringay pointed out, "and Mr. Arbuckle is going to have to decide what to do about our quick-witted sleuth and his brilliant deductions.

No brilliant deduction was necessary to guess that the unknown Arbuckle was somehow involved. "Who is . . . ?"

Alec started to ask. He fell silent as the butler returned with a short, slight, long-faced man in evening dress.

Long-faced in both senses of the phrase, Alec noted. Between the lantern-jaw and the receding hairline was as careworn a countenance as he had ever seen.

While the butler set a seventh place at the table, Petrie introduced Alec—as *Mr.* Fletcher—to Arbuckle. Another surprise: the man was an American. He didn't look at all pleased to meet Alec, even though he was unaware of the police connection.

The footman, Ernest, and a parlour-maid brought in several dishes. During the serving of loin of veal with broad beans and sauteed potatoes, the conversation stuck strictly to the weather. Arbuckle reported lightning over the Malvern Hills. No one mentioned the possibility that Daisy might get caught out in a storm. On the contrary, the prospect of the end of drought and heat was welcome with much false-ringing enthusiasm.

"All very well," Bincombe said gloomily when the servants had withdrawn, "but if it really sets in to rain it's not going to make things any easier."

"Never mind that," Arbuckle said flatly, with a dismissive gesture. "There's two things I wanna know: Where's Miss Dalrymple and what the heck is this gennelman doing here?" He glared at Alec, then transferred his glare to Petrie.

"Daisy's missing," said Mrs. Pearson, a catch in her voice. Her husband pressed her hand.

"Missing?" Arbuckle groaned, sinking his head in his hands. "I knew I shouldn'ta let that little girl. . . ." Recalling Alec's presence, he raised his head and frowned.

"Mr. Fletcher is a friend of Daisy's," Miss Fotheringay told him. "He came to see her, and we could hardly conceal her absence."

"But he don't know . . . ?"

"He's guessed a good deal," Pearson said bluntly. He

gave Alec an apologetic glance. "Deduced, I should say. Mr. Fletcher happens to be a Scotland Yard detective, don't y'know."

Arbuckle looked appalled. "How much has he figured out?" he demanded.

"That someone has been kidnapped," Alec said. "I must assume, someone close to you." Which meant the man was wealthy enough to make extortion worthwhile. What the connection with Petrie was, Alec could only conjecture.

"No dice, you won't get another thing out of me," Arbuckle said fiercely. "Nor my young friends, I hope."

"Not a word," vowed Petrie.

"Daisy's missing," Miss Fotheringay reminded them with equal fierceness.

"Oh lord!" Petrie groaned.

The American shook his head despairingly. "I know, I know, and I feel real badly about it, you can bet your sweet life. I've taken to that young lady in a big way."

His patent wretchedness somewhat assuaged Alec's rebuilding fury. "I'm going to go on guessing," he said. "Deducing, if you will. For a start, I believe the victim is your daughter, sir." A pretty girl was the only possible explanation for Petrie's predicament, the only possible rival for his loyalty to his dead chum's sister. Arbuckle's dropped jaw confirmed it. "Further, you have been warned not to contact the police if you want her safely returned."

That was too obvious to surprise Arbuckle, though Petrie was impressed.

"By Jove, Fletcher," he said, "I don't know how you fellows do it. Didn't I tell you, sir," he went on, turning to the American, "that Scotland Yard knows what's what?"

"You did, son, and I don't doubt it, though I'm doggone sure they don't have much experience at dealing with kidnappers. But anyways, what can they do except join the search? There's no way to keep a posse secret, and the moment word gets out, it's all up with Gloria."

"Sir," said Alec, "I do appreciate your position, believe me. But are you so sure there's nothing else I could do if I knew all the facts? I'm trained and experienced in deciphering the way criminals think and in drawing conclusions from inadequate data."

"Sure, but . . ."

"In any case, I must insist on being given any information which might conceivably help in finding Daisy—Miss Dalrymple. I take it you all suspect she's in the hands of the kidnappers?" He looked around the table, garnering general agreement. With an effort, he managed to keep his tone calm and reasonable. "If they are as ruthless as you believe, she's in danger too. You can't imagine I'd do anything to add to the risk?"

Miss Fotheringay cast a half apologetic, half defiant glance at Arbuckle. "I'll tell you anything you need to know, Mr. Fletcher. Anything *I* know, at least. Daisy's safety comes first, and we haven't the foggiest what to do."

Her taciturn boyfriend nodded.

"Oh yes," cried Mrs. Pearson.

"Sorry, old man," her husband said gruffly to Petrie, "but she's right, you know. We'll try to give away as little as possible."

Alec shook his head. "I can't tell what will be useful until I've heard everything. Nor can I know what will need to be done." He turned to the American. "I'm prepared to say I shan't approach the local force unless I consider it absolutely vital, but that's as far as I'm able—and further than I ought—to go."

Sagging in his chair, Arbuckle yielded, his face becoming an old man's as the tension left it. "Okay, okay, I guess I know when I'm beat. Tarnation take it, I owe Miss Dalrymple something for the gutsy way she's gone to bat for my girl. If you'll just not spread the word about being a gumshoe, I'll tell you everything. Where shall I start?"

"First things first. Let's see if we can work out where Daisy went today."

13

Like the man who had brought their bread and marge, tinned corned beef, and mushy, greyish tinned peas, the kidnapper who fetched their plates wore a scarf across nose, mouth, and chin. In the increasing gloom, his features would have been practically invisible anyway. Daisy wondered whether she would be able to identify the one she had seen in full daylight at the front door.

She rather doubted it. Not only had she seen him very briefly, what attention she could spare from her plight had been concentrated on his black eye and Phillip's probable role in its creation.

He left. The bar thudded into place.

"Will he come back?" she asked Gloria, whose face was no more than a pale smudge beside her.

"I guess not. They never have after . . . dinner."

"Dinner!" Daisy sighed. Not particularly hungry after Mrs. Barnard's tea, she had eaten the bully beef but had not managed to swallow more than a mouthful of the rest. She suspected she might regret it later. "Well, it will soon be night outside as well as in here. I'd better get on with it. Help me move the mattress under the hole to deaden the sound if any big bits fall."

As, blundering in the dark, they hauled the pallet into the other corner, Daisy heard a faint rumble. She could not imagine what their captors were doing. About to ask Gloria whether she had heard a similar noise before, she was forestalled by a second rumbling growl, which she recognized as distant thunder. The weather had broken at last.

She was glad she had not mentioned the sound to her companion. Gloria did not seem to have noticed the far-off drum-roll; if she happened to be afraid of thunderstorms, the longer she remained unaware the better.

"Tell me about the kidnapping," Daisy invited, feeling for their makeshift plug and giving it a tug. It came loose in a shower of plaster, pieces of lath, and musty, mouldy straw. Coughing, she was pleased to see that the hole, an irregular patch of dark grey in the blackness, had nearly doubled in size.

"I thought Phillip told you. Can I help?"

"There isn't enough room. I'm having to stand with my neck crooked as it is. Phil did tell me, of course, but you might have noticed something he didn't. By the way, I don't suppose you've learned anything more about the kingpin, the man they call the Yank?"

"No," Gloria said, sounding puzzled. "They didn't talk in the room below this again. Maybe they realized Phillip overheard them. Does it make any difference who he is?"

"You never know, it could. Phthoo!" Daisy spat out crumbs of plaster, suddenly wondering how many insects made their homes in the thatch, and what sorts. Not that she really cared whether it was spiders or earwigs which landed in her hair, as long as they stayed out of her mouth. "I can't talk while I'm doing this," she mumbled through half-closed lips.

Gloria obligingly began to recount the kidnapping and everything that had happened since, which was little enough. Listening, to her disappointment learning nothing significant, Daisy continued to demolish the roof. It was hard work chiefly because she had to reach up to do it. The plaster and straw came down easily, and the lath was not much solider, though she had to pull and twist to break some pieces.

In one way that was most satisfactory. On the other hand, she had no greater desire to fall *through* the roof than *off* it.

A gust of wind blew a flurry of bits of straw in her face. Feeling a sneeze coming, she snorted.

"Shall I take a whack at it?" Gloria asked.

"Would you? It shouldn't take much longer." Fumbling around each other, they changed places. Daisy heard a closer growl of thunder and began to talk about Phillip and Gervaise's boyhood.

After a few minutes, Gloria interrupted her in a small voice. "It's beginning to rain, and I think I can hear thunder."

"So do I," Daisy admitted. "Are you afraid of it?"

"N-no. Not exactly, but I don't like it. At least, it's the lightning. We have terrible electric storms at home."

"They're not so bad here," Daisy assured her, as though she had a basis for comparison. "In fact I rather enjoy all the banging and crashing and flashing. Shall I take over again?"

"No, I'm okay. Oh, there's something big and hard here."

"A proper rafter, or beam, or whatever?"

"I think so."

"Good, it'll give us purchase. The hole must be about big enough, isn't it?"

"It's hard to tell in the dark. Let me feel."

A momentary flood of light silhouetted Gloria's head against the hole. She gasped.

"One, two, three, four, five," Daisy counted, "six, seven. . . ."

Crash, bump, bump, mutter, mutter, mutter.

"G-golly gee!"

"It's still a long way away. Seven miles." Or was it a count of five to the mile? She couldn't remember and hoped Gloria couldn't either. "Any noise we make they'll think is thunder," she said encouragingly, "and the lightning will help us get our bearings. Let's go."

"Y-you first."

"All right. We'll roll up the mattress to stand on, and then you'll have to give me a boost, I expect. I'm no gymnast."

Wobbling on top of the mattress, Daisy stuck her head out into the open. Her shoulders brushed the thatch. Refreshing rain hit her face in dots and dashes, and odd gusts of wind frivolled through her shingled hair. She felt for the beam Gloria had reported.

Luckily, it was on the downward side of the slope. With a bit of a struggle, Daisy managed to raise her arms through the hole and dislodge some of the straw resting on the beam. Then she was able to get her elbows on top of it.

"Give me a shove," she requested.

A jerk and a heave and a moment later she was on the roof, careful to keep her weight over the beam. The still-dry thatch prickled through her thin linen skirt, but at least it wasn't slippery. She was afraid it soon would be once the rain really got going.

"Come on!"

Hauling Gloria out was more difficult. At last she sat beside Daisy on the beam. Daisy heard her take a deep breath of fresh air and let it out on a sigh.

"What next?" she asked.

A sheet of lightning let Daisy look up, hopefully, into the sycamore tree above. The nearest branches were within reach, but too thin to support anything larger than a squirrel. A pity—climbing down the tree would be the easiest way to the ground.

The next flash, which followed almost at once, showed Gloria with her hands over her ears and her eyes screwed shut. It also showed Daisy what she had forgotten: the lean-to behind the cottage. Its roof was directly below them, not more than a couple of feet lower than the edge of the eaves, and at its lowest point only four or five feet above the ground.

The heavens crackled and roared. The moment the din ended, in a hush as if the world held its breath waiting for the next onslaught, Daisy reached out unseeing to pull Gloria's invisible hands away from her invisible ears.

"Listen!" she hissed. "All we have to do is slide straight down. There's a two-foot drop, then another slide, and then a drop of about four feet. Can you manage it?"

"I th-think so."

"Good. We'll both go at once; we'll be less likely to land on top of each other. Keep still when you reach the ground and I'll find you."

"Okay."

"Ready . . . steady . . . go!"

Thatch rasping her skin, Daisy found it quite frightening to let herself slither into the blackness—and she had seen what lay below, however briefly. Gloria could only trust her blindly. Already afraid of the storm, was she spunky enough to obey?

Daisy's feet met thin air. A moment later she *thunked* on her bottom on the lower slope. She had just time enough to wonder if she'd have done better facedown when her feet flew out again. She landed, arms swinging for balance, on something that crunched, a cinder path perhaps.

Gloria landed beside her with another crunch, loud in the unnatural stillness. It didn't sound at all like thunder. It sounded, in fact, like feet on a cinder path.

"Wossat?" The voice came clearly from the cottage. No betraying gleam of light showed, but the men were there and awake.

"Better 'ave a dekko. Coulda bin . . ." The rest was drowned out by a stupendous thunderclap. The lightning was almost simultaneous.

Daisy grabbed Gloria's hand and tugged her away from the building.

Speed was impossible, so there was no advantage to aiming for the comparatively clear ride in front of the cottage, even if they were not starting from the back. They would do better losing themselves quickly in the tangled thickets of the wood, Daisy had decided. Hand-in-hand, lightning-dazzled eyes sightless, they stumbled forward, hands groping ahead for obstacles.

Behind them electric torches sprang to life.

They were spotted immediately, but the long beams spilled past them, illuminating a green wall of leaves. Daisy saw a rabbit path opening to their right.

"Quick!" she cried, and broke into a run.

Footsteps and curses followed. Within a few paces, the twisting path hid the men, but they had the torches to light their way. Once out of range, Daisy and Gloria were blind again.

The skies came to the rescue. Flare after flare banished the dark, amidst continuous blasts and booms and long, rattling rolls. Unable to hear or see their followers, sure they must be gaining, Daisy dived into the nonexistent gap between two bushes, dragging Gloria with her.

They emerged in a space free of undergrowth beneath a larch. Rather, they were more or less in the middle of the larch, for the branches started less than a yard from the ground, continuing up the trunk in what looked to Daisy practically like a ladder.

As the next flash arrived, in a momentary hush, she grabbed Gloria's arm, pointed upwards, and said in her ear, "Climb!"

In pitch darkness she started up, feeling her way, testing each branch before she put her weight on it, childhood skills taking over just like riding a bike. Thunder rumbled sullenly, but the next flash of lightning was pallid, the storm already moving on.

Glancing down, Daisy realized Gloria had not followed.

The thunder ceased. She heard a crashing in the bushes and swearing voices, then a shout of triumph.

"Got 'er!"

"What abaht the uvver one? Keep looking!"

"Blimey, we'll never find 'er in this, mate."

The rain was pouring down in earnest now, breaching the leafy canopy in trickles, streams, and torrents. The larch's needles were no protection. Uncomfortably seated on a narrow branch, clinging to the trunk, Daisy was soaked through in no time. She shivered.

They had Gloria again. All Daisy's efforts were for nothing—unless she could get back to Fairacres in time to send the men to the rescue before the kidnappers moved their victim elsewhere.

Yet she dared not descend until she was certain they had given up searching. Fortunately, the thunder was distant now. Through the hiss and plop of falling rain, she listened to the sounds of the hunt dying away.

"Bloody 'orrible!"

Daisy would have jumped a mile if she hadn't been hemmed in by branches.

"Gawd, I can't wait to get back to the Smoke!"

The voices sounded as if they were just below the tree, but through leaves and branches she saw the glimmer of torches and realized the men were on the path. She watched the lights bob away towards the cottage, having kindly helped her find her bearings.

She waited what seemed like an age, then clambered down, though she could not be sure the others were not lying in wait. Pushing through the bushes, she turned away from the cottage and plodded gingerly into the inky night.

Alec scowled at the map spread out on the desk in the viscount's den. "Here and here and here, Mrs. Pearson?" He pointed to the three villages Daisy had telephoned from.

"Yes." The pretty young woman consulted her list. "And she said she had covered these others in between. She didn't ring from each place."

"So she could have gone on to any of these three, or beyond if she made good time. Has anyone any reason to favour a particular direction?" He glanced around the circle of intent faces.

"She was heading generally back towards Fairacres," Pearson pointed out hesitantly. "I shouldn't imagine she'd turn away again."

"A good point," Alec approved. "These two are most likely, then, Astonford and Little Baswell."

"Astonford's a tiny hamlet," Petrie put in. "Doesn't even have a pub, let alone a shop."

"The shop in Little Baswell will have closed long since," said Miss Fotheringay, "but the pub will be open for another half hour."

"Heck, what does it matter?" Arbuckle asked. "We might figure out which village she went to but she could be anywheres now. We can't comb the countryside."

"And if we could," Bincombe gloomed, punctuated by a rumble of thunder, "if we had a hundred men, we might pass within a yard or two of her without seeing or hearing her in this weather."

Unfortunately he was right. Alec bowed his head in defeat, then squared his shoulders and said reluctantly, "Yes, we'll have to wait till daylight. Maybe by then I'll have come up with a brilliant plan to find her."

"Maybe she'll be back," Mrs. Pearson consoled him wearily. "You're not waiting up to see, my pet," her husband informed her. "Beddy-byes time."

"You'll all want to be rested for tomorrow," Alec said. "You'd better all go to bed, except you, Petrie, if you please. I want to hear everything you can tell me about the kidnapping. And from you, too, Mr. Arbuckle, if you don't mind staying a while, sir."

"No sirree. But Lord and Lady Dalrymple may be a mite surprised to find us here when they get home."

"Great Scott, I'd forgotten all about them! We could go down to the Wedge and Beetle, but I haven't booked for tonight and I don't know whether they can accommodate me."

"You'd better stay the night here, Mr. Fletcher. I expect we can square it with Daisy's cousins." Miss Fotheringay eyed him sardonically. "We'll just tell them she forgot she had invited you. *They* don't know that's inconceivable."

Acknowledging her mockery with a half-smile, Alec agreed, "It would be much more convenient to stay. I shan't go to bed anyway, in case Daisy turns up."

"You need your beauty sleep too," she told him. "We'll take it in turns sitting up, won't we?" she appealed to the others.

"Not Madge," Pearson said firmly, "but I'll take my turn. I'll make out a schedule." He sat down at the desk and searched the drawers for paper and pencil.

Alec did not argue. His eyelids felt heavy and gritty after the drive from London following a long day at the Yard, clearing up paperwork so that he could take an extra day off.

"Someone wake me when it's my turn," Miss Fotheringay drawled, "or if the missing sheep returns to the fold. I'm for bed. Come on, Madge, darling. If we're gone when the cousins get back they'll assume Daisy's gone up, too, which will spare all sorts of complications—for tonight at least."

"Good thinking, Miss Fotheringay."

"I can when I try. I'll tell Lowecroft to have a bed made up for you. Good-night all."

The ladies departed just in time. Pearson had barely finished writing out his schedule when from the front hall came the sound of voices and a door shutting.

Petrie turned to Alec. "I'd better introduce you right away, Fletcher."

"I'll lie low," Arbuckle said promptly.

Alec followed Petrie out. As they emerged from the passage into the hall, the gentleman handing his dripping umbrella to the footman said irately, "Dash it, Geraldine, I know a copper when I see one!"

Taken aback, Alec hesitated. Lord Dalrymple could not have caught more than a glimpse of him, was now not even looking their way. Besides, Alec was seldom if ever recognized as a policeman. Not that he himself objected to his profession being known, but he had promised Arbuckle to keep it quiet.

"The small copper is common," his lordship continued didactically, to Alec's further bewilderment; though not particularly tall, he was above regulation height. Lord Dalrymple, bending to give an absent pat to the spaniel who lolloped to greet him, went on to assert, "What I saw was a Queen of Spain, a rare visitor. The man was talking through his hat. I should hope I can tell *Issoria lathonia* from *Lycaena phlaeas!*"

"Yes, dear," soothed Lady Dalrymple, "but the man *is* a noted authority. That was why he was invited to meet you."

"Authority!" her husband snorted. "Ass!"

Petrie turned his head. "Butterflies," he murmured, then moved on. "Lady Dalrymple, will you allow me to present Mr. Fletcher? I'm afraid Daisy forgot to mention to you that she had invited him. He wasn't able to make it until today."

"How do you do, Mr. Fletcher," her ladyship said severely, and at once turned back to Petrie. "Where is Daisy? She missed tea and had not come in when we left."

"The ladies have gone up to bed," Petrie told her misleadingly. "They had a tiring day."

"Indeed! This treasure-hunting nonsense of Daisy's has gone on long enough. I shall tell her so in the morning."

Meanwhile, Lord Dalrymple introduced himself to Alec, and continued eagerly, "Are you acquainted with the *Lepidoptera,* by any chance?"

"I'm afraid not, sir. I can tell a Peacock from a Cabbage White, but that's about it.

"Large White, my dear sir, Large White. You refer to *Pieris brassicae,* I take it. A pest, to be sure, but not unattractive in its way."

"Are you coming, Edgar?" said his wife. "It is late and you *will* insist on going out at dawn."

"I was going to offer Mr. Fletcher a night-cap, dear."

"I'm sure you can rely upon Mr. Petrie to do the honours."

"Please do, my boy. You'll excuse me, Mr. Fletcher. It's true I like to rise early and go out before the heat of the day. Good-night."

Forbearing to point out that tomorrow was unlikely to be hot, Alec bade him good-night.

At the bottom of the stairs, the viscount turned and said earnestly, "It *was* a Queen of Spain, I'd take my oath on it. A fritillary, you know."

Alec rather liked him, but he could see why Daisy didn't choose to make her home with her cousins.

He and Petrie rejoined Arbuckle, Pearson, and Bincombe in the den. The footman came in a moment later with decanters of brandy and whisky.

"*I* knows Miss Daisy's not come in yet," he said in a hushed, enigmatic voice, with a significant look. "Mr. Lowecroft's gone to bed. I'm the only one on duty. If there's aught I can do to help, just ring, and you knows, Mr. Petrie, sir, I can keep mum."

"Good fellow," said Petrie, turning to Arbuckle. "Whisky, sir?"

"I could bear to take a drop."

More appreciative than Petrie of Ernest's offer, Alec soberly told the youth, "It doesn't look as if there's anything to be done now. Tomorrow's another matter. If Miss Daisy isn't home yet, we may need every man we can get."

14

Pearson declined a night-cap. Handing Alec the schedule for the night watch, in an unstated acceptance of his authority, he went upstairs to join his wife. Alec took his seat at the desk and accepted a spot of brandy. Arbuckle sipped his Scotch and muttered something blasphemous about the Prohibition.

Petrie supplied himself and Bincombe with whisky and soda. "All right, Fletcher," he said, "what can we tell you?"

Lord Gerald interrupted in a burst of unwonted loquacity. "Look here, old man," he said to Alec, "Lucy may not show it much but she's deucedly fond of Daisy. Do anything for her. And I'd do abso-bally-lutely anything for Lucy, don't you know. Do a good deal for Daisy, come to that. So you've only to give the word."

Alec gravely thanked him.

"I mean," the large young man persevered in his laborious effort to explain himself, "we all rallied round for Miss Arbuckle, but after all, we don't know her." He cast an apologetic glance at the kidnapped girl's father. "Except Petrie, what? But Daisy is . . . well, Daisy, if you know what I mean."

"I do indeed," Alec agreed, with a painful clenching of his heart. Where was she? Was she lost, hurt, helpless in the hands of villains?

"That's all right then," said Bincombe, relieved. "Wake

me when it's time." Swallowing his whisky in a single gulp, he silently departed.

Turning to Arbuckle, Alec said, "I'll have your story first, sir. Just a minute while I find some paper to make notes."

"Nothing in writing! It's too damn dangerous."

"I find going over notes of a conversation often brings to one's attention points one had not previously noticed."

"No!" said the American adamantly. "You want me to play along, you do it my way."

Alec conceded the point, hoping his memory would prove less fuzzy than his tired eyes. He let the touchy gentleman tell the story without interruption, making mental notes of questions to be asked, points to be clarified.

Arbuckle produced the notes he had received from the kidnappers, which he carried on him at all times. They were printed in pencil in block capitals on ordinary notepaper available anywhere. The wording was uneducated, but in an awkward way which could well be faked. Though Alec had never worked on a kidnapping—they were rare in Britain—he knew such was often the case.

Several instances of American slang, spelling, and phrasing, though possibly also faked, suggested that "the Yank" Petrie had reported to Arbuckle was in fact American. There was always a chance he was some English criminal whose copied methods had earned him the nickname, but Alec was sure he'd have heard at least a rumour of such a man.

"I guess me telling you about the Yank's just hearsay," said Arbuckle as Alec pored over the notes, "but Petrie will confirm it."

"I'm not concerned about hearsay," Alec assured him. "You're not giving a formal statement or evidence. I want to know everything: hearsay, opinion, conjecture, distant possibilities."

Rather red in the face, Arbuckle said, "Waal, there's something I told Miss Dalrymple that I've kept from Petrie here. I'm sorry, son, but I didn't want you thinking Gloria's poppa was the kind to go stepping on people's corns on purpose. The fact is, I've made a few enemies in my time."

"Which of us hasn't?" said Alec, and Petrie nodded solemnly. His blank look suggested he was trying hard to recall any enemies he had made in his time.

Arbuckle explained how, in the course of his business dealings, he had inevitably offended various people. Asking him to make a list of names, Alec turned to Petrie.

His account, where it covered the same events, coincided closely with Arbuckle's, allowing for different viewpoints.

"Any comments or ideas?" Alec invited.

"Well, there is one thing, Chief Inspector."

Arbuckle sat up. "Chief Inspector? That's real high up, isn't it?"

"Pretty high up," Petrie assented in a modest tone which suggested he accepted the credit for providing a police officer of superior rank.

"Swell! I guess that means you've got some leeway, Mr. Fletcher, when it comes to acting on your own?"

"A certain amount," Alec said cautiously, trying not to envisage what his Super, let alone the A.C., would think of his present activities. "What were you going to say, Petrie?"

"Oh, it's just something that's rather puzzled me. If you don't mind my saying so, sir," he said to Arbuckle, "I was a bit surprised that the Studebaker had no spare radiator hose in its tool-kit. They're always splitting or getting punctured, or even just falling off. Crawford knowing all about motor engines, I'd have expected him to keep such a basic spare part to hand."

"Crawford's my technical adviser, not my chauffeur, son. He keeps an eye on the Studebaker but I don't hold him responsible. I left Biggs back home, seeing I mostly drive myself anyhow."

"Gloria—Miss Arbuckle—drives too," Petrie told Alec proudly.

"Yet Mr. Crawford was driving you on this occasion," Alec said to Arbuckle. "Why was that?"

"Gloria wanted to show me Hereford." He pronounced it Her-ford. "When Petrie took her there, she found out Nell Gwynne was born in the city and thought I'd be interested. I'm not real hep when it comes to history—like Henry Ford says, history is bunk—but I took a fancy to that old story of Nell Gwynne, the orange girl, and your King Charles. Now Crawford, he's almost as keen on your history and the countryside as Gloria is. Spends all his weekends exploring. So when he hears we're going to Herford, he says he'd like to come along and he'll drive."

"It was his idea to go with you, then?" Alec asked.

Arbuckle pondered. "Gee, I couldn't swear to it. He was interested when we were talking about it, all right, but I've a feeling Gloria asked him along. She was pleased, anyhow, because him driving let her and me admire the scenery. I guess she doesn't pay much attention to the scenery when she's out with Petrie," he added slyly.

Petrie blushed, confirming Alec's surmise as to the reason for his concern over Gloria Arbuckle.

"So you think Miss Arbuckle invited Crawford to go." Alec hated to see a promising lead evaporate. "Tell me, what happens when a radiator hose goes? Am I right in supposing it's quite spectacular?"

"By Jove, yes!" said Petrie. "The remaining water boils and there's clouds of steam hissing all over the place. You jolly well know it's happening, which is just as well because if you don't stop right away, the engine overheats and can be ruined."

"Steam?" Arbuckle frowned. "I'll be darned if I recall clouds of steam."

"You don't recall whether there was steam," Alec asked sharply, "or you do recall that there was not?"

"There was not," the American said in a flat voice. "Crawford said over his shoulder something was wrong.

He pulled into the gateway and opened the hood. The bonnet, you call it. Then he muttered about the radiator, took some piece out—the hose, I guess. He put it in his pocket and I didn't see it. He said he'd have to find a garage, and off he went."

"He didn't look in the tool-box?"

Arbuckle shook his head, reluctantly. "He musta known there wasn't a spare there."

"You didn't hold him responsible for the Studebaker. He might assume the tool-kit was complete and not check it beforehand, but if so, you'd expect him to look there for a spare hose when it was needed. On the other hand, if he was aware of a deficiency, wouldn't you expect him to replace it?"

"Y-yes. Maybe he just hadn't gotten around to it."

"I assume in fact there was no spare hose. Petrie, did you look in the Studebaker's tool-box?"

"No. I saw it on the running board, a topping mahogany chest, which would practically hold my whole engine," Petrie said enviously. "But Crawford being an engineer, I took it he'd have used the spare if there was one. It's a simple repair. Besides, I was pretty sure I had a piece I could use."

"So the . . ." Alec started.

Arbuckle interrupted. "Listen, I know what you're suggesting. But this guy's been with me ten years, my right-hand man. Maybe he did see changes coming, like Miss Dalrymple said, but he knew I'd see him right."

"Changes?" Much as Alec deplored Daisy's penchant for meddling, anything which raised her suspicions was worth investigating.

With a sidelong glance at Petrie, Arbuckle shrugged. "A business that doesn't change dies," he said unhelpfully.

Alec appeared to go along with him. "You drove the Studebaker here tonight?" he asked. "Petrie, may I ask you to go and take a dekko in the tool-box?"

"Right-oh." Petrie caught the keys Arbuckle tossed him and departed.

"Changes?" Alec pressed.

"Waal, now, you'll have maybe figured out that that young man is sweet on my girl. Gloria's nuts about him, and I've found no reason to think he wouldn't treat her right, nor that all he cares for is her pocketbook."

"You've made enquiries?"

"You betcha! I'm not saying he's the smartest cookie in the jar, but he's a decent guy and willing to work, no lounge lizard, and he knows automobiles. That's my business, see, investing in automobile manufacturers, but I'm a real simp when it comes to the technical side."

"That's Crawford's contribution?"

"As of now. My notion is to train Petrie to take his place. That's if him and Gloria get hitched, if his snooty family doesn't throw a monkey-wrench in the works."

Mentally translating—if Petrie's blue-blooded family didn't throw a spanner in the works—Alec sympathized. He took a swallow of the superb Cognac Daisy's blue-blooded family had no doubt laid down generations ago.

"Is Miss Dalrymple right about Crawford foreseeing the possibility of losing his job?"

"Could be, but like I told her, he knows I'd see he didn't lose by it."

"Not financially, perhaps, though I imagine he'd lose opportunities to invest knowledgeably. By the by," Alec added parenthetically, "he may resent your having utilised his expertise to make a fortune he can't hope to match. But I was going to suggest he'd lose in status, in closeness to the boss."

"You may have something there," Arbuckle said slowly. "Tarnation, I've wondered. . . . Not close to the boss so much as close to Gloria? You see what I'm getting at? I've wondered if Crawford hadn't set his sights on my girl."

"Or—forgive me—her money. I don't mean to suggest

your daughter is not attractive in herself, but your wealth must be an added attraction."

"Brother, you've said a mouthful. If I had a sawbuck for every fortune-hunter I've seen off . . . ! I can spot 'em at a hundred yards. Petrie isn't one. Crawford . . . waal, I gotta admit Crawford could be."

"Whether the attraction's money or love, he'd see his chance of winning Miss Arbuckle going down the drain when Petrie came along," Alec observed. "What made you think he had hopes?"

"Little things. Lately, this business of suddenly he's so keen on history and the countryside. I had a hunch that was just because of Gloria's interest." He stopped, looking appalled. "Aw, jeez!"

Alec had no difficulty following his train of thought. "You said he'd taken to spending his weekends exploring the countryside. He had every opportunity to find a deserted cottage such as Petrie describes, and to learn the back lanes. And another point: London and Hereford are in opposite directions from Malvern, yet Petrie came across you stranded by the roadside when you were on your way from one and he from the other."

"He was aiming for his parents' place," Arbuckle said dubiously, "not Great Malvern, like us. I gotta say I was a mite puzzled seeing the Malvern Hills first getting closer, then further away. Still and all, you gotta go round, not over, and these lanes of yours twist and turn like a rattler."

"The kidnapping had to have been arranged in advance for a certain place, though there might have been some leeway as to time."

Petrie loped in, the ring of keys dangling from his forefinger clinking like castanets. "I say, that tool-chest has the whole caboodle, sparking plugs, inner tubes, hand pump, patching kit, fan-belt, even lamp glasses. Just about anything you could need—except hose."

"That doesn't prove anything," Arbuckle growled.

"No," Alec agreed, "it's just another possibly significant fact to add to the pile. Petrie, can you pinpoint on the map the exact spot where the kidnapping took place? Just there? You're sure? That's quite a way off the direct route from Hereford to Great Malvern, isn't it?"

"Miles. It was a pretty good choice, come to think of it, with all hayfields around, already mowed and stacked so no farmer was likely to come along. It looks as if Crawford's our man, doesn't it? I never did quite cotton to him."

"Why not?"

Brow furrowed, Petrie thought. "He was an oily, smug sort of b . . . chap," he said slowly, "not exactly pudgy, just sort of too well-fed-looking, like an old maid's cat, but that's hardly . . . No, by Jove, I have it. I never nailed it down before. It was the way he looked at Gloria!"

"Mr. Arbuckle has just told me he suspected Crawford had ambitions in that direction."

Surging to his feet, Petrie pounded with his fist on the desk. "By Jove, if the bounder has laid a finger on her . . . !"

Alec laid a calming hand on his arm. "We must hope he's chiefly motivated by money."

"I can't believe it." Arbuckle shook his head. "Sure, things look real bad for Crawford, but I just don't believe he'd do a low-down, lousy thing like this."

"As I said, sir, we don't have anything like proof." Alec had few doubts that he was on the right track, but he would see things clearer after a good night's sleep.

Part of a night's sleep, he corrected himself, glancing at the brass clock on the mantelpiece. "I want to know more about his movements these past few weeks," he went on, noting that Arbuckle looked as exhausted as he felt, "and just what you've said to him about the kidnapping, but that can wait until the morning."

"I have to go to Lunnon to collect the dough, but I'll come by on my way. I would've anyways, to see if Miss

Dalrymple's back. I'll be off, now, and see you in the morning."

"Will you see Crawford in the meantime?"

"At breakfast, probably, before he goes off to Oxford."

"Don't say anything to him," Alec warned. "Not a word of our suspicions, and try not to alter your manner to him."

He and Petrie went out to the hall to see the American off. Ernest appeared from nowhere with an umbrella and accompanied the small, somehow crumpled figure down the steps to his motor.

The rain was belting down. Was Daisy out in it somewhere?

Consulting Pearson's list, Alec said, "You've got the first watch, Petrie."

"The drawing-room, I should think. There are French windows. If she comes and sees the light, she'll be able to get in easily. I say, Fletcher, I don't want you to think I'm not frightfully cut up about Daisy going missing. It's just that Gloria. . . ." Words failed him.

"I know." Walking with him to the drawing-room, Alec wondered if Petrie could possibly be feeling the same agony of apprehension. "Look here, I imagine you're known at most of the garages hereabouts? I'd like you to go in the morning and make enquiries at any Crawford might have made his way to that day."

"Right-ho, old chap." Petrie opened a door and flicked on a light switch. "If no one's heard of him, we'll know for sure, won't we?"

"It would be awfully hard for him to argue his way out of it," Alec agreed grimly, following him into a long room in which the finest furniture of two centuries melded into a harmonious elegance. He waved at floor-length blue brocade drapery on the far wall. "Is that the French windows? I'll draw the curtains back and make sure they're unlocked." Opening the curtains, he reached for the handle.

"They're locked, sir." The footman came in behind them,

bearing the tray of decanters and glasses. "The key's in this here drawer. There you are. Will you be wanting another night-cap, sir?"

"Not for me, thanks, but you might leave it here. Mr. Petrie's staying up. Is the front door bolted and barred?"

"Yes, sir, but it's a Yale lock, the kind you can open without a key from inside."

"Good. You can show me the way to my room, then, if you will, and go to bed yourself. Oh, here's the schedule, Petrie. You'll wake Bincombe in an hour or so."

"Right-ho. Sleep well, old man. I must admit I'm dashed glad you turned up."

He held out his hand, and Alec was shaking it when from the corner of his eye he saw the handle of the French window move. As he strode towards it, it opened, and over the threshold tottered a tatterdemalion mudlark.

"Alec, thank heaven!" croaked Daisy, and fell into his arms.

He picked her up and sat down on the nearest sofa with her on his lap, holding her tight, disregarding completely the effect on himself, the sofa, and the Aubusson carpet.

Streams of murky water ran from her bedraggled hair and torn clothes. Her face, turned up to his, was scratched and daubed with mud. As he kissed her chilly lips, all he was conscious of was the joyful singing in his heart.

Daisy snuggled against Alec's chest and felt safe for the first time in hours. She could have happily stayed there for just as many hours to compensate, but the reason for her struggling on to Fairacres, resisting the appeal of shelter in barn or haystack, still stood. She was safe. Gloria was not.

Reluctantly she raised her head from Alec's shoulder, and saw Phillip's anxious face.

"Phil, she's all right." Daisy felt it was most improper to be cuddled on Alec's knee with Phillip, and the footman behind him, looking on, but she wasn't going to move until she absolutely had to. "They've got her in the witch's cottage in Cooper's Wood."

"Little Baswell? By Jove, we ought to have thought of it! Right-oh, I'm off."

"Don't be an ass, Petrie," Alec said sharply. "You said there are four bruisers, at least. It'll take all of us."

"Me too!" said the footman, all agog. "I knowed there were something up. I knowed it!"

"You too, lad. The two of you go and roust out Bincombe and Pearson, and ask Miss Fotheringay to come and take care of Daisy. Try not to wake her cousins." As they rushed out, he looked down at her and smiled. "A hot bath is called for, I'd say. Is there anything else we need to know, sweetheart?"

"Not that I can think of. She's in the upstairs room on the right. At least she was until we escaped through the roof, and I don't expect they have another room secured. She couldn't get out that way without help. You see, I. . . ."

"I see you went rushing into danger when you were supposed to be merely asking questions, without even the elementary precaution of telephoning your whereabouts first!"

"The only public 'phone was out of order," Daisy said indignantly. "And I did take precautions. I hid my bike—I hope we can find it—and borrowed a dog for camouflage."

"A dog!" Alec laughed and hugged her. "My darling idiot."

"There speaks a townsman. The wood is far too overgrown for cycling, and the day far too sultry to walk for pleasure, but dogs always have to be walked. They wouldn't have suspected a thing if Tuffet hadn't gone snooping around the side of the house."

"And you snooped after? Just as I thought. The wood's very overgrown, is it?"

"Even the ride. There's a path of sorts trampled through the thickets, though the beginning of it may be hard to find if they've bothered to conceal it. But Phillip will find it.

He knows the wood well, he'll be able to lead you straight to the cottage."

"Good."

"You'd never find it otherwise. They have the windows well covered so no light escapes, and they don't let Gloria have a light at all. Poor Gloria! I hope they didn't hurt her when they caught her. She didn't follow me up the tree, you see. I suppose she must have panicked."

"Maybe she just doesn't know how to climb trees. Not everyone is as resourceful as you, sweetheart."

"Oh Alec, I do like it when you call me sweetheart!"

He responded in a most satisfactory fashion, but their kiss was interrupted when Lucy swept into the drawing-room. She was as elegant as ever in fawn silk pyjamas and matching dressing-gown, even with her hair in a towelling bandeau.

"Daisy darling, what *have* you been up to? Too, too squalid! You'd better come along and have a bath."

Reluctantly slipping down from Alec's lap, Daisy reeled. He caught her up.

"I'll carry her," he said to Lucy.

On the landing they met the men. Phillip was still in evening dress but carrying boots, Ernest in his livery, Binkie and Tommy apparently dressed in whatever had come first to hand.

"Well done, Daisy!" said Tommy softly, grinning.

"I'll join you in a minute," Alec told them. "Don't forget electric torches, one each if possible. Have we another motor? Five would be a squeeze in mine."

"I'll get the Lagonda out. It's bigger than Bincombe's Alvis."

"Ask Bill Truscott to go with you," Daisy advised, thinking of the four roughs they would be facing. "Tell him it's by my request."

"Good idea," said Phillip. "He's a good chap. Take care of yourself, old bean. Come on, fellows."

Alec carried Daisy to the bathroom where Lucy was already running a steaming bath. He deposited her on a chair and stood for a moment gazing down at her, shaking his head.

"Squalid is the word. Straight to bed and I'll see you in the morning."

"Right-oh, Chief," said Daisy. "Alec, you will take care, won't you?"

"You can count on it, love," he assured her with a grin. "The last thing I want is to meet your mother for the first time sporting a black eye!"

15

On Daisy's arrival, now that there was something to be done, all desire to sleep had left Alec. Nonetheless, having picked up the Dalrymples' chauffeur at the lodge, he let the man take the wheel of the Austin. Truscott knew the way to Cooper's Wood—and the rain was still coming down by the bucketful.

Peering through the opened windscreen, the chauffeur followed the red tail-lights of the Lagonda down the lane. Petrie, also familiar with the route, was at the wheel of the car in front. Its owner, Pearson, sat beside Alec in the back of the Austin.

"The others may think I should be in on the planning," he said self-deprecatingly, "but I'm quite prepared to leave it to you, sir, don't y'know. This show's a bit different from storming a French village held by the Boches. We couldn't very well go in with machine-guns blazing in the middle of Worcestershire, even if the girl weren't there."

Alec blenched. "Ye gods, no! I trust none of you has a service revolver hidden in his pocket?"

"No. Bincombe said something about shotguns but I soon set him straight."

"You have my eternal gratitude, Mr. Pearson. My superiors are not going to be happy about this caper at best. If someone got shot, I'd be in the soup over my head and swimming for my life with no land in sight."

"You'd be back on the beat and I'd be struck off the

roll," said the solicitor wryly. "No firearms. Right-oh, what's the scheme?"

"Dammit, I wish I'd asked Daisy more about her hole in the roof."

"Her *what?*"

"She and Miss Arbuckle escaped through a hole in the roof, I gather. Knowing Daisy, she probably made the hole."

"But how did they get down from the roof?" Pearson queried, sounding stunned.

"I don't know," Alec said regretfully. "If there's a ladder, we might use it to climb up and abstract Miss Arbuckle before we tackle her captors." He raised his voice to be heard above the tattoo of raindrops dancing on the hood. "Do you know the cottage, Truscott?"

"No, sir, that I don't." The chauffeur shook his head, silhouetted against the headlamps' light reflected off water sheeting from the sky. "If you don't mind me asking, sir, what's this about Miss Daisy escaping? From what Mr. Phillip said, I thought we was going to rescue her. I'd do a lot for Miss Daisy, but if she's safe I've the missus and the nippers to think on."

Letting Pearson explain the situation, Alec tried to devise a plan. Again and again he wished he had asked Daisy more questions. He had been so thankful to see her safe and sound, however filthy, that he hadn't been able to think of anything else.

"So it's Mr. Phillip's young lady's to be rescued?" said Truscott. He gave a philosophical sigh. "Ah well, I'll do my bit. The missus wouldn't hear of aught else. What was you wishing me to do, sir?"

"We'll all follow Mr. Petrie through the wood to the cottage, with only his torch lit if at all possible. If he directs it at the ground, it shouldn't be visible very far off. Then we'll surround the cottage. I'm assuming it's pretty small, so we shan't be too far apart. If anyone finds a ladder, we'll try to get the girl out first."

"I take it, sir," said Pearson, "your aim is to bag the kidnappers as well as rescue Miss Arbuckle?"

"Ideally," Alec agreed, unsure whether the "sir" was addressed to him as a superior officer for the nonce or because of his age. It made him feel ancient, though Pearson could not be more than five or six years younger. "We'll do our best to take them in," he continued, "but the girl's safety must be paramount. Otherwise I'd wait and try to catch the ringleader, as well as his minions."

"Of course."

"It means we absolutely must take them by surprise, so that they don't get a chance to use Miss Arbuckle as a shield. They'll have a man on look-out, especially after Daisy's escape. No lights as we get near the cottage. We'll have to work by touch."

"This rain will cover a certain amount of noise."

"Yes, we're lucky there."

"Are you going to invoke the name of the law, sir?"

"I hadn't thought. Given that I'm here strictly in an unofficial capacity, what would you advise?"

"Hmm. In view of the threats against Miss Arbuckle, and the possibility, however remote, that they might get away with her, I'd say not."

"You're a copper, sir?" Truscott asked. "A policeman, I mean?"

"Detective Chief Inspector Fletcher," Pearson introduced him, "of Scotland Yard. But keep it under your hat. What next, Mr. Fletcher? Say we have the place surrounded but haven't got the girl out. Shall we try to break in or try to draw them out with some sort of sound?"

"The downstairs doors and windows may be barred or reinforced. If we haven't got the girl, we'll try to draw them out. What shall we do? We can hardly just knock on the door."

"Daisy could, pretending she was lost and cold and preferred shelter at any cost."

Alec shuddered. "Thank heaven you didn't come up with that little notion back at the house! She'd have done it."

"One of us could fake it. I've done some amateur theatricals in my time."

"Let's hear you."

"Let me in," Pearson begged in a high voice. "I'm freezing!"

"Lor, sir, that's Miss Daisy to the life!"

To the discriminating ear of a lover it didn't sound in the least like Daisy, but Alec supposed it would do for a bunch of Cockney criminals. "Throw in a bit of a stutter," he suggested. "Teeth chattering."

"P-please let me in. I'm f-f-freezing."

"Not bad. You can perform if we decide to go that way. Any other ideas?"

They discussed other possibilities but came back in the end to the pseudo-Daisy. The men must be eager to recapture her so her voice would bring at least one to the door.

"I'll give you a choice of back-up," said Alec. "Petrie, who's the keenest, or Bincombe, who's the best with his fists, I'd guess."

"Petrie. Deprive him of the chance to get to his girl and he might go off half-cocked and take it anyway."

"All right. For the rest of us, I'll have to talk to him first about whether there's a back door, and the positions of windows. We shan't be able to see so I hope he remembers."

"Looks like the rain's lightening up a bit, sir," Truscott reported. "Nearly there."

Before Alec had time to consider the effect on their plan of the end of the downpour, the Austin pulled in behind the Lagonda. Truscott doused the lights. Alec had caught a glimpse of tree-trunks, unobscured by curtains of water. The rain had decreased to the point of no longer penetrating the foliage above.

He stepped out of the car. A chilly douche promptly hit

his hatless head and trickled down his neck. He swore silently.

An electric torch snapped on. By its light, the six men gathered in a huddle, and Alec questioned Petrie about the cottage and its immediate environs.

"There's a back door. We once watched the witch coming out of it to feed her chickens. No windows in the end walls downstairs, only upstairs, I'm pretty sure. Well, almost sure. I haven't been near the place since I was a boy, remember. The other windows are small enough to make it dashed difficult for a man to climb through. I think."

On that shaky basis, Alec ordered the disposition of his troops.

"All right, Petrie, how do we get there?"

"The beginning of the ride is back here. It's so overgrown I nearly missed it."

They followed him back along the lane a dozen yards. In the torch's narrow beam, the mass of bushes and small trees seemed to Alec unbroken, impenetrable, but Petrie soon found a path.

He extinguished the torch. "It's light enough to find the way without," he said, and plunged between two thickets.

Alec realized the clouds had parted and the first faint light of midsummer's early dawn was painting the world in tones of grey and charcoal. A crow's sleepy caw came from the tall trees edging the ride, and nearby a small bird twittered.

"Wait! That's torn it. I was relying on darkness for surprise," he explained as Petrie returned, "as well as heavy rain to cover any sounds." He held out his hands palms up. The only falling water was dripping from the surrounding leaves.

"We'll just have to storm the place," Petrie said impatiently, already turning back to the path.

"That's the most risky for Miss Arbuckle. You go ahead, but don't rush in. Pearson and I will study the lay-out and see if we can't come up with a better scheme. All right, fellows, let's go."

Close behind Petrie, Alec stayed ready to grab him if he seemed about to run amok. He found himself dodging scarce seen branches which whipped back into his face, jerking his trouser turn-ups from the determined grasp of brambles, squidging through ankle-deep mud. His admiration for Daisy, who had traversed this jungle in pitch darkness in a thunderstorm—and in a skirt—grew by leaps and bounds.

Petrie stopped so suddenly Alec nearly ran into his back. "I think the cottage is under that sycamore," he whispered, pointing at a tree towering over the brush choking the ride. "Yes, there's the chimney, see?"

"Good man." Alec turned his head. "Pearson, come and have a look."

They squeezed past Petrie and picked their way forward. The only sound they made was the squelch of the mud beneath their feet, hidden by a rising ground mist, but all around the birds were singing now. Greys paled and hazy colours emerged. The air smelled richly of green, growing things.

The path curved around a gorse bush speckled with yellow blossoms. Alec stopped dead as one end of a thatched roof came in sight.

Motioning Pearson to keep still, he inched ahead. A blotchy wall, a broken window. . . .

He halted, heart in mouth, but nothing stirred.

Another step.

The door stood open, a black hole like a missing tooth in a decaying face. "Too late," said Alec with a sigh. "They've cut and run."

Warned by the maid who answered her bell that "her ladyship's in a proper taking," Daisy toyed with the notion of breakfast in bed.

She dismissed it as cowardly. Geraldine was *her* cousin's wife, and the whole show had been her idea. It was up to her to smooth ruffled feathers.

Besides, she had to find out what had happened last night. Worry had stopped her going back to sleep, though it was still quite early. She had a sinking feeling that if Gloria had been rescued, she would have heard about it by now; but the others might hesitate to disturb her after yesterday's ordeal.

Actually, she felt perfectly well. The stiffness was not much worse than after the first day's bicycling. Some of the scratches smarted a bit, in spite of Lucy's free hand with the boracic. The ones on her face she smothered with a good coating of face-powder before she went down.

In the dining room she found Edgar and Geraldine finishing their breakfasts, and Lucy and Madge in the middle of theirs. The men must still be asleep after the activities of the night.

Lowecroft came in with fresh tea as Lucy shook her head at Daisy, her mouth—already vividly lip-sticked despite the early hour—turned down. No Gloria.

"Lord Dalrymple has caught a lobster," Madge said brightly. A vision of Edgar in oilskins hauling in lobster-pots crossed Daisy's mind even as she asked, "Moth or butterfly?"

"A moth, *Stauropus fagi*." Edgar beamed at her apparent interest.

"A particularly spectacular one?" Daisy queried, crossing to the sideboard and loading a plate with everything in sight.

"The adult form is not spectacular," her cousin admitted regretfully. "In fact, it may be mistaken for a bundle of dead leaves. However, I obtained some eggs which I believe it had just laid, and which I hope to hatch. The larva is quite ostentatious. It may be said to resemble a lobster in some respects. Its head, for instance, looks somewhat like a lobster claw."

The diversionary tactic worked only until the butler left the room. Then Geraldine ruthlessly interrupted.

"Yes, dear, I am sure the caterpillar will be a fascinating sight. Daisy, what is this my maid has been telling me? While delighted to welcome your friends, we cannot approve of the sort of high jinks, to use a vulgar phrase, you young people indulged in last night."

"No, indeed," Edgar seconded her with a stern frown, changing instantly from the dotty lepidopterist to the censorious schoolmaster. "Such frolics may suit modern notions, but we choose to preserve the old-fashioned proprieties at Fairacres."

"Frolics!" Daisy easily suppressed her guilt at having taken advantage of her cousins as she recalled the exhausting, uncomfortable, and at times frightening events of the past twenty-four hours. "Of course, you couldn't guess, but everything we've done has had an extremely serious purpose."

"What?" Geraldine asked bluntly, but Edgar looked thoughtful, perhaps remembering the condition in which he had found Phillip.

"I can't tell you the details."

"Indeed!"

In the face of Geraldine's justifiable scepticism, Daisy decided the moment had come to blow the gaff, at least in part. Sooner or later they would find out that Alec was a police detective, so she might as well make use of him.

She cast a deliberately exaggerated glance at the door, then leaned forward and said in a low, mysterious voice, "You mustn't tell anyone, but we're helping the police. Mr. Fletcher is from Scotland Yard, a Detective Chief Inspector *incognito,* and we came here to act as camouflage for him when he arrived. Last night he asked the chaps to do something more for him, I don't know quite what. I do know it's absolutely vital to keep his profession secret."

"Gosh, yes," said Madge solemnly.

Lucy, the abominable Painted Lady, prudently opened her mouth only to insert a forkful of kedgeree.

"So, please," Daisy continued, "if you don't believe me, ask to see his warrant card, but do it discreetly. I'm truly sorry we've upset you. We felt it was our duty to do what we could to uphold law and order."

Geraldine's face was a study in doubt.

"My dear," said Edgar, "perhaps I should have mentioned to you that when I came across young Petrie the other morning, he had clearly not been injured in a motor accident. As a matter of fact, his wrists and ankles were bound."

"Really, Edgar, you might have told me!"

"I do beg your pardon, dear. I didn't want to alarm you, but I must also confess my mind was distracted by wondering whether it was remiss of me not to have secured the blood vein."

The four ladies gaped at him. "Phillip wasn't badly injured," Daisy said uncertainly.

"Do you mean to say, Edgar, that there was another victim of whatever nefarious business is afoot, and that you let him expire from loss of blood?"

"No, no, good heavens no! The Blood Vein moth, *Calothysanis amata*. Mr. Petrie had an excellent specimen of the larva crawling up his neck when I found him."

Madge and Daisy burst out laughing, and Lucy smiled.

Geraldine shook her head in despair. "I should have guessed. Well, I cannot pretend I find it anything but distasteful to be involved in a police matter, however peripherally, but I suppose it is our duty to aid the authorities."

"I'm sorry," said Daisy. She was saved from further grovelling as the butler came in.

"Mr. Arbuckle is here, my lady."

"Good gracious, what ails the man to call at this time in the morning!"

"He asked for Mr. Fletcher, my lady," Lowecroft informed her with a hint of sympathy.

In response to Geraldine's glance of exasperated enquiry, Daisy nodded.

"Show Mr. Arbuckle in, please, Lowecroft," said Geraldine, sighing, "and you had better inform Mr. Fletcher of his arrival. Well, Daisy, we shall take ourselves off. I only hope you know what you are about!"

"So do I," said Daisy.

16

"Quick," said Daisy, as the butler followed her cousins from the room, "what happened last night? I take it Tommy told you, Madge?"

"The birds had flown. They went upstairs and saw the hole in the roof, which I gather you made? Tommy was frightfully impressed."

"A fat lot of good it did in the end. We're back where we started, with no idea where Gloria is."

"Oh no, darling," said Lucy, "your disappearance persuaded Mr. Arbuckle to confide in your pet copper, and we have a suspect."

Madge nodded. "Phillip told Tommy Mr. Fletcher suspects Mr. Arbuckle's chauffeur."

"Chauffeur?" Daisy asked eagerly. "You mean Crawford, his engineer? I thought there was something fishy about him, but I've never met him. I have no sense of his character."

"Phillip doesn't like him, I gather," Lucy informed her.

"Phillip's no judge of character. But he takes people at face value, and tends to like them, all things being equal, so if he dislikes Crawford there must be a reason. And if Alec thinks there's good reason to suspect him, we must follow him, in case he contacts. . . ." She stopped as Lowecroft showed Arbuckle in.

The American's face brightened as he caught sight of Daisy. Only greetings and offers of breakfast could be voiced until the butler left again, but the moment the door shut, Daisy jumped up and demanded, "Where is Crawford?"

"My dear Miss Dalrymple!" Arbuckle took her hands in his. "I'm mighty happy to see you safe. I was . . ."

"Thanks, but never mind that. Is it true Alec—Mr. Fletcher—suspects your Mr. Crawford? Someone must follow him!"

"Jeez, of course. He's supposed to go to Oxford today, to Morris's factory. Cowley, that is. I guess it's a little town near Oxford."

"Had he left the hotel when you did?"

"No, he hadn't come down yet. He's nearly finished up over at Morris's, figures a few more hours is all he needs to give me a recommendation."

"We'll go," announced Madge, "Tommy and I. There's not much I can do to help, but I can sit in the car and keep an eye out for Crawford while Tommy drives. I'll go and get him up, poor dear. They didn't get in till after three."

She dashed out. Lucy poured a cup of coffee for Arbuckle, and Daisy asked him what Alec had concluded about Crawford. He explained, reiterating—though without much conviction, Daisy thought—his belief in his employee's innocence.

Arbuckle was eager to hear why Daisy had gone missing yesterday evening. She did not want to tell him about seeing Gloria until Alec was there to describe the abortive midnight raid on the witch's cottage. He came in sooner than she expected, remarkably alert after so little sleep, if a bit bristly about the chin.

She had never seen him in flannels and a tweed jacket before, since he had always been on duty and thus formally dressed when they met in the country. He looked simply spiffing—or would when he'd had time to shave. Mother would never be able to guess he was a policeman if she wasn't told.

With an apologetic glance at her and Lucy, he stroked his chin. "Your pardon, ladies. I didn't want to keep Mr. Arbuckle waiting. You've heard about last night, sir?"

"No, sir, I have not," Arbuckle said anxiously. "I was just asking."

Daisy and Alec between them were breaking the news of her capture and escape and Gloria's new disappearance when Madge and Tommy arrived.

"I gather we're off"—Tommy yawned enormously— "Sorry . . . to Oxford?"

Alec looked at Daisy, his dark, thick eyebrows raised, obviously jumping to the instant conclusion that this was her doing.

"To follow Crawford," she explained.

"Good thought!"

"Cowley, not Oxford. Mr. Arbuckle, what car does he drive?" Daisy asked, delighted by Alec's approval.

"He has a maroon A.C. Six."

"Right-oh." Taking off his glasses, Tommy blinked at the lenses, then took out his handkerchief to polish them. "We'll try to pick him up in Great Malvern. If the A.C. isn't parked at the hotel, we'll just tootle off towards Oxford, hoping to spot it on the way. And failing that, we'll look around for it in Cowley."

"The Morris motor-car works," said Arbuckle, "that's where he's supposed to be."

"Do you happen to know which route he generally takes?" Tommy asked. Arbuckle shook his head. "Never mind. If we miss him, we'll do Cheltenham and the A40. It's fastest."

"If you're stopped for exceeding the speed limit, I'll pay the fine," Arbuckle assured him.

"Telephone from Cowley," Alec put in, "whether you find him or not."

"Right-oh. Thanks, darling," he said to Madge as she

presented him with a large roll, hastily buttered and stuffed with bacon. "We'll buzz off, then. Toodle-oo."

As they left, Daisy followed her example and went to the sideboard to fill a plate for Alec. On the way, she said to him, "The men will be bound to contact Crawford after last night, don't you think? And he'll want to see where they've taken Gloria."

"It seems likely, always assuming he's our man—and we have no better prospects. Mr. Arbuckle, where else has your business taken Crawford?"

"Since we came to Malvern, to Austin's at Longbridge, Sunbeam in Wolverhampton, and a whole bunch of factories in Coventry: Swift, Lea & Francis, Hotchkiss, Humber, Daimler, and Hillman, I think. I guess that's the centre of your auto business, like Detroit."

Alec groaned. "So he might have found a place anywhere in the central Midlands, or on the way there, as an alternative hiding place."

"He wouldn't want them to be too far away," Daisy argued, setting a heaped plate before Alec, "or he would have chosen somewhere farther away for the first hidey-hole. He must need to be within reasonably easy reach of both them and Mr. Arbuckle. And he can't move his own base from Malvern without arousing suspicion."

"Not that it helps how close they are," Lucy pointed out. "Wherever it is, we'll never find it unless he leads us to it. So your brain-wave about following him was a work of absolute genius, darling."

Daisy tried to look modest.

Alec grinned at her, swallowed a mouthful of scrambled egg, then turned to Arbuckle to ask what he had told Crawford about the kidnapping.

"Mighty little, as little as I could get away with, just because I figured the less anyone knew the better. I couldn't keep the kidnapping secret, what with Gloria vanishing without notice and me having the willies, and him getting dumped. Like I told Petrie, he was real mad at being left to walk home. He acted mad enough to fool me, at any rate. He asked was I going to contact the police and I told him no sirree."

"Do you recall his response?"

"He approved."

"Did he!" Alec exclaimed.

"No big deal," Arbuckle insisted. "He thought I was right for Gloria's sake, and he advised me not to mention it to anyone at all because things have a way of getting out."

"True enough. Did you follow his advice? You didn't tell him Petrie had turned up again, or about his friends searching for your daughter?"

"Not a word."

"Good. Anything else?"

"Lessee." Arbuckle pondered, then said in dismay, "Rats, yes, I almost forgot. He offered to deliver the ransom for me. If you're right, Mr. Fletcher, that would be handing it to him on a plate!"

"Did you agree?"

"Nah. I said if anyone but me turned up with the dough, it could mess things up but good. I told him to go on same as usual, like nothing had happened, so's not to make anyone nervous."

"How did he react to that? Did he seem relieved?"

"Not so I noticed. Why?"

"Oh, you might have wanted him to stick close to you, which would have cramped his style. As it is, he's been free to meet his henchmen whenever he wants. He knows you're off to town today to fetch the ransom?"

"I mentioned a coupla days ago I'd have it by today."

"All right. Just one thing more, unless you have any questions, Daisy? Miss Fotheringay?"

"Yes," said Daisy. "Mr. Arbuckle, I realize it goes against the grain to think a trusted employee might have turned on you like this. But it's better than if it was someone out for revenge, isn't it? I mean, at least Gloria's safe? You haven't actually done anything to make Crawford hate you, whatever he may fear for the future."

"I have not, Miss Dalrymple, not consciously," Arbuckle said heavily, "though, like Mr. Fletcher said, it maybe sticks in his craw that I've made more from his know-how than he can ever hope to. But—and believe me, I lay awake half the night thinking about this—if I'm right that he's carrying a torch for my girl, and he knows she prefers young Petrie, waal, that opens up a whole new can of worms."

Even as she wrinkled her nose at the graphic idiom, Daisy acknowledged the validity of his fears. The rejected lover, the mutation of love into hate, had been the basis of uncountable tales of rape, murder, and mayhem throughout the ages.

Lucy had lost her usual blasé expression, and Alec's grave face showed his concurrence.

"I'm afraid you're right," he said, "which may make you look more kindly on my last point. I most strongly advise calling in the local force and setting up a proper search for Miss Arbuckle."

Arbuckle stood up, impressive despite his lack of inches as he leaned forward with both fists planted on the table. "Nope," he said inflexibly. "I don't believe they'd find her, and it just might be what sends the guy over the edge. I can't risk it." He held up one hand as Alec opened his mouth to argue. "You tell 'em and I'll deny it. I'll say Gloria's gone back to the States. No, sir, we have to play it his way, whether it's Crawford or some other bastard. I'm going to fetch the ransom."

His resolute march towards the door turned to a tired trudge before he reached it, but he left, nevertheless.

Alec watched him go, sighed, and turned back to his almost untouched breakfast. Cutting into a sausage, he said, part sour, part admiring, "Obstinate old so-and-so. I do feel for him, poor chap, but . . . !"

"What are you going to do?" Daisy asked. "Phillip and I are eyewitnesses to the kidnapping, so his denial won't carry much weight."

"None, even if Petrie won't cooperate. But I'm caught between the devil and the deep blue sea." He glanced at Lucy.

"I shan't tell tales out of school, Mr. Fletcher," she said dryly.

"Thank you." He gave her a wry smile. "You see, I have to agree with Arbuckle on several points. For a start, he's correct in saying the British police are not well versed in handling kidnappings. We have very few, whereas I gather there's quite an epidemic in America. In the second place, a search is not likely to succeed when the area to be covered is so enormous."

Daisy feelingly agreed. "It was pretty hopeless when we could be fairly sure she was nearby. I only found her by sheer luck."

"Exactly. And the associated problem is that she may very well not be in Worcestershire any longer. The Met doesn't have the manpower or the local knowledge to mount a detailed search, and I haven't the authority to call out the forces of half a dozen counties!"

"Who does?" Lucy asked. "Your superiors?"

"Only the Home Secretary," Alec told her bluntly. "Even the Commissioner would have to try persuasion, and before that I'd have to talk the Assistant Commissioner, the head of the C.I.D., into. . . . Well, suffice it to say it's a long chain of persuasion, and all in the face of Arbuckle's denials. By the time anything was done, the chances are the ransom would be paid and the whole thing over."

Lucy nodded. "More than likely. Too, too maddening!"

"There's another thing." Alec hesitated. "I hope I'm not letting it influence my decision. The fact is, whenever I report the kidnapping, I'm going to face some awkward questions about why I didn't report it sooner. Especially after last night. The only thing which can save my bacon is a successful outcome."

"You only found out about it late last night!" cried Daisy, outraged on his behalf. "I don't see what else you could do when I came in and told you where Gloria was but go and see if she was still there! Any delay would have been madness."

"So your delinquency only begins this morning, Mr. Fletcher," Lucy observed. "Which means the prospect of awkward questions actually weighs on the other side, that is, *for* reporting in now."

"Confound it, Lucy!" Phillip burst into the room, his usual diffidence towards her in abeyance. "You're not trying to persuade him to spill the beans!"

"Take a damper, Petrie," Alec advised him. "I'd already decided it was more or less pointless to contact my colleagues at this stage, and I wouldn't save my skin at the expense of Miss Arbuckle's, believe me. Not that I'm ungrateful for your *caveat,* Miss Fotheringay."

"Lucy," she murmured.

Alec smiled at her. Daisy could have kissed her. If Lucy unbent so far as to invite him to call her by her Christian name, it was a good omen for the Dowager Lady Dalrymple's eventual acceptance.

"Sorry," said Phillip, abashed. His face was drawn, dark circles beneath his eyes. The hopes raised last night, only to be dashed, must have been harder to bear than his previous state of despondency.

He needed something to do, Daisy decided. "So it's all up to us now," she said. "Tommy and Madge have gone to follow Crawford . . ."

"Tommy! Dash it all, why not me? Why didn't you wake me?"

"We'll all have to take a turn, or he'll get suspicious of

the same car always being behind him, don't you think, Alec?"

"Certainly," Alec said promptly, continuing with his breakfast and leaving present matters to Daisy.

She knew, however, that he would not hesitate to jump in if he disagreed with her proposals. A husband who always knuckled under would be as bad as one who never let her use her own brains, she thought. "So you can relieve the Pearsons, Phil," she said.

"I haven't got a car," Phillip pointed out disconsolately.

"Binkie will lend you the Alvis," Lucy promised. "Won't you, darling?" she added as Binkie came in.

"Right-ho. What?"

"Is that an interjection or a question, darling?"

"What will I do?" Binkie asked with a belated touch of trepidation.

"Lend Phil the Alvis."

"Oh, right-ho! Why?"

"Because the kidnappers pinched the Swift," Daisy reminded him, glaring the nascent grin off Alec's face. "Tommy and Madge have followed Crawford to Cowley. When they telephone, Phillip will take over the pursuit."

"Oh, right-ho. Er, who's Crawford?"

Binkie had somehow been missed out of the general enlightenment. While Phillip, unmoved by doubt, explained that Crawford was the confounded ugly customer who had grabbed his girl, Daisy turned to Lucy.

"I don't think Phillip should go alone," she said in an undertone. "The poor chump's bound to do something silly. Binkie had better go with him."

"Binkie will never stop him. Besides, a mixed couple will look less suspicious than two men, don't you think? I'll go, unless you want to?"

"No!" Alec swallowed a mouthful. "Daisy's still rocky from last night. I'd take it as a favour if you'd go, Miss . . . Lucy."

"I'm perfectly all right," Daisy insisted. Battling the infuriating blush she felt rising in her cheeks, she went on, "But actually, if you don't mind going, Lucy, I'd rather like to take Alec to meet Mother later on. Unless there's something else you need to do, Alec?"

"Unfortunately, I can't think of a thing." It was his turn to flush. "Unfortunately for Miss Arbuckle's sake," he said hastily. "I'm looking forward to meeting Lady Dalrymple."

Lucy laughed. "Daisy's mother doesn't actually bite," she commiserated.

"No, but Geraldine jolly nearly does," Daisy said guiltily. "I'm afraid I had to tell her and Edgar that you're a detective—and that we're all here at your request to provide cover for your investigation."

"Great Scott!" Alec groaned. "You could at least have confessed that it's I who am embroiled in your affairs, not the reverse! Lord and Lady Dalrymple must think the police . . ."

"What's that?" Phillip demanded. "The Dalrymples know you're police?"

"I told them, Phil."

"Hang it all, Daisy, the more people know, the more risk for Gloria!"

"I had to say something. Geraldine was on the verge of throwing us out after what she described as our 'frolics' in the early hours of the morning."

"They'd know who Alec is sooner or later," Lucy said, "and they'd have been fearfully offended to have been kept in the dark earlier."

"Why the deuce should they ever know?"

"Because Edgar's Daisy's cousin," Lucy explained patiently, with a sly look at Daisy, "and when Alec joins the family they can hardly keep his profession secret."

"Joins . . .? Oh! It's come to that has it?" Phillip looked faintly disapproving. Daisy scowled at him.

"Should have guessed, old man," said Binkie. "Invited

Fletcher down to meet her mater and all that, what? Have
to tell one's people first."

"Actually," Daisy fumed, suddenly unexpectedly near
tears, "nothing's settled. Alec hasn't even proposed and after the m-mess we've landed him in, perhaps he never will."

Alec reached for her hand. "This isn't quite how I'd en-
visaged it," he said wryly, "but I can't leave you in suspense, my love. This isn't the first mess you've landed me
in, and somehow I doubt that it will be the last. Will you
marry me?"

"Oh, Alec!" The tears flowed then. He enfolded her in
his arms.

The others tactfully disappeared. As the door closed behind them, Daisy was distantly aware of Binkie's plaintive
voice: "But Lucy, I haven't had my breakfast!"

Madge telephoned. She and Tommy had followed Crawford
all the way from the Abbey Hotel to the Morris factory.
Tommy was sitting in a perfectly ghastly cafe opposite the
works, drinking simply poisonous coffee and keeping an
eye on the maroon two-seater, while she reported in. What
next?

"I advised her to try the tea," Alec told Daisy and Lucy,
"to follow if he leaves, and otherwise to hang on until relieved. Bincombe and Petrie should be back soon."

Phillip and Binkie came in a few minutes later.

"We tried three garages," Phillip announced. "The nearest to the kidnap spot's a mile and a half away, and the others
four or five miles. They all swore they'd never been asked by
an American to go searching the lanes for a Studebaker."

"Not the sort of thing they'd forget, eh, what?" said
Binkie.

"I hardly think so," Alec agreed. "I can't see how even
Arbuckle will be able to doubt now that Crawford's our
man."

17

"I've just remembered," Daisy said in dismay. "Crawford's met Phillip. What if he recognizes him?"

"Not likely." Lucy adjusted the cloche to a jaunty angle on her smooth, dark head. "I won't let Phil get too close, and I'll see he keeps his hat on. With the Alvis's hood up he'll be practically invisible."

"Having the hood up will look suspicious."

"Hardly, darling, when it's drizzling."

"Oh, is it?" Daisy looked out of Lucy's bedroom window. A light but steady rain was falling. Odd; for the past couple of hours she'd have sworn the sun shone. "That's lucky. Phillip really needs something to keep him busy."

With quick, expert fingers, Lucy touched up her makeup. A last dab of powder on the nose and they went downstairs. The men were waiting in the front hall, Phillip twitching with impatience.

Alec smiled at Daisy but addressed Lucy. "I've asked Petrie to ring up at once if Mr. and Mrs. Pearson are gone when you reach Cowley. They'll be following Crawford, so don't waste time trying to find out if he's still there. Bincombe will stay within reach of the 'phone."

"Hold the fort, darling." Lucy kissed Binkie's cheek, then turned and kissed Daisy. "Good luck, darling. Cheerio. All right, Phillip, you can stop fidgeting. Let's go."

Alec gave Binkie a few last-minute instructions about

what to do in various contingencies. "Don't telephone the Dower House unless you absolutely have to," he finished.

Binkie grinned and nodded. "Right-oh. Best of luck, old man."

"Anyone would think Mother was an ogre," Daisy said crossly as she and Alec went out under a shared umbrella to the Austin, brought round from the stable-yard by Bill Truscott. Everyone's good wishes had the perverse effect of making her more nervous than she already was. "She may be a bit difficult at times, but I've seen you cope with much worse."

"And cope I shall," he soothed her, opening the passenger door. She was grateful for his forbearance in not pointing out that she had never seen him dealing with a prospective mother-in-law.

He went round, got in beside her, and saying, "First things first," he kissed her.

"First things" thoroughly accomplished, Daisy settled back in her seat with a satisfied sigh as Alec pressed the self-starter, engaged the gear, let off the brake, and started down the avenue.

"When we're married," she said, just for the sake of saying the words, "will you teach me to drive?"

"I'm not sure its a good idea for husbands to teach wives."

"Binkie taught Lucy."

"They're not married. We'd better not wait for the wedding. Daisy, are you quite sure your mother really invited me to lunch?"

Daisy melted at the evidence that he was nervous too. "Of course," she assured him. "When I rang up to see if it was convenient for us to pop in today, she actually offered of her own accord."

"She wants to vet my table manners," he said with conviction, adding ruefully, "Fairacres is rather larger and more impressive than I'd expected."

"There's nothing wrong with your table manners, dearest. Fairacres is a bit different from the house in Chelsea, isn't it? I dare say that's why it came as a shock."

"What I don't understand is how you came to be penniless when your father owned so much. The house and land are entailed on the male heir, of course, but still . . ."

"It's because of Gervaise dying in the War. Father had always assumed he'd take care of me, you see, until I married or if I didn't marry. When he was killed, Father was too heartbroken to think about changing his will, and then he died in the 'flu epidemic before he got around to it."

"I know how it took people by surprise," Alec said softly. "Joan left things undone. Dear love, you mustn't mind if I speak of Joan now and then. I love you differently, but just as much."

"I don't mind. I know Belinda will need to talk about her mother. Alec, I have to tell you about . . ." She stopped as the car turned into the Dower House's short drive. "Oh, bother, here we are. It will have to wait."

He put on the brake and turned to her, his grey eyes serious. "I hope you will always feel able to tell me absolutely anything."

She squeezed his hand. "Oh, Alec, I do love you. No, don't kiss me. Mother wouldn't do anything so vulgar as peer through the window, but she might just happen to be standing by it. Alec, when Edgar inherited Fairacres, he offered me a home, and when I refused he offered to settle some money on me. I refused that, too, but I'll tell him I've changed my mind if you want me to."

"Great Scott, no! I shall expect you to help support the family by writing, not by cadging off your relatives."

Laughing from sheer lightness of heart, Daisy waved gaily to the gardener, who was pulling the crop of weeds already springing up after the rain.

"You remember Owen Morgan, from Occles Hall?" she

asked Alec. "If we need another man to help rescue Gloria, I'm sure he'd do it."

"Not another one who finds an appeal from you irresistible?" Alec said indulgently. "Whatever it is in those guileless blue eyes that persuades people to jump through hoops for you, I hope you'll try it on your mother."

"Mother's proof against it," Daisy said with regret.

The Dowager Lady Dalrymple acknowledged her daughter's introduction of the undistinguished stranger with a haughty nod and a cool "How do you do." But Daisy saw her eyes widen.

Fearing a penniless intellectual, a wealthy upstart, or even, heaven forbid, a foreigner, her ladyship obviously didn't know what to make of Alec. He was neither scruffy nor over-smartly dressed; his voice, while not Eton-and-Oxford, was accentless; he was, in fine, the very picture of a perfectly respectable gentleman.

Unfortunately, where a prospective son-in-law was concerned, respectability was a damning word. Lady Dalrymple had set her heart on nobility, or, at worst, the upper ranks of the landed gentry.

"Sherry, Mr. Fletcher," offered her ladyship stiffly, "or do you prefer one of these modern cocktails? Cook has some gin, I believe."

"Sherry, please, Lady Dalrymple," Alec said, and bit his lip. Catching his eye, Daisy was relieved to see he was biting back amusement, not chagrin.

"Alec prefers medium dry, like me, Mother," she said. "Shall I pour? Sweet for you?"

"Thank you, dear. You are staying at the Wedge and Beetle, I understand, Mr. Fletcher. I trust you find it comfortable?"

"As a matter of fact, I haven't tried it yet. I spent last night at Fairacres."

"Indeed! Of course, Edgar and Geraldine have not yet quite found their feet in their new position." The dowager's tone said clearly that she doubted they ever would, as evidenced by their inviting someone like Alec to stay.

Her mastery of the veiled insult had to be admired, but Daisy wasn't going to let her bully Alec. Not that he was exactly bullyable. He still looked amused, she noted, handing him his glass.

"Edgar and Geraldine seem to have settled in very nicely," she said brightly.

Her mother sniffed, but she was not to be deflected from her primary target. Sitting down, and inviting Alec to do likewise, she said, "Who are your people, Mr. Fletcher? I don't believe I'm acquainted with anyone of that name."

"My earliest ancestors of whom we have any record," Alec expounded, "were medieval arrow-makers and bowmen. By the sixteenth century, the family took a literary turn. I regret to say we cannot claim John Fletcher, of Beaumont and Fletcher fame, but you have heard, perhaps, of Giles Fletcher the Elder? No? He was a poet and author of a book on Russia, and he passed on his gifts to his sons, Giles the Younger and Phineas, both noted poets and churchmen in their time. Giles's sermons were much admired, and Phineas's poems attacking the Jesuits were very well received, though for my part I prefer his delightful descriptions of rural scenery."

Daisy felt almost as dazed as her mother looked. Continuing, Alec managed to appear to take pity on them.

"I shan't bore you with the next few centuries," he said with a sweeping gesture which seemed to unjustly exclude swarms of distinguished forebears. "My father had no literary aspirations. His vocation lay in the world of finance."

Mr. Fletcher the Elder had been the manager of a North London branch of the Westminster Bank, Daisy knew. Her suspicious glance at Alec was answered with the suspicion of a wink.

Thinking back over what he had said, she realized the "record" of his early ancestors could well be no more than the name itself. Nor had he actually claimed to be descended from the poetical Fletchers. Oh, the tortuous mind of a detective!

"Finance?" The dowager was at least slightly impressed. "You have followed in your father's footsteps?"

"No, I decided to dedicate my modest talents to the protection of society."

"The Army?" Lady Dalrymple asked eagerly. The Army was a perfectly acceptable profession.

"The police," Alec said blandly.

"Good gracious!" Aghast, Lady Dalrymple stared at him, apparently trying to picture him in a blue helmet, swinging a truncheon. "I must say, I'd never have guessed," she admitted in a weak voice, looking daggers at Daisy.

"He's quite presentable for a bobby, isn't he?" Having thrown this provocation into the ring, Daisy decided her mother was ripe for the dénouement. "As a matter of fact, Alec is a Detective Chief Inspector at Scotland Yard."

"Oh, *plain*-clothes!" The elimination of the awful prospect of a son-in-law in police uniform mollified her, just as Daisy had hoped. In comparison, a high-ranking detective was endurable. *"Chief* Inspector? Your father was on very good terms with the Chief Constable, Daisy. Colonel Sir Nigel Wookleigh, a charming man. Perhaps you know him, Mr. Fletcher?"

"Not yet, Lady Dalrymple, but I have every expectation of making his acquaintance very shortly."

Since he didn't mention that he was going to have to explain to the Worcestershire C.C. why he had been operating on his patch without permission, the dowager was pleased. At least her daughter's friend moved in the proper circles. The rest of the visit took place in an atmosphere of astonishing cordiality.

Daisy didn't go so far as to announce that she was engaged to Alec. It was better if Mother believed her approval had been sought in advance. They would break the news before returning to town on Sunday.

If they returned on Sunday! Daisy's mind, otherwise occupied, had lost sight of the kidnapping and Gloria Arbuckle's plight. Remembering, she was anxious to get back to Fairacres, though Binkie would have telephoned if anything urgent had come up. She extricated Alec from her mother's laments over the parlous state of the world and left her grumbling about the shortness of their visit.

"We could have stayed a little longer," Alec protested mildly as they drove off. "It seems a pity to have upset her when we were getting along swimmingly."

"You did charm her, darling! But in just another few minutes she'd have found cause for complaint in our staying too long. I'd rather she had too little of us than too much. Besides, I'm simply dying to find out whether Phillip and Lucy have picked up Crawford's trail."

Phillip peered through the rain-smeared windscreen at the dingy building: ERT'S CAFE said the sign painted on the steamed-up windows.

"Surely this can't be the place?" he said uncertainly.

Lucy sighed. "I'm afraid it must be, old thing. It's right opposite the factory entrance, it only needs a 'B' to make it 'Bert's,' and it looks as if it serves poisonous coffee. And there's the Lagonda, down that alley. Bite the bullet, hold your nose, let's go."

Jamming his hat down further on his forehead, Phillip stepped out into the drizzle. In the forecourt of the Morris factory, behind the wire fence, he saw a maroon A.C. Six.

He ducked his head back into the Alvis. "Crawford's still here," he hissed.

Lucy stopped powdering her nose for long enough to say, "I should jolly well hope so, or Madge and Tommy really botched it."

Opening his umbrella, Phillip went round the pointed, "duck's back" rear of the polished aluminum two-seater and opened the door for her. In her smart, high-heeled strap shoes Lucy perched on the running board, gazing down with dismay at the muddy puddles between her and the café.

"Perhaps I'll just wait here."

"He may stay for hours yet. Do come along."

She sighed again, cautiously stepped down, and picked her way to the door. As Phillip opened it, a hot, moist blast of air saturated with stale grease and cigarette smoke hit them.

"Faugh! Hours, you said? I shan't survive five minutes."

Phillip ignored her moaning. "There are Tommy and Madge," he said as every head in the room turned towards them. There were few customers at this time, shortly before the lunch hour. He led the way, squeezing between the close-packed, oil-clothed tables, each with its bottle of HP Sauce, to where the Pearsons sat by the window.

"Thank heaven you've come," said Tommy, standing up. "Madge is feeling sick."

"Poor darling, I'm not in the least surprised," Lucy commiserated. "You could cut the atmosphere in here with a knife."

"How can you make such a fuss," Phillip burst out angrily, "when Gloria's in danger?"

"Here, I say, old boy," Tommy protested. "Steady! We're all doing everything we can to help."

"Sorry." Staring down miserably at the grubby tablecloth, Phillip wished he had never fallen in love. His calm, ordered world, its extremes of emotion the boredom of the office and the pleasure of working on the Swift, had vanished. The joy of knowing Gloria and the hope of winning her had turned into this awful emptiness of dread.

He didn't think he could cope with it much longer.

Madge took his hand in both hers. "It's all right, Phillip," she said gently. "You must feel as I did when Tommy first went to France; you haven't had time to grow numb. Just remember we're with you through thick and thin. You mustn't mind what Lucy says. It's just her way."

"That's right, darling," Lucy drawled. "Tommy, you'd better get Madge out into the fresh air quickly. She's turning green. You might move the Alvis round the corner for us, if you don't mind. It's rather conspicuous and I'd prefer not to be left alone in this frightful place."

The Pearsons hurried out. Lucy sat down beside the window and, with her handkerchief, retouched the clear circle Madge had wiped in the condensation. Taking the opposite seat, Phillip did likewise.

"The A.C.'s still there," he said with relief.

"That red car inside the fence? Lucky it's that colour. I'll be able to spot it quite easily when we get going."

"Yes. Look here, Lucy, I'm sorry I blew up."

"Not another word on the subject. Are you going to buy me tea? Blast, I forgot to ask Madge if it was any more drinkable than the coffee."

To a request for a pot of China tea, the slatternly waitress responded that all they had was TyPhoo in the urn, milk and sugar already added. Lucy shuddered. They finally settled on a bottle of ginger-beer apiece.

Before long, mechanics from the works opposite streamed in for their midday meal. Phillip and Lucy garnered many a curious glance, but no one disturbed them. After the first rush, though, the waitress was not too busy to demand that they order something to eat if they insisted on taking up a table.

Lucy decided tinned tomato soup was the safest item on the menu. Phillip ventured upon sausage and mash, which he ate without tasting, his eyes glued to the clear spot on the glass.

The maroon motor-car continued to sit unmoving across the road. The workmen left, streaming back through the gate in the wire fence, past the A.C. Six, into the buildings.

Lucy opened the copy of *The Queen* magazine she had brought with her and flipped idly through it. Time passed.

"Suppose he's gone out a back way," Phillip said, beginning to despair. "Suppose he's taken a Morris for a spin and he stops off to see his men."

"Someone from the factory would go with him," Lucy told him firmly, "to make sure everything runs smoothly. Anyway, there's nothing we can do about it."

The waitress reappeared. "Was you wanting anythin' else? 'Cause I got to sweep the floor afore the next lot comes in," she said in a disgruntled voice. Phillip saw she had already up-ended the chairs on most of the other tables. "You been here going on four hours."

"No wonder I'm stiff." Lucy stretched. "I'll have another ginger-beer and some plain biscuits, please, Rich Tea or Marie."

"Same for me," said Phillip, massaging the crick in his neck as he turned back to his peephole.

"Let's switch seats so you can bend your head the other way," Lucy suggested.

"Good idea." As Phillip sat down on her chair he wiped the window. Applying his eye, he saw two men standing beside the A.C. Six.

He jumped up. "Come on! He's leaving at last."

"At last!" Lucy closed the magazine and stood up.

"Hoy!" exclaimed the waitress. "You going? What about this stuff you ordered?"

"Never mind that," Phillip cried.

"We'll take it," Lucy contradicted him. "Who knows when we'll get another chance to eat?" She stuffed the biscuits into her handbag.

Phillip tossed a florin on the table, grabbed the bottles and his umbrella, and ran through the forest of chair-legs to the door. He opened it and held it for Lucy, gentlemanly instinct prevailing, but he beat her to the Alvis although she quickly abandoned her attempt to preserve her shoes from puddles. By the time she wrenched open the door and jumped in, he had the engine started, the hand-brake off, and first gear engaged.

She slammed the door. "Creep forward till we can see around the corner," she advised.

Instinct now shrieking at him to move fast, he had to acknowledge the common sense of her suggestion. Slowly letting out the clutch, he inched forward.

"Stop!" said Lucy. "Damn, if you go any farther the bonnet will stick out and I still can't see the gate. Can you?"

He craned his neck. "Not quite."

She groaned. "All right, I'll get out and stand on the corner. Where's the umbrella?"

"Here. Leave the door open."

Lucy had barely peeked around the building when she ducked back. "He's coming this way," she said breathlessly, closing the umbrella and hopping in.

"Back into Oxford. Dash it, I hope he's not going to stop in the town."

"Gosh, yes. We could easily lose him there."

But Crawford drove steadily through the town centre, turning north at Carfax, then branching left on the Woodstock Road.

"At least he's not heading for the Midlands," Phillip observed with relief. "This is the way home via Chipping Norton and Evesham. Oh Lord, do you think he's just going to drive straight back to Malvern?"

"I haven't the foggiest. We'll see, if you don't get too close so you have to overtake or look suspicious."

Phillip eased up on the accelerator.

Through the village of Woodstock, past the gates of Blenheim Palace; up the long slope into the Cotswolds: then Chipping Norton, Moreton-in-Marsh, Bourton-on-the-Hill—Phillip's spirits sank lower with every mile they followed the maroon motor-car.

"He's not going to stop."

"We're only half-way. Phillip!" Lucy clutched his arm. "He's turning off! No, don't slow down, drive on past. He might glance back."

Reluctantly, Phillip obeyed. Crawford had turned into a narrow, unpaved lane, its entrance half obscured by hedges and overhanging trees on either side. The A.C. Six was already out of sight. Phillip stepped on the brake and put the Alvis into reverse. Lucy closed her eyes, crossing her fingers as he backed along the main road.

A Napier swerved around the Alvis; its chauffeur shook his fist.

Just past the lane, Phillip stopped again and engaged forward gear. They plunged into the green tunnel beneath the trees.

18

The Alvis squelched, sloshed, and jolted along muddy ruts with grass growing in between. Phillip hoped the suspension was up to it. He wouldn't have chosen to drive his Swift this way.

He remembered sadly that he might never see the Swift again.

They emerged from the tree-tunnel and started uphill. The drainage was better though the potholes were just as bad. The hedges gave way to high banks topped with drystone walls. An occasional gateway showed steep hillsides of short-cropped pasture, where fleeing sheep added to Phillip's impression of the rarity of motor-vehicles.

"No side turnings," Lucy observed.

"Thank heaven."

"And I think the rain's stopping."

The bank on their right ended. Now they could see the sheep-dotted slope rising beyond the low wall. The few trees were scattered, twisted thorns or clumps of oaks in the hollows of the hills.

"There, I saw his hood," Lucy exclaimed in triumph. "He's not far ahead, just around a bend or two. Slow down."

Phillip caught a glimpse of something moving less than a quarter of a mile ahead, before a particularly vicious pothole made him clutch the steering wheel. He returned his attention to his driving. If they had a puncture or broke a spring, they would lose Crawford for good.

A moment later Lucy leaned forward and peered round Phillip. "There's what looks like a farm track up to the right," she said. "A pale streak winding back round behind the hill. I don't think it's the lane. Gosh, he's turned up it. Phillip, stop! If I can see him, he can see us. Go back a bit."

"Are you sure it's not the lane?" Phillip asked in an agony of doubt even as he braked.

"Pretty sure. I can see what I think is the lane curving round to the left between the hills. See, over there. There's a double line of walls. It must be this lane. Go back, he'll see us!"

"No, with no sun shining to reflect off the glass we'll be less likely to catch his eye if we're not moving, and we can watch him, too. Where . . . ? Oh yes."

The maroon A.C. crept up the track, crossing the slope at an angle. As the car disappeared around the hillside, Phillip started the Alvis forward again.

Around a couple of bends, they came to a gate. As Phillip slowed, Lucy said, "That's it. Look, you can see the tyremarks in the mud, and there's the beginning of the track. No!" she exclaimed as he turned the wheel. "We can't follow him up there. He'd be bound to see us, or even meet us face to face. It looks to me as if the track circles the summit."

Something tugged at Phillip's memory. Frowning, he got out of the car and went to lean against the gate, staring up at the crest of the hill. An odd shape, as if a handleless frying pan had been set down upside-down on top, it was vaguely familiar.

He turned back to Lucy. "I have to go and look. Crawford's got to have Gloria hidden up there, somehow. Why else should he go up?"

"There's something fishy up there all right, but you can't drive up and you can't leave the car here for him to find. You're not planning anything asinine, are you, Phillip? Trying to rescue Gloria single-handed will just mean two people for the rest of us to rescue."

Flushing at the accuracy of her guess, he returned to the driver's seat. "What shall we do, then?" he asked a bit sulkily.

"Drive on until we find somewhere to hide the car, behind a wall or something. Then you can go off and reconnoitre. At least *you* had the sense to wear walking boots." She glanced down ruefully at her muddy footwear. "I can't go slogging cross-country in these, though they're already ruined."

"I'm sure Mr. Arbuckle will pay for a new pair," Phillip consoled her, driving on.

The lane continued to rise for a few hundred yards, curving to the left between a shoulder of the odd-shaped hill and a lower ridge to their left. Then it abruptly swung right and began to descend. Still nowhere to conceal the Alvis. Phillip was starting to fret when Lucy cried, "Oh, perfect!"

"By Jove, a quarry!"

The flat floor of the abandoned slate-pit was level with the road and thickly overgrown. Phillip pulled over among the trees and bushes.

Lucy took out her vanity-case and powdered her nose.

Between the trees, the ground was stony. Getting out, Phillip saw that the Alvis had left no tracks. He strode back to the lane and turned. The car was invisible.

Returning a few paces, he called to Lucy, "I'm off. Give me a couple of hours, and if I'm not back you'd better go and tell the others."

"For pity's sake, don't do anything idiotic," she responded. "Don't let them see you."

Phillip did not deign to retort. For one thing, he knew Lucy could easily squash him in a contest of words. For another, he was in far too much of a hurry. Somewhere on that hill his girl was being held against her will.

His long legs took him at a fast lope up the lane until

he had a clear view of the hilltop. Then he clambered over the wall and set off across the short grass.

In spite of his resentment, he was mindful of Lucy's parting injunction. The men probably had a look-out, but he was pretty sure there weren't enough of them to watch in all directions and the chances were they kept an eye on the track Crawford had used. As Londoners, they might well discount the likelihood of anyone approaching cross-country. So Phillip, despite his impatience, headed around the hill.

From every angle, the summit had the same peculiar, truncated appearance. Now Phillip knew where he was. That was Brockberrow Hill, once a favourite place to bicycle for a day's outing.

The excrescence on top was the remains of an Iron Age fort, unless it was Stone Age or Bronze Age or something. The Picts, or Early Britons, or whatever, had chosen a good viewpoint for their fortifications. From the top of the circular mound one could see forever. Inside, one was sheltered from the wind. There was even a ruined shepherd's hut for refuge from showers.

That, of course, was where they had Gloria. How Crawford had ever found the place was a mystery, but Phillip would bet his bottom dollar on it.

He cast his mind back to the old days. The bicyclers—he and Gervaise and various friends and siblings—had always left their cycles at Brock Farm, on the far side of the hill from the track. Buying picnic supplies from the farmer's wife, they used to walk up a footpath to the top.

It had not been much of a footpath, more of a sheep trail. The kidnappers could easily overlook it, or discount its significance, especially as trees hid the farm buildings from the top.

Quite a few stunted hawthorns grew on the upper slopes on that side, Phillip recalled. There were criss-crossing drystone walls, too, dividing pastures and sheep-pens, all good cover for a clandestine approach. And, come to think of it, a clump of thorn trees—more bushes, really—had taken root on the shallower inner side of the fortification mound. If they had survived the years, he could wriggle in amongst them to watch and listen in perfect safety.

Perfect safety, he assured himself, dismissing the faint echo in his mind of Lucy's warning.

Climbing a wall, he saw down to his left the tall beeches around Brock Farm. Ahead was the slope—sheepless at present—scattered with hawthorns, just as he had pictured it. From the shelter of the nearest he scanned the hilltop, wishing he had brought binoculars.

No head protruded above the level brow of the mound; no sign of movement; no sound but the cawing of rooks in the valley behind him, the trill of a lark above, and an occasional far-off *baa*. All the same, Phillip avoided the path itself when he found it, and took full advantage of the cover of trees and walls as he made his way up the gentle slope.

Before tackling the last, bare stretch up to the track encircling the base of the ancient fortification, he paused for another survey. Nothing had changed.

He set off again at a jog-trot.

Pity it had stopped raining. Not only did rain obscure the vision, the discomfort distracted sentries' attention from their business—one of the lessons learnt in Flanders which Phillip had never expected to think of again. He wouldn't be surprised if it was raining again before nightfall, though. Here on the exposed upper slopes, a gusty wind was blowing, warm and damp, from the south-west.

Dashing across the track, he tried to remember the layout inside the fort. The one-time gateway, now just a narrow gap, was round to his left, he thought, a quarter circle from the head of the track, perhaps for some obscure, prehistoric defensive purpose. The thorn bushes, fortunately, were slightly to his right. He hoped.

He scrambled diagonally up the steep bank. Lying prone

on the damp grass, his elbow in a patch of scarlet and yellow ladies' slipper, he took off his hat and raised his bare head inch by inch.

No outcry greeted the appearance of his hair on the horizon. He moved up a little farther and found he had perfectly judged his position. The hawthorn thicket hid him from those below. They hid the men from him, too, but he heard their voices.

Listening, he slithered over the top and under the spiky branches.

". . . don't fink we're gonna let yer pick up the bunce on yer own and scarper back to the States wiv it, do yer? Not bloody likely!"

"Come off it, would I vamoose and leave you guys holding the baby?" Crawford's voice was not so much oily as slimy, Phillip decided with loathing. His chuckle was still more repulsive. "Still and all, by golly, she's a baby worth holding, which is one reason I won't skedaddle with the dough. I'll be back to . . ."

Phillip missed his next words. Seeing red, he forgot his good resolutions and rose to his knees, prepared to rush down and strangle the bounder whatever the consequences.

A thorn raking down his cheek brought him to his senses. Joining Gloria would not help her. With a silent groan he moved a little further down the slope to where he could see the men and glare his hatred at their oblivious heads.

Crawford and three others stood in a group to the left of the one-room, tumbledown stone shepherd's hut, between it and the gateway.

"Blimey, guv, we don't none of us hold wiv none of that!" one of the men was protesting. Phillip recognized his anxious tone. "You swore . . ."

Crawford cut him off with an unconvincing laugh. "That's so. I guess I must have gotten a bit carried away. Oh, well, that's all right. Now, how can I convince you I don't plan to make a get-away without you?"

"Two of us goes wiv yer, or yer can 'and over yer passport, mate, that's what," the biggest man said menacingly.

In the momentary silence Phillip noticed, beyond them, an Army tent pitched against the bank. At least Gloria did not have to suffer their company all the time, he thought with gladness.

Of course, though it seemed an age since Daisy staggered into the drawing-room at Fairacres, Gloria had only been here since the middle of last night. Phillip vowed that she should never spend an entire night in the hut. He must get back to Lucy and organize the rescue party.

But he didn't dare leave until Crawford had driven off. Besides, he might hear something useful, might even catch a glimpse of Gloria. He checked his wrist-watch: still time enough before Lucy started worrying.

"My passport?" Crawford said uneasily, his hand moving to cover his breast pocket.

" 'Sright, mate. Long as you're stuck in England, we've gotcha by the short 'airs."

"Reckon we oughta 'ave one or two of us watching the pickup, too," said another. " 'Case anyfing goes wrong, they can get back 'ere and warn the others."

"Rats, nothing's going to go wrong." Crawford sounded distinctly irritable now. "These plutocrats have nerves of steel when it comes to playing the market, but hit 'em with something like this, and by golly, they crumble faster than a stale cookie. I've jollied Arbuckle along and he's fallen for it, no if, and, or but about it. You should see him. He's in a dandy funk! The old coot hasn't gone within a mile of a cop."

The men continued to wrangle over collecting the ransom, then, without a decision, moved on to complaints about their quarters. Crawford told them it was their own fault they had to leave the gamekeeper's cottage. They were lucky he had found them a fall-back, pure curiosity having led him to investigate the significance of the word CAMP on a map.

"It won't be for long, anyhow," he added. "Tonight's the night."

"Then 'and over that there passport!"

Tonight! Phillip glanced at his watch again. If he didn't hurry, Lucy would assume he'd been caught and leave without him. He couldn't wait for Crawford to clear out. He'd have to rely on hearing the A.C. Six start up to give him time to take cover.

Voices raised in a row over the passport allowed him to make a hasty withdrawal from the hawthorns without worrying about rustling leaves. Hat in hand, he crawled back over the crest of the mound and slid down the bank. Bounding down the hillside, he headed directly for the quarry.

Behind him a motor-car engine coughed to life. He raced for the nearest wall, dived over it, and lay flat.

A pair of inquisitive sheep turned their heads to stare, then ambled over to take a closer look. Phillip twitched as one nibbled hopefully at his hair.

"Pa-aa-ah!" it said in disgust, and started on the grass two inches from his nose.

Hearing the engine noise grow louder as the A.C. rounded the hilltop, he didn't dare raise a hand to push the beast away.

The sound of the engine retreated. Phillip rose to a crouch and peered over the wall. The maroon car was halfway down the track, heading away from him at an angle, but the driver's side was towards him. He must not move on yet.

He watched the A.C. Six reach the bottom. Crawford climbed out to open the gate, drove through, shut it again, and zipped off back towards the main road.

Phillip rose, sparing a regretful glance for the muddy, grass-stained knees of his flannels. Another pair of bags ruined! He set off at a steady run for the quarry.

The Alvis was gone.

He gazed around, hoping he'd come to the wrong spot, but no, there were the broken, wilting branches he had half noticed before. His watch showed he was five minutes late. Lucy might have given him a few minutes extra! She was on her way back to Fairacres to tell the others he had gone and done something idiotic. Fletcher would think the kidnappers knew they'd been found. What he'd decide to do, goodness only . . .

"Pssst! Phillip, is it all clear?"

"Lucy! Yes. What the deuce . . . ? Where's the Alvis?"

She emerged from the bushes, brushing her skirt vigorously. "I moved it. There's a van hidden behind those branches and I was afraid someone might come for it."

"A brown Ford van? With a butcher's name on it?"

"Green, unmarked. It could be a Ford for all I know."

"Never mind, it must be the one because it's them all right. They'll have painted it, to disguise and camouflage it. I say, suppose I disable it, so they can't get away?"

"No, better not. If they try to go somewhere before we're ready, they'd be forewarned. Come on, we must get back to Fairacres. The Alvis is over here."

Phillip took two steps after her and stopped. He had been torn from Gloria's side before. He found he simply could not bear to leave her voluntarily, even if she was not aware of his presence.

Across his mind flashed Crawford's description of her: "a baby worth holding," and his vow to return for her, ambiguously retracted.

"I'm staying," Phillip announced. "If something goes wrong, perhaps I'll be able to help Gloria."

"Oh bosh!" Lucy turned, exasperated, hands on hips. "If she's still all right now, nothing frightful's going to happen at least till they have the ransom."

"That's tonight. What if Fletcher can't get things organized in time?"

"I'm sure he will. I'm coming to have considerable respect for Detective Chief Inspector Alec Fletcher. All the same, he's going to need all the men he can get, and if you go and get yourself caught before the rest arrive. . . ."

"I shan't," he said obstinately, "unless I absolutely have to try to protect her. Crawford said. . . ." His voice got tied in a knot in his throat. He tried again. "They talked of harming her even after getting the money."

"I see. But Phil, I'm not at all sure I'll be able to find the way here again. All these hills look alike to me."

"Daisy knows it. Tell her they're at the ancient fort on Brockberrow Hill, where we used to picnic. Listen, you'd better tell Fletcher they don't trust Crawford so they may have more than one man fetching the ransom."

"Where from?" she asked, tacitly agreeing to pass on the information, and thus to Phillip's staying.

"I don't know. They'll tell Arbuckle where and when to drop it off, and with luck he'll pass it on to Fletcher."

"How many men are there?"

"I only saw three, but there was probably one watching the track, and maybe one in the hut with Gloria. Oh, there's a tent, too, besides the shepherd's hut. Don't want anyone falling over the guy-ropes."

"Draw a diagram," Lucy suggested.

Her fountain pen ran dry before he had done more than inscribe the broken circle of the mound in the margin of a page of *The Queen.* A search in his pockets produced a handkerchief, two pound notes, small change, a Scout knife, and a propelling pencil with no lead.

"Damn! I mean, dash it."

"Damn, by all means." Delving into her handbag again, she sighed. "Lipstick. It'll be wrecked. Do you think Arbuckle will replace it, as well as my shoes?"

"Give him a list." With the clumsy implement, Phillip drew the fort on top of an advertisement for a Charity Ball at the Royal Albert Hall. XT showed the position of the tent, XH of the hut, and a dotted line the beginning of the track. He studied his handiwork, dissatisfied. "Oh well, Daisy knows it. The tent's pitched just round to the left from the gateway."

"I still think you should come back with me, to tell them yourself."

Phillip shook his head. "I'm staying," he said firmly, and strode off before she could confuse him with useless arguments.

Behind him the Alvis started up. It caught up with him and stopped as he climbed over the wall. Lucy beckoned.

"Here, you'd better take the biscuits and ginger-beer. Toodle-oo, old chap. Do take care!"

He watched the motor-car's duck's back rear disappear up the lane. As soon as it was out of sight, he dashed back towards the quarry. He'd be damned if he was going to let those swine make a clean get-away if he could help it.

His first notion was to remove the van's radiator hose, as an act of poetic justice. But if one of them left for some reason, he would discover the tampering as soon as the radiator boiled, which would be too soon to stop him warning the others. Whatever Phillip did must look like a natural occurrence, he thought as he reached the slate-pit.

No wonder Lucy had found the van. The conspicuous wilting leaves on the broken branches hiding it were another sign of the Londoners' lack of familiarity with the countryside. It was a Ford all right, its green paint spanking new but applied in a decidedly slapdash fashion.

Phillip tried the rear doors, finding them unlocked. There was no tyre pump to be seen, and the tool-box contained no patching kit—in London, of course, such things were readily available.

He let the air out of the spare tyre, then stabbed one front tyre with the corkscrew on his pocket-knife. Considering the state of the lane, a puncture should come as no surprise, and spares often went flat just sitting. They would have no reason to suspect sabotage.

Grinning, Phillip sang softly to himself as he returned to the lane: " 'He had to get under, get out and get under, to fix his automobile!' "

A swirl of wind spattered his face with spots of rain as he climbed the wall again, jumped down into the meadow, and set off for his own private thorn-patch.

19

"Mr. Arbuckle, my lady." The butler's air of long-suffering suggested he was becoming accustomed, if not resigned, to the American's habit of arriving at hours when no real gentleman would call uninvited.

"Show him in, Lowecroft," said Geraldine, equally long-suffering. "Edgar, we shall go up and dress for dinner. The rest of you. . . ." She paused, and sighed. "The rest of you and Mr. Petrie and Miss Fotheringay, should they condescend to return, will no doubt forgo that nicety if pressed for time. Daisy, you had better invite Mr. Arbuckle to dine with us."

"Thank you, Geraldine. You see, he's . . ."

Geraldine held up her hand. "No, I don't wish to know."

Edgar looked rather wistful, as if he wouldn't have minded a little elucidation, but he followed his wife from the drawing-room, only pausing to greet Arbuckle as he came in.

"It's sure swell of your folks, Miss Dalrymple, not to shoot off their mouths about all this to-ing and fro-ing," Arbuckle said. Waving a sheet of blue notepaper, he advanced on Alec. "Mr. Fletcher, I've gotten the instructions for dropping off the dough. I found this in my suite at the hotel when I got back from Lunnon."

Alec took it. "Plain Basildon Bond, like the others, but this one is in ordinary handwriting, rather shaky."

"Gloria's," said Arbuckle heavily, dropping into a chair. "At least she's still alive."

Daisy, beside Alec on the sofa, craned her neck to read over his shoulder.

"Do tell," Madge begged.

"It's directions to a quarry in the Cotswold Hills," said Arbuckle. "I'm to go alone, at sunset, and leave the dough in the back of a van I'll find parked there."

"And then they'll let Miss Arbuckle go?" Tommy asked hopefully.

"It's more complicated than that." Alec frowned. "Mr. Arbuckle is instructed to go away as soon as he's dropped the money, then return at dawn to pick up directions explaining where to find his daughter. I don't like it."

"If I do anything different, I'll never see Gloria again."

"She says they'll be watching him," Daisy put in.

Restlessly on edge, Arbuckle stood up again. "So things have got to go their way. I'm doing what I'm told tonight, and I better get back to the hotel so if they're watching they see me leave from there."

"Won't you stay for dinner? My cousin asked me to invite you."

He shook his head. "Please tell her ladyship I'd be tickled to death some other time, Miss Dalrymple, but I'm not fit for company right now, even if I could spare the time. Mr. Fletcher, I sure hope I can trust you not to call out the troopers."

"Much as I'd like to, it's far too late to organize a police presence."

"And you won't none of you go near this here quarry." Arbuckle glanced around. "Hey, where's young Petrie?"

Bincombe, silent so far, opened his mouth.

Alec gave him a warning look. "Petrie and Miss Fotheringay went to keep an eye on Crawford. Since they haven't telephoned, we assume they haven't seen anything significant."

"At this point, it don't matter a hoot if it's Crawford or some hoodlum. There's damn-all to do but follow instructions."

"All the same," said Alec, "you'll telephone if they change your instructions, won't you? Or if you think of anything we can do to help?"

"Surely." Arbuckle took back the letter and shook Alec's hand. "Don't think I don't appreciate the support you folks been giving me."

Daisy jumped up and gave him an impulsive hug. "Gloria will be all right," she said. "This is England, not America."

He gave her a weary smile. Alec walked with him to the door and closed it behind him.

"I say, Fletcher, what about Lucy?" Binkie burst out at once. "It's all very well agreeing with Arbuckle, but they've been gone since before lunch. Are we just going to sit on our hands?"

"Steady, old man," Tommy soothed. "No sense getting the poor chap upset about Lucy as well as his daughter, don't y'know. And if I'm not mistaken, Fletcher's one step ahead of us."

"I wish I were," Alec said ruefully. "There really isn't much we can do without more information. I don't imagine you know that bit of country, Daisy. It's rather far from here."

"I don't know the quarry," Daisy admitted unhappily. She had brought her friends into this thoroughly nasty business by claiming her knowledge of the countryside would help. A fat lot of use it had been so far. "We used to cycle that way sometimes, but it's on the outer edge of our range. Oh, blast, I should have copied down the directions. I can't remember them properly."

Alec promptly recited them.

"Map," said Binkie, and disappeared.

He returned a few moments later and they were all poring

over a map of the north Cotswolds when Lucy sauntered in.

"Don't let me interrupt," she drawled.

Binkie bounded to her and engulfed her in a hug which made her squeak. "Where have you been?" he demanded.

"Let me breathe, darling, and I'll tell you." Released—though Binkie kept her hand in his—she joined the others and gazed down at the map. "The Cotswolds? You already know?"

"Only where Mr. Arbuckle's to take the money," said Daisy. "Lucy, where's Phillip?"

"All in good time, darling. Now let me see. No, it's no good. I never could read a map. Phillip swore you'd remember the place, Daisy: Brockbarrow Hill."

"Brock*berr*ow."

"Here," said Tommy, planting a forefinger on the map. "It's right next to the slate-pit I'm sure must be the quarry."

"At least half a mile," Lucy protested, subsiding with languid grace onto the nearest chair and kicking off bespattered shoes. "More to the top. Daisy, I'm simply ravenous. You're none of you dressed. Is dinner going to be late?"

"No. Lucy, for pity's sake, what's this about Brockberrow Hill? Did Phillip go there? Without you?"

"Let's hear the story, please, Lucy," Alec seconded Daisy with a smile. "If you've brought the information we need, time is of the essence."

Lucy grinned at him. "Oh, very well, Chief Inspector, though I was rather enjoying keeping you all in suspense. What it boils down to is that we followed Crawford from Cowley to Brockberrow Hill and Phillip found the kidnappers in some sort of ancient fort at the top."

"And Miss Arbuckle?" Alec asked sharply.

"He didn't see her, but from the way they talked, he was sure she was there."

"She'd be in the shepherd's hut," Daisy said.

"That's right." Lucy waved the magazine she had brought

in with her. Opening it, she said in dismay, "Oh gosh, it's frightfully smeared. I hope you remember the place well enough to make sense of this, Daisy."

"Let's see."

Both pages were a mess of lipstick, but between Daisy's memory and Lucy's and what they could make out, Daisy reconstructed Phillip's diagram.

"This is the fort itself," she pointed out to the others as they clustered around. "All that's left is a high bank, of course."

"How high?" Tommy wanted to know.

"Gosh, I don't know. You couldn't see out from the inside, only sky, but then it's the highest point for quite a way."

"Could you see the roof of the hut from outside?" Alec asked.

"N-no, I don't think so. No, I'm sure the bank's higher than the hut, so it's much higher than a man. Perhaps ten feet?" she hazarded. "Twelve? Fourteen?"

"Good enough. How steep?"

"Steep enough to persuade one to go round and through the gateway—here—after bicycling from here and tramping up the hill. But we used to climb it after the picnic, for the view."

"Phillip must have climbed it," Lucy said, "because he saw inside the circle and I hardly imagine he'd have trotted through the gap like a lamb to the slaughter."

"You didn't go up with him?"

"You're joking, Alec. In those shoes? No, he came down to tell me what he'd found and overheard, then went back to keep an eye on Gloria."

Alec groaned. "Understandable, I suppose."

"I tried to stop him. He did promise not to try any solo attempt to rescue her unless she was in immediate danger."

"Which means, I take it," said Madge, "he expects a mass rescue attempt."

Tommy nodded. "If we don't go, goodness only knows what he'll do."

"He heard them threaten to harm Gloria even if the ransom's delivered as instructed."

In shocked silence, everyone turned from Lucy to Alec.

"We'll go," he said crisply. "I said I don't like this business of Arbuckle having to return to the quarry at dawn to get directions for finding his daughter. I meant it, and now we know Crawford's our man and that threats have been made, I like it still less. Lucy, what else did Petrie overhear?"

"He didn't tell me much. He saw three men besides Crawford, but he thought there were probably at least four. More than one man will go to pick up the ransom, because they don't trust each other. It's to be delivered tonight, but I gather you know that."

"At the quarry at sunset," Alec confirmed. "When does the sun set?"

"Nine thirtyish," Tommy said, "with Summer Time."

They all looked at the clock. Quarter to eight.

"It'll take an hour to get there," Lucy said uneasily. "Maybe more if this rain gets any worse. The lane's in a frightful condition, and then there's the hill to climb. Phillip said there's probably a man watching the track, so you'd have to go round. That's assuming you're heading for the hilltop, not the quarry."

Alec thought for a moment. "If they have hidden men watching the drop-off, it's too risky to try to grab Crawford there, besides leaving Miss Arbuckle in danger from the others."

"Start from this side of the hill," Daisy advised. "Take the path from Brock Farm. That's the way we always used to go. It could cut off ten or fifteen minutes."

"All right, Daisy," said Alec, "I'll take your word for it. You can explain later. First, does Morgan live in at the Dower House?"

"Yes. I'll go and telephone. Do you want Truscott, too? If he's not up here I can get him on the extension to the lodge."

"Please. Pearson, find that young footman, Ernest."

"Was you wanting me, sir?" Ernest advanced eagerly, tray in hand. "Her ladyship said to bring sherry."

Daisy hurried out, leaving Alec to recruit the footman and deal with the question of sherry.

In the hall she met Lowecroft, coming from the direction of the family sitting room, where Edgar and Geraldine must have taken refuge.

"Will Mr. Arbuckle be dining, miss?" he asked, obviously put out. "And do you expect Mr. Petrie to return in time for dinner?"

"No, and no, and I should think Mrs. Pearson and Miss Fotheringay will be the only ones joining my cousins. If you could organize sandwiches for eight in a big hurry— say ten minutes?—it would be much appreciated. Oh, and we'll be taking Ernest with us, I'm afraid."

She dashed on to the 'phone, leaving the butler with his mouth opening and closing like a goldfish.

Truscott promised to be ready to be picked up at the lodge in fifteen minutes, and Morgan would wait at the Dower House gates. Daisy sped up to her bedroom and flung on a warm tweed skirt and jacket and walking shoes. Alec was bound to try to stop her going along. After all her efforts she was determined to see the thing through, and Gloria would surely be glad to see a female face. Daisy refused to be left behind because they would not wait while she changed.

She had other cards up her sleeve.

Grabbing her mac, she headed for the drawing-room. She entered on the heels of Ernest, whose arms were full of electric torches.

He glanced back at her with a grin. "Sandwiches coming

up, Mr. Lowecroft says, miss. I never seen him in such a pother." He laid the torches on a table.

"Thanks, Ernest," said Alec. "Go put on your oldest clothes and stout boots now. Hurry."

"Yessir!"

"You two bring the Lagonda and my Austin round to the front, please," he directed Tom and Binkie, who strode out. They had already changed, as had Alec. "Daisy, come and show me. . . ." He stopped as he noticed her costume. His fearsome eyebrows lowered. "Oh no, you're not coming with us!"

"I can't show you on the map. It's too complicated. I'm not even sure I remember the way to Brock Farm well enough to describe it, but I know I'll recognize it when I see it."

Alec turned on her the piercing grey eyes which made crooks quiver and subordinates leap to attention. Daisy was glad she was telling the truth. Nonetheless, she brought out another ace.

"Even if you found Brock Farm without me," she said persuasively, "the farmyard's the only place to leave the cars and the people there don't know you. They'll remember me. Besides, you'd never find the path without help. It's easy to get lost in the wood before you get to the hillside."

"Oh no, if you come as far as the farm, you go no further. Someone there will show us the way."

"How long would it take to explain the situation to them?"

Alec glanced at the clock and grimaced.

Ten minutes later, Daisy sat in the front passenger seat of the Austin as Alec drove down the avenue. The little car shuddered as wild gusts of wind hit it. Though dark, ragged clouds raced overhead against the paler grey overcast, the rain had stopped for the moment.

The Lagonda was close behind, Tom driving, Binkie next

to him, Ernest in the back. At the lodge, Truscott stood at the door with another man, older grizzled, but still robust.

"Carlin," said Daisy. "Father's gamekeeper."

The chauffeur stepped up to the Austin. "Mr. Carlin dropped by for a chat, sir, and wants to know can he go too?"

"The more the merrier. You two join the Lagonda—the extra weight won't slow it. We'll take Morgan."

They picked up the gardener at the Dower House gates and drove on. Daisy fed sandwiches to Alec as they continued through Pershore and Evesham and up the flank of the Cotswolds to Broadway.

"Turn right at the church," she said as they entered the village, its amber stone drab dun in the gloom of the early twilight beneath the clouds.

"Off the main road already?"

"There might be a quicker way turning off further on, but I don't know it. We'd only get lost."

"You're in charge. Morgan, the Lagonda's still there?"

"Chust behind us it iss, sir."

Alec stuck out his hand and turned. They plunged into a labyrinth of serpentine lanes. For a while Daisy was frightfully afraid she had bitten off more than she could chew, but as crossroads and forks fell behind them, she grew more confident.

"Sharp left at the end of this hamlet," she said as they came to a huddle of cottages, "and then the first right. There used to be a finger-post. . . . Yes, there it is! 'Brock Farm Only.' "

"Well done! I can see why you couldn't have explained the route."

The farmhouse and its outbuildings stood close to the edge of the wood where dwelt the badgers which had given the farm its name. The moment the Austin pulled up next to the barn, Daisy jumped out and ran to the house. Barking dogs announced her before she knocked.

A hefty young man came to the door. Daisy didn't recognize him, but he knew her at once in spite of the years and the shingled hair.

"Why, it's Miss Daisy! Mother, Dad," he called, "it's Miss Daisy."

"Good gracious, you can't be little Charlie?"

He grinned. "That's me, miss, and not so little no more, neither. Step in, do."

"Not just now, if you don't mind. Good-evening, Mrs. Clay, Mr. Clay," Daisy said to the couple who came up behind Charlie. "I've brought my fiancé and some friends to see the old camp. We're running late and it'll be dark soon. May we leave the cars in the yard and cut through your wood?"

"O' course, Miss Daisy," said the farmer's wife. "You just hurry along afore the rain come down again, and stop in for a glass o' cider on the way back, if ye've time enough."

"Spiffing," said Daisy.

With a wave, she dashed off, but not before she heard Mr. Clay observe sagely, "They'm all barmy as new beer, the gentry."

An ominous splatter of rain struck Daisy's face. Shivering, she turned her mind at last to their real errand. If the farmer knew they were out not for a jaunt but to tackle a vicious gang of kidnappers, would he think them less barmy—or more?

20

"All right," said Alec, coming to a halt at the edge of the dank, dark wood, "show us the way through and set us on the right path up the hill, then come back to your friends at the farm."

Brock Wood was very different from Cooper's Wood. The beeches stood tall and straight, well spaced, with little undergrowth. Instead of narrow, twisting paths which came to dead-ends, the difficulty lay in distinguishing a path from the general openness.

Daisy took Alec's hand and they led the troops under the trees. To hide her uncertainty, Daisy enquired meekly, "How are you going to find Phillip?"

"That's what I've been wondering," Tommy said, coming up on Alec's other side. "If he doesn't know we've arrived, we not only lose a man to help carry out your plan, Fletcher, he'll very likely wreck it."

"It's a problem," Alec admitted. "We can't go hunting for him without the risk of alerting the kidnappers."

"He'll be hiding in the hawthorns," said Daisy. "It's the only place he can watch from without being seen. You'll never find him without me."

"You're not coming, Daisy," Alec said firmly and patiently. "With your facility with words, I'm sure you can describe his position well enough for us to follow."

"If you manage to stick to the direct path up the hill. There are countless sheep paths to lead you astray, so that you come out at a different point on the circle. Ah, here we are," she said with relief.

Just ahead their path was crossed by a shallow ditch and low bank, perhaps once part of the fortification on the hill above. They climbed over, turned right, and followed the bank, barely visible in the gloom. Alec and Tommy discussed tactics, with Binkie listening in and the four servants following.

They came to a stile in a post and rail fence. Daisy climbed over. Alec followed, then stopped on the top step.

The fence marked the end of the wood. Beyond it rose the bare hillside, its truncated summit standing out against a darkening sky.

"We can find our way without you, love," said Alec. "Tell me where to find Petrie and you go on back to the farm."

Glancing back, past the pale faces of the men to the murk beneath the trees, Daisy remembered her lonely trek from the witch's cottage to Fairacres. She shivered. "Don't make me go through the woods alone."

"Make you?" The tender laugh in his voice caused a quite different sort of shiver to run down Daisy's spine. "When have I ever succeeded in making you do anything? All right, come with us, but *please,* I beg of you, stay close to me until we storm them, and then stay behind. If you insist on going in with us, you'll get in the way and divert our attention to protecting you."

"I'll keep out of the way," Daisy promised.

"Good girl." Alec turned to face his troops. Raising his voice to be heard above the patter of rain on leaves, the sough of tossing branches, he said, "I take it you all know by now what we're here for. The idea is to rescue Miss Arbuckle while at least one of her captors has gone to fetch the ransom, improving the odds on our side."

"Already in our favour," Tommy put in.

"As far as we know. What we don't know is whether

someone has already left, and whether they have a look-out watching the track on the far side of the hill. I'm hoping to learn that from Mr. Petrie, who's up there somewhere."

"If so be there's a guard to be took out, sir," said Carlin, " 'e'll not find a better man nor I at creeping up on poachers."

"Thank you, Carlin, I'll remember that. I'll give you all further instructions when we see what Mr. Petrie has to say. For now, we follow Miss Dalrymple up the hill. If you must speak, keep your voice down. Let's go."

Outside the shelter of the trees, the blustering wind swooped upon them, flinging random salvoes of rain. Daisy grabbed her hat. As she tugged it down further over her ears, a mighty gust sent her tottering. She clutched Alec's arm.

Hanging on to him, she slogged up the hill at his side. Wetter and wetter, chillier and chillier, she tried to remember why she had insisted on coming.

The path, never more than a stripe of sparser grass across the close-cropped turf, was hard to make out in the dusk. For the most part it led straight up the slope, with here and there a zigzag around a stunted hawthorn. Daisy began to wonder whether her memory of the thorn thicket within the fort was accurate, and whether she was right to assume Phillip would have taken shelter there.

She pictured the interior of the circle as viewed from the gateway, where they had always entered. The hut was somewhat to the right of the centre, she thought, with the hawthorns visible beyond it to its right. According to the lay-out she and Lucy had pieced together, that meant the thicket would be to her right when they reached the track at the top.

"Which way?" said Alec.

"To the right. Oh, you mean now?" Rounding a tree, they had come to a fork. The right-hand branch led away around the hillside, the left-hand upward. "No, left here."

They trudged between two more hawthorns and faced a bare slope to the top. Alec stopped.

"If they're watching in this direction, they can't miss us." He looked back. "Pearson, do you see any alternative approach?"

Tommy came up beside him. Hand sheltering his eyes from the rain, he scanned the surroundings. "No," he said baldly, "but at least it's no Vimy Ridge. I presume they're not waiting with artillery and machine-guns. In any case, I rather doubt they have a sentry out in this foul weather, not being disciplined troops."

"Let's hope not." Alec glanced at his wrist-watch. "We can't wait for it to get any darker. In spite of this gloom, the sun's only just setting and the half-light may linger for another hour. We'll have to risk it."

There was no way to tell whether they were observed as they moved out into the open. For all they knew, a look-out could be rushing to the hut. By the time they reached the top, perhaps the kidnappers would be hustling Gloria down the track on the far side of the hill.

Might they even mistake the amateur rescue-party for police and kill her?

Daisy forced her weary legs to move faster. She strained her ears: surely Phillip would attempt to save Gloria if they tried to move her, and surely he'd shout as he attacked— before they knocked the poor, gallant chump out again.

The only sounds were the wind and the rain, and the distant, sleepy bleating of sheep settling for the night.

At last they reached the level track circling the base of the mound. Daisy walked round to the right. "It must be about here," she said doubtfully. "I can't be quite sure."

She eyed the steep bank without enthusiasm, without the least desire to climb. However, after her insistence on coming, it would be too frightfully shabby to back down now. Moving forward, she reached for a handhold.

Alec instantly pulled her back. *"You're* not going up, Daisy."

Equally instantly, perversely, she was determined to do it. She racked her brains for reasons why she was the best choice.

"The first thing Phillip sees will be a silhouette. If it's a man, he may think it's one of the villains and raise an outcry."

"Someone can wear your hat."

As he spoke, Daisy pulled away from his grasp and started up the bank. After a couple of feet, she promptly slid down again.

"Blast, it's fearfully slippery in the rain. You'll have to give me a boost. And as I'm the lightest, I'm the one to do it."

The others had gathered round by then. "I am not hefty, look you," said Owen. "It's glad I'd be to go, sir."

"Phillip might refuse to budge for Owen," Daisy pointed out, silently berating herself for persisting in the face of any number of excellent excuses. "I can talk him into joining the rest of us."

"Daisy's right," Tommy said reluctantly. "Petrie won't be happy to be asked to abandon his vigil at the crucial moment. He'd quite likely disregard a servant."

Alec conceded. "All right, but Daisy, if you get up there and see anyone but Petrie, you slide straight back down. Or if you don't see him right away. Don't hunt around for him. Promise?"

"Promise."

"Bincombe, you're tallest and strongest. See if you can get her to the top."

It was a fearfully undignified scramble, in the course of which Daisy managed to kick the uncomplaining Binkie in the face. At the last, one of her feet in each of his hands, he gave her a great heave. She shot upwards and only just stopped herself slithering head-first down the reverse slope.

The electric torch in her mac pocket thumped her hip painfully.

Gasping for breath, she lay on the ridge, peering down into the bowl. Not a soul in sight, though soft lamplight glowed between the chinks in the stone walls of the shepherd's hut. The wind seemed to have died, and she heard a murmur of voices but failed to make out any words.

The hawthorn-patch was still a bit further to her right. Alec could not have meant she was not to look for Phillip in the thicket just because she had miscalculated its position. She wriggled along the top of the bank, silently cursing the torch, till she was able to peer down among the tangled, spiky branches.

She couldn't see Phillip, but there was only one hole in the thick growth large enough for the passage of a large body, a few feet ahead of her.

Daisy squirmed forward, cupped her hands around her mouth, and hissed, *"Philip!"*

A rustle and a squeak might have been a frightened rabbit. Daisy hoped it was Phillip—being stabbed by a thorn? A moment later, the soles of a pair of boots came into view. They vanished; there was more rustling; and Phillip's fair head appeared.

"Daisy!" He mouthed the word, or spoke in a whisper too low to be heard over rain pelting on leaves. Her name was followed by what looked like, "Confound it, what the deuce are you doing here?"

She beckoned. He cast a glance backward, then crawled up to her.

"What the deuce are you doing here?" he repeated in an audible whisper.

"Never mind that. Come on down and explain what's going on."

Phillip shook his head. "Something might happen while I'm not watching."

"Listen, old dear, you can't do anything to help Gloria

on your own, and Alec can't plan the most effective help with you playing the loose cannon."

"Fletcher's here?"

"Of course. A fat lot of use I'd be to you on my own. Alec, Tommy, Binkie, and four servants—eight men with you. Enough to rescue her. Do come on. Time may be important."

He cast another longing glance in the direction of the hut, then raised himself the last few inches to look down the other side. The others had moved along the track and now stood directly below Daisy and Phillip. Tommy gestured urgently.

"Oh, right-oh," Phillip sighed.

Daisy was already so sodden she simply sat on the grass and whooshed down the bank. Alec broke her fall, catching her hands and pulling her to him.

"He argued," she said, breathless but smug, as Phillip landed beside her. "He wouldn't have come for Owen."

Alec's smile was maddeningly sceptical. He let her go and said, "Petrie, have any of the men left yet to pick up the ransom?"

"No. They're all in the hut with Gloria, all four of them. The fellow on watch over the track refused to stick it out in the rain. We can easily bag the lot. Let's go!" He took a step forward.

"Hold on," said Alec, not budging.

"Steady, old chap." Tommy put out a restraining hand. "We need to know a bit more about what we're getting into."

"Carlin," Alec addressed the gamekeeper, "can you sneak around and keep an eye on the gateway without being seen?"

"Aye, sir."

"Off you go, then." He eyed the wiry gardener. "Morgan, you look pretty nippy on your feet. Go with Carlin but keep back, well out of sight. If he sees anyone, you run back to tell us."

The two went off. Alec turned back to Phillip. "The hut has only one door, I take it?"

"Yes, doesn't it, Daisy? A narrow opening, round the other side. I couldn't see it from here."

"So you don't know whether there is an actual door or only a doorway?"

"There never used to be a door, just old, rusty iron hinges sticking out of the wall."

"They haven't had much time to rig one up," Daisy said. "It seems like forever but it was only last night they left the witch's cottage."

"Could have brought one with them," Binkie put in. "Knew they might have to come here, what? Had a tent."

"True. Damn—sorry, Daisy!—I wish I knew. What about windows?"

"Not even window-holes," Phillip said promptly, and Daisy nodded agreement. "No holes in the walls. Actually, though one thinks of it as dilapidated, it's pretty solid except for the chimney. The bit sticking up fell into the inside bit and blocked it up an age ago."

"No big holes in the walls," Daisy corrected him, "but whatever was used to stuff up the gaps between the stones is gone. I saw their light through dozens of little holes."

"By Jove, you're right! We can peep through and see what they're up to before we burst in. Let's go, Fletcher. We outnumber them two to one."

"Good odds," Alec acknowledged, "but they have Miss Arbuckle. With three, say, to fight us off in a narrow doorway, leaving one to threaten her—no, I don't like it. Pearson?"

"I have to agree. What's more, if we go in through the gateway to spy on them through the chinks in the walls, we risk being seen by whoever comes out to go for the money. All he has to do is run back to warn them and they become virtually impregnable."

Phillip groaned. "What do we do then?"

"Wait," said Alec. "With one or more gone, we can surround the place unseen and have a much better chance of dealing with the rest. I'd hoped to station men all around on top of the bank, but it looks as if that's out."

"Impossible," Daisy confirmed. "The grass is too short for handholds and much too slippery for footholds. Even Binkie couldn't shove all of you up there."

"So I'll leave Carlin watching the gateway. Let's see, who's the best runner besides Morgan?"

"Me, sir," said Ernest eagerly. "I always win the egg-and-spoon race at the church fête."

"I'm not so bad myself," Phillip protested.

"Then both of you go round the other way and keep an eye on the track down to the lane. In case Carlin misses something, see which of you can get back here fastest if anyone goes down."

Phillip and the footman hurried off around the bend. "All right," said Alec, "with Petrie safe out of the way—Bincombe, do you think you can put Pearson on top of the mound?"

Binkie surveyed Tommy's middling-tall but stocky form. "Give it a try," he grunted.

Even with Truscott helping on one side and Alec on the other, Tommy proved too great a weight for Binkie to boost to the crest. After three attempts, Alec turned with a rueful face to Daisy.

"Aren't you glad I came?" she said tartly.

"I could fetch Owen back. He can't weigh much more than you."

"That would waste time. I'm ready. I just wish I'd thought to bring some chocolate."

Truscott delved into his pocket. "Here, Miss Daisy. Never go anywhere without it."

"Angel!"

This time, tired by his efforts to hoist Tommy, Binkie gave her just enough impetus to reach the top safely. She lay there, nibbling chocolate, her gaze fixed on the hut. Nothing moved.

The murmur of voices came from both the hut and the track below, where Tommy and Alec were no doubt discussing a plan of attack. Every now and then, Alec called up softly, and Daisy responded with a wave to show she was still alert.

She was too damp and chilly to feel the least drowsiness, despite insufficient sleep last night. Though she would have liked to sit up and huddle with her arms around her knees, that would make her stand out silhouetted against the skyline. Still, the temptation grew as the risk waned with the daylight.

It was growing dark. Nothing moved.

And then came the growl of a motor engine and a light in the sky, headlamp beams glinting off a thousand raindrops. Footsteps pounded along the track as Phillip and Ernest arrived from one direction, Owen Morgan from the other.

Daisy strained her ears to hear their excited but hushed voices. Not that she couldn't guess what was going on: Crawford had arrived.

A flicker of light crossed the gateway and the engine's rumble was suddenly louder before it cut off. At the same moment Daisy noticed the appearance of a glimmer of light reflected from the rain falling directly beyond the hut. Twisting, she leaned as far down the slope as she could without losing her balance.

"Alec! They have a door!"

"Thanks, love. You have your torch?"

"Yes."

"Flash once if Crawford goes to the hut, twice if he's carrying a bag, three times if anyone comes out and goes to the car. Got it?"

"Got it."

She hauled herself back up, just in time to see a torch-beam start to bob along from the gateway towards the hut. While trying to keep an eye on it, she extricated her own torch from her pocket, reached down the bank, and flashed the button on once.

As Crawford came a little closer, the back-scatter of light from his torch revealed a bulging attaché-case in his other hand. Daisy flashed twice.

"Right, miss." Ernest's low voice, then his footsteps, running.

Daisy glanced down. The rotters had gone and left her!

She looked back at the hut. Crawford's figure stood out momentarily against the dancing raindrops, then vanished. The light from the doorway vanished too, as the makeshift door thudded shut.

The voices within were louder now, but still unintelligible. The only light was the flecks glowing through the chinks between the stones in the wall, a galaxy of irregular stars come to rest on earth.

A shadow eclipsed a patch of stars, a man-shaped shadow. As it moved on, another took its place and then a third.

They were surrounding the hut. Daisy could not decide whether she was sorry or very, very glad she had promised to keep well out of the way. It was agony not to be able to tell what was going on.

For what seemed an age nothing appeared to happen. Then everything happened at once.

Light flooded from the opening door. A man yelled. Alec cried out, "Police! Come out one by one with your hands raised." Someone shouted. Gloria squealed.

A few moments of ominous quiet were followed by an urgent voice. Then came a gunshot, and a scream of pain.

Alec? Her heart choking her, Daisy slid down the bank and ran towards the hut.

Alec was pleased with the silently efficient way his men flitted across the grass and took up their posts surrounding the shepherd's hut. The light spilling from the nooks and crannies was just enough for him to make them out.

He had stationed Morgan and Ernest on either side—both were slightly built and too young to have seen combat—and Carlin, strong but slowed by age, at the rear. Their responsibility was to yell for help in the unlikely event of the kidnappers battering their way out through the walls, or to lend their aid if called.

That left the odds even. Surprise was essential.

Petrie, Bincombe, Pearson, and the hefty chauffeur, Truscott, lurked in a semi-circle between the hut and the gateway, beyond the reach of the light when the door opened, by Alec's reckoning. Their eyes were accustomed to the dark. Those emerging from the hut would be framed against the doorway and virtually blinded for a few moments when they moved away from it.

His ear to one of the crevices in the front wall, Alec listened to the hasty counting of rustling banknotes. Turning his head to peep through the hole, he saw the back of a frayed and grimy coat collar, the nape of a still grimier neck, and a chequered cloth cap.

He didn't dare move to another cranny in hopes of a better view for fear of making a noise. In any case, listening

was more likely to tell him what was going on, he thought,
and once more he pressed his ear to the cold stone.

"You guys satisfied I haven't pulled anything on you,
huh?" The American drawl dripped sarcasm.

"Looks orright, mate."

"Then give me my passport and get out of here!" Crawford snarled.

"Aincha gonna give us a lift down to the van?"

"In a two-seater? Come off it! 'Sides, I plan to spend a
while alone with Miss Gloria Arbuckle." His tone was now
smoothly complacent.

Miss Arbuckle's frightened squeak must have drowned
out Petrie's gasp of outrage, quickly silenced by Pearson's
hand across his mouth.

A different Cockney voice said irresolutely, "You swore
you wasn't going to do nuffing to 'er."

"Just a little chat, to give her a message for her poppa.
Scram, fellas, and don't worry your little heads about us.
It's been swell working with you." The sarcasm was back.

Not for a second did Alec believe the American's dis-
claimer. As he listened, he wondered briefly whether to let
the London roughs pass unmolested, at the risk of losing
them, for the sake of concentrating his forces on Crawford.
Petrie said he had disabled their van, so it was no great
risk.

It was, however, too late to change the plan of campaign.
Even as he reached that decision, the door opened and a
large man stepped out, turning up his coat collar against
the rain.

"Gorblimey, it ain't fit for a dog out 'ere! Can't see a
bloody fing."

"Use yer bloody torch, cock."

Fumbling in his pocket, the first man walked into the
darkness and Bincombe's fist. All Alec heard was a soft
thunk.

The second man, torch already in hand, moved towards a similar destiny as the third crossed the threshold.

Alec couldn't tell what went wrong. A muffled squawk alerted the third man. With an inarticulate yell he jumped back through the narrow doorway.

Springing forward, Alec cried, "Police! Come out one by one with your hands raised."

The door started to close. Alec thrust his torch into the gap. As he leaned his weight against the splintery wood, someone shouted.

The girl screamed.

Petrie and Bincombe arrived neck and neck. Brushing Petrie aside, Bincombe charged the door, an irresistible force Alec only just managed to dodge. He burst into the hut, Alec and Petrie on his heels.

Two scruffy villains faced them, hands reaching for the roof. Behind them, visible between them, a well-dressed, pudgy man with oiled-back hair had his arm around Miss Arbuckle. His other hand held a pistol to her bedraggled blond head.

"Get out or I'll kill her," he said, quietly vicious. "Now!"

"Oy!" One of the Cockneys swung round. "You said she wouldn't come to no 'arm!"

The American was staring at Petrie. "You!" he exclaimed with loathing, and turned on his henchmen. "You said you'd disposed of him!"

"We got rid of 'im, but like we told you, we don't 'old wiv murder. Let the girl go." The man took a step forward. "We're done for anyways."

"You dumb yahoos, if we're done for it's your fault!"

"Come on, mate, let 'er go. Least we done nuffing to dangle for."

Crawford shot him.

His shriek cut through the reverberation of the shot as he fell. Miss Arbuckle wrenched herself away from Crawford, who cringed back, his gun dangling, looking sick.

"Oh God," he babbled, "I didn't know it would be. . . . I've never seen. . . ." He turned away and vomited in a corner as Petrie caught the girl in his arms.

An amateur crook, Alec thought in disgust. Often more dangerous than the pros, because they didn't know what they were doing. He left Crawford and the uninjured Cockney to the others and dropped to his knees beside the wounded man.

Blood welled from his shoulder. His face was deadly pale. " 'Ave I 'ad it, guv?" he asked faintly. "Din't know 'e 'ad a shooter, honest."

"I believe you. Don't try to talk now." Alec pressed his handkerchief to the wound. It soaked through alarmingly fast.

He needed help. He looked round to see what the others were doing, just as Daisy burst into the hut.

"Alec . . . Oh, thank God it wasn't you!" She glanced down at the victim and gulped. "Wait just half a mo and I'll take off my petticoat. Luckily it's a waist one."

She dashed out again, to return with a wad of white cloth. A glimpse of lace edging brought a twinge of untimely desire as Alec took it and exchanged it for his blood-soaked handkerchief.

"Can you hold it while I take off my shirt to tie it in place? Press hard."

Pale but game, she took his place. "Who shot him? Crawford?"

"Yes." He took off his raincoat and jacket and unbuttoned his shirt, glad he had put on a clean vest this morning. "You feel all right?"

"I can manage. It's not like in Occleswich, when I'd hit that dreadful man and you were hurt."

Alec smiled at her. "I seem to remember you coped very competently then, however frightful you felt. Here, let's tie it round as tight as we can. There's not much else we can do, I'm afraid."

"He'll be in shock. We must try to keep him warm."

As he helped Daisy bind the man's shoulder and wrap him in both their coats, Alec spared a fragment of his attention for the goings-on around them. Pearson was competently directing the rounding-up of the prisoners. Petrie still had his arms around Gloria Arbuckle and appeared to be whispering sweet nothings in her ear.

"Petrie!" Alec grinned as the young man started and blushed.

"Oh, er, by Jove, let me introduce . . ."

"Later. I'd like you to take Crawford's motor and send us a doctor. Then notify the police, and Mr. Arbuckle. You'd better take Miss Arbuckle with you."

"Gosh, thanks. I mean, yes, of course, old man. Police? Local or the Yard?"

"Scylla or Charybdis. It hardly matters," Alec clarified as Petrie looked blank. "I'm in hot water either way."

"The Chief Constable," said Daisy. "Sir Nigel—at least, let's assume we're still in Worcestershire, though it could be Gloucestershire. We must be right on the border. A Dalrymple and a Petrie, and throw in *Lord* Gerald Bincombe for good measure, and between us we should be able to talk Sir Nigel Wookleigh round."

"Right-oh," said Petrie. Tenderly supporting Miss Arbuckle, he moved towards the door.

Pearson stopped him. "Just a minute, old fellow. There's no need to tell Wookleigh that Fletcher was in charge of the operation. Say he's here, by all means. That will make the man sit up and take notice. But try to contrive to give the impression that he arrived at the last minute and was dragged along willy-nilly."

"Right-oh."

"Hurry, Phillip," Daisy urged. "This chap needs proper medical attention. Toodle-oo, Gloria. See you later."

* * *

Not for a fortnight did the entire cast of characters—minus the villains—meet again. The occasion was a double engagement party thrown by Mr. Arbuckle at Claridge's Hotel.

The millionaire had not only asked Daisy, Alec, and Phillip for guest lists, he invited everyone who had anything to do with rescuing his daughter. Thus, in the true democratic tradition, the Dowager Lady Dalrymple rubbed shoulders with her gardener, Owen Morgan; Colonel Sir Nigel Wookleigh, Chief Constable of Worcestershire, with Detective Sergeant Tring of Scotland Yard; Lord and Lady Petrie with their neighbours' gamekeeper, Carlin.

Nonetheless, Daisy was not a little startled when her cousin Edgar came up to her and announced, "I've seen a chimney sweeper, black as the ace of spades."

"A chimney sweeper?" she enquired cautiously, trying to resist craning her neck and peering around.

"Not uncommon, but they turn brown a day or two after emerging so one rarely sees one sooty black."

"Butterfly or moth?" said Alec.

"Moth, my dear fellow. *Odezia atrata*. Next time you come down to Fairacres, you must stay longer and see whatever specimens I have on hand at the time."

Daisy's family had accepted Alec as a future member—her mother and Geraldine with reluctance, Edgar and her sister Violet with equanimity, Vi's eldest boy with sheer joy. His chums at prep school, the nine-year-old confided to his aunt, were bitterly envious of a prospective uncle who was a Scotland Yard detective.

He and Alec's daughter Belinda, the same age and allowed to attend the first hour of the party, were soon thick as thieves. The Dowager Lady Dalrymple and Mrs. Fletcher, though loath to abandon suspicion of each other, at least found common ground in mutual censure of marriage between the classes.

As for the Petries, they were so relieved that Phillip was

to be an engineering adviser, not a motor-mechanic, that they welcomed Gloria and endured Arbuckle with gratitude.

Gloria, Daisy decided upon better acquaintance, had not much more sense than Phillip. However, once recovered from her ordeal, she proved a cheerful, good-natured girl, and her father's money would shield them from the world.

Half-way through the evening, Daisy and Alec, Lucy and Binkie, and the Pearsons came together by chance.

"Darling," Lucy drawled to Alec, "I've been wondering what's become of the villain Crawford shot."

"He survived," Alec assured her, "thanks to Daisy's first aid. That's all I know."

"He's recovering," said Tommy.

"Mr. Arbuckle has retained Tommy to represent him," Madge explained.

"He'll get off lightly then," Alec said with a grin. "Pearson's eloquence is wasted in a solicitor's office. He belongs at the Bar."

"Tommy persuaded the Assistant Commissioner to forgive Alec," said Daisy. "Without ever telling an outright lie, he gave the impression that Alec didn't even know a crime had been committed until he reached Brockberrow Hill. I shall never again believe anything a lawyer says."

"He did an excellent job of putting the A.C. in the right frame of mind," Alec confirmed, "though if anyone can see through legal verbiage, the Assistant Commissioner for Crime is the man. What really saved my bacon, however, and led to complete forgiveness, was his discovery that Daisy was involved. Living in terror of her unorthodox methods of 'helping' the police, he relies on me to restrain her."

"Beast," said Daisy, but she didn't really mind. Tonight she felt as light as the bubbles in her champagne glass, with only her hand tucked under Alec's arm to anchor her to the earth.

Please turn the page for an exciting sneak peek of
Carola Dunn's next Daisy Dalrymple mystery

DEAD IN THE WATER

coming in July 2002
from Kensington Publishing Corporation

Daisy paused at the top of the brick steps leading down from the terrace. The negro butler had said Lady Cheringham was to be found in the back garden, but there was no sign of Daisy's aunt.

On either side of the steps, roses flourished, perfuming the still air. From the bottom step, a gravel path cut across the lawn, which, shaded in part by a huge chestnut, sloped smooth as a bowling green to the river. The grey-green Thames slid past around the bend, unhurried yet relentless on its way to London and the sea.

Upstream, Daisy saw the trees on Temple Island, hiding the little town of Henley-on-Thames. Downstream, the white buildings of Hambleden Mill and the pilings dividing the boat channel from the mill-race marked the position of the lock and weir. Beyond the towpath on the far bank of the river, the Berkshire side, Remenham Hill rose to a wooded crown. On the near side, at the foot of the lawn, was a long, low boathouse half-hidden by shrubs and a rampant lilac-flowered clematis. From it, a plank landing-stage ran along the bank, with two bright-cushioned skiffs moored there side by side. On the landing-stage stood two hatless girls in summer frocks, one yellow, one blue.

Daisy took off her hat with a sigh of relief. The water-cooled breeze riffled through the honey-brown curls of her shingled hair.

The two girls were gazing upstream, hands shading their eyes against the westering sun, still high in a cloudless sky. From her vantage point, Daisy followed their gaze and spotted a racing eight emerging from the narrows to the north of the island. Foreshortened by distance, the slender boat crawled towards them like an odd sort of insect, oars rising and dipping in unison on either side. The cox's voice floated across the water.

"Got you!" The triumphant exclamation came from nearby, in a female voice.

Looking down, Daisy saw a spotted brown-linen rear end backing cautiously out of the rosebed, followed by a broad-brimmed straw hat.

"Hullo, Aunt Cynthia."

"I keep telling him chopping off their heads won't kill them." Lady Cheringham, straightening, brandished a muddy-gloved hand clutching a dandelion with a twelve-inch root. Her lean face, weathered by decades of tropic climes, broke into a smile. "Hullo, Daisy. Oh dear, is it past four already?"

Daisy started down. "Only quarter past. The train was dead on time and your man was waiting at the station." On the bottom step, she nearly fell over a garden syringe.

"Careful, dear! I was spraying the roses, dealing death to those dratted greenfly, when I noticed the dandelion."

"Not deadly poison, I hope? It seems to have dripped on your blouse."

"Only tobacco-water, but perhaps I'd better go and wash it off. It does stain horribly." Lady Cheringham dropped the dandelion's corpse by the sprayer. "Bister sumply won't admit that hoes are useless against these brutes, but that's what comes of having a chauffeur-cum-gardener-cum-handyman."

"I rather like dandelions," Daisy confessed.

"Never fear, however many we gardeners slaughter, there will always be more." She stooped to pick up a trug, loaded with pink and yellow cut roses, which lay on the grass at her feet. "As a matter of fact, I really just came out to deadhead and cut some roses for your room—you're sure you don't mind sharing with your cousin? The house is packed to the rafters."

"Not at all. In fact it's spiffing. It will give me a chance to get to know her better. Now that Patsy's grown-up, that five-year gulf between us won't seem so vast."

"Tish, dear. Patricia insists on being called Tish these days, Heaven knows why. I dare say I should be thankful they don't address each other by their surnames, she and her friend Dottie." Lady Cheringham waved at the two girls by the river. "I gather that is the custom at the ladies' colleges, apeing the men. So unsuitable. I can't help wondering if it was quite wise to entrust Patricia's upbringing to Rupert's brother while we were abroad." She sighed.

"I suppose being brought up in the household of two Oxford dons must have inclined Pat . . . Tish to academic life."

Daisy hoped she didn't sound envious. Neither family nor school had prepared her for university studies. In fact, the idea had never dawned on her until the newspapers reported Oxford University's admission of women to degrees, just three years ago, in 1920. Already twenty-two and struggling to earn a living, she had recognised that her chance was past.

Her aunt said cheerfully, "Oh, Patricia has to swot like mad. She isn't really any more intellectual than I am. Luckily—since I suspect she has an understanding with Rollo Frieth. A charming young man but not brainy, though he's an undergrad at Ambrose College."

"That's the crew you're putting up for the Regatta, isn't it?"

"Yes, Rupert's nephew rows for Ambrose. Christened Erasmus, poor boy, but everyone calls him Cherry."

"I've met him, I'm sure, more than once but years ago."

"Very likely. He's practically a brother to Patricia. You'll see him at tea, and meet the rest."

"I think I saw them rowing this way."

They both turned and looked at the river. The boat was a couple of hundred yards off, drifting downstream towards them, the rowers in their white shirts and maroon caps resting on their oars. Sounds of altercation reached Daisy's ears, though she could not make out the words.

"I must go and change, and deal with these flowers," Lady Cheringham said hastily. "Do go on down and say hullo to Patricia, since she stayed home especially to welcome you. That's Dottie Carrick with her."

Daisy walked down to the landing-stage. At the sound of her footsteps on the gravel, Patricia—Tish—and her friend looked round.

Tish was a pretty, fair-haired girl, just turned twenty. Slim in pale blue pique, a dark blue sash at the low waist, her figure was admirably suited to the bustless, hipless fashion of the day, Daisy noted enviously.

She didn't know her cousin well. Sir Rupert Cheringham, in the Colonial Service, had left his only child to be brought up by his brother and sister-in-law, both lecturers at Oxford University. Visits between that academic family and Daisy's aristocratic family had been few and fleeting, though Lady Cheringham was Daisy's mother's sister.

To Daisy, Oxford was a railway station, or a place one motored through, between London and her ancestral home in Gloucestershire, now the property of Cousin Edgar. Daisy's brother, Gervaise, might have gone to Oxford had the War not intervened. His death had eliminated that connection. The death of her fiancé had left her uninterested in any men who might otherwise have invited her to May Balls after the War, when demobbed officers flocked to the universities.

Gervaise and Michael were five years gone. The new

man in Daisy's life had taken his degree at the plebeian University of Manchester.

"Hullo, Daisy!" Patricia greeted her. "You haven't brought Mr. Fletcher with you? Alec Fletcher is Daisy's fiancé," she explained to her friend.

"He can't get away till Friday night. He's booked at the White Hart."

"Just as well. Mother would have to stuff him into the attics. Half the men are on camp-beds already, sharing rooms, with the cox in the linen-room because he's the only one short enough! Oh, you don't know Dottie, do you? Dorothy Carrick, a college friend—and she's engaged to Cherry. Dottie, my cousin, Daisy Dalrymple."

Miss Carrick, round-faced, bespectacled, rather sallow, her painfully straight, mousy hair cut in an uncompromising short bob, looked every inch the female undergrad. A frock printed with large, yellow cabbage roses did nothing for her stocky form. Daisy, always at odds with her own unfashionable curves, felt for her.

"How do you do, Miss Carrick," she said. "Mr. Cheringham's rowing, isn't he?"

Dottie smiled, a boyish grin revealing even, very white teeth. "That's right. In both the Thames Cup and the Visitors'—the eight and the coxless four, that is." Her voice was a beautiful, mellifluous contralto. "The four won their heat this morning, and we're waiting to hear about the eight. You're here to write about the Regatta, Tish said?"

"Yes, for an American magazine. Harvard and some others often send crews over so the races get reported, especially when an American boat wins, but my editor wants an article on the social side of things."

"Champagne and strawberries in the Stewards' Enclosure?" said Tish.

"Yes, that sort of stuff. Ascot hats, and watching the fireworks from Phyllis Court. A friend of my father's is a member, and the husband of a friend of mine is a member of the Stewards' Enclosure, and they've both kindly invited me. I'm going to throw in a bit about the fun-fair, too."

"*Hoi polloi's* share of the social side," Dottie observed. "Jolly good. I'll help you do the research. I've been dying to go on the Ferris wheel."

Tish shuddered. "Rather you than me! But I'm a dab hand at a coconut shy. Let's talk Cherry and Rollo into going with us after tea."

"Rollo?" said Daisy disingenuously.

"Roland Frieth." Tish's fair skin flushed with delicate colour, as good as confirming her mother's report to Daisy. "He's Cherry's chum."

"And the Ambrose captain," Dottie put in. "Here they are now."

"Keep out of their way while they get the boat out," Tish advised. "It's serious business."

Head bobbing, a solitary moorhen scurried for the safety of the middle of the river as the boat nosed gently in alongside the landing-stage, behind the two skiffs tied up there. The cox, short and wiry, with bare, sun-tanned knees knobbly beneath his maroon rowing shorts, jumped out. He held the stern steady while his crew counted off.

"Bow." Daisy recognised Tish's cousin, Erasmus "Cherry" Cheringham, a fair, serious-looking young man much larger and more muscular than she remembered him.

"Two." Another large, muscular young man, dark-haired. He gave a quick, cheerful wave. Daisy assumed they had won the heat.

"Three."

"Four."

"Five."

"Six."

"Seven."

"Stroke." In contrast to the rest, the stroke looked sulky. Otherwise, apart from varying hair colour, they could have been septuplets for all the difference Daisy could see.

On the cox's command, eight large, muscular, perspiring young men stepped out onto the planks, making them bounce beneath Daisy's feet. She hastily moved backwards onto solid ground.

Bow and stroke held the boat while the other six laid the oars out on the grass. Then all eight oarsmen bent to the boat.

"Hands on," ordered the cox. "Ready. Up!"

With one smooth motion, the boat rose from the water and swung upside-down over their heads.

"Ready. Split!"

The elongated, many-legged tortoise tramped towards the boat-house. "We took the trick," it called gaily as it departed. "Be with you in a minute, ladies."

Tish and Dottie each picked up one of the maroon, green, and white banded oars and followed. Eyeing the twelve-foot length and dripping blades of the remaining sweeps, Daisy decided against lending her aid.

The cox also stayed behind, staring after the rowers with a scowl on his face.

"I thought you won?" Daisy said with puzzled sympathy.

"What? Oh, yes, we won all right." Orotund Oxfordian contended uneasily with a flat, nasal whine straight from the Midlands. "We may be a small college and we wouldn't stand a chance in the Grand, but we've a good shot at the Thames Cup."

"You don't look very happy about it. Oh, I'm Daisy Dalrymple, by the way, Patricia's cousin."

"Horace Bott. How do you do, Miss Dalrymple? Of course I'm glad we took the heat," he went on gloomily, "but even if we win the final, I'll still be an outsider."

"Because you don't row?"

"Because I haven't got the right family, or accent, or clothes, or instincts. When I won the scholarship to Ambrose, I thought all I had to do was prove I'd earned it, but

I could take a hundred First with Honours and my father would still be a small shopkeeper."

"There's nothing wrong with being a shopkeeper," Daisy encouraged him. "Napoleon said the English were a nation of shopkeepers, but we beat him all the same."

"Nothing wrong as long as we know our place." Bott groused, "which isn't at Oxford competing with our betters. 'Betters,' my foot! Half the stuck-up snobs who treat me like dirt only got into Ambrose through their family connections, and with all the private tutoring in the world they'll be lucky to scrape by the Pass Thirds."

Daisy didn't care for his peevish tone, but she suspected he had reason for his disgruntlement. If Gervaise had gone up to Oxford, it certainly would not have been on the basis of academic brilliance, nor with the intention of excelling academically. She rather thought he would have scorned those who did, and he had certainly not shared her willingness to hobnob with the lower classes.

"Do you join in the other stuff?" she asked, adding vaguely, "Acting, and debating, and rags, and sports, and so on . . . Oh, sports, of course."

"I thought sports'd do it, coxing, and I play racquets— got my Blue in that last year, actually."

"You play racquets for the university, not just the college? Congratulations."

"All very well, but the toffs still don't choose to hoist a pint with me after a match," Bott said resentfully.

His lack of popularity might have less to do with his birth than with the way he wallowed in his grievances, Daisy guessed. She nearly said so, then thought better of it. He would be sure to take advice amiss, however well-meant, and though she felt sorry for him, she did not like him.

He took a packet of Woodbines from his shirt pocket. "Smoke?" he offered.

"No, thanks."

He lit up the cheap cigarette, flicking the match into the river. "I suppose you never touch anything but Turkish."

"As a matter of fact, I don't smoke at all. I don't care for the smell of cigarettes." Pipe smoke was another matter, especially Alec's pipe.

Bott moved a step away, wafting the smoke from her with his hand. "Sorry. My girl doesn't like it, either. She's coming down this evening—booked a room in the town—so once I've finished this packet, I won't buy another for a few days." His momentary cheerfulness at the prospect of his girl's arrival faded and gloom returned. "Can't really afford them, anyway."

Tempted to start listing the things she couldn't afford, Daisy was saved by the return of the others from the direction of the boat-house. Beside it, the racing shell, too long to fit inside, now rested upside-down on supports.

Three of the men started up the lawn towards the house, a Georgian manor built of age-mellowed red brick with white sash windows. A shout followed them: "Don't hog all the hot water!"

Tish, Dottie, Cherry, and four others came towards Daisy and Bott.

"Daisy, you remember Cherry?" said Tish.

"Yes, of course."

"How do you do, Miss Dalrymple?" the fair-haired bow-oarsman greeted her.

"Daisy, please. We're practically cousins, after all."

A grin lit his face. "Daisy it shall be, if you promise never to call me Erasmus."

"I promise!"

During this exchange of social amenities, two of the men picked up a pair of oars each and returned towards the boat-house, while Daisy heard the dark number two rower say to the cox, "Jolly good show, Bott."

"Thanks to St. Theresa's hitting the booms," the fifth oarsman said sarcastically. He was dark-haired, like Number

Two, but his hair was sleeked back with pomade. Daisy thought he was the sulky stroke.

"Lots of boats are hitting, with this experimental course being so deucedly narrow. Bott's steered us dead straight. We'll beat the tar out of Richmond tomorrow."

"Not if we're all poisoned by those filthy things he smokes."

Bott gave the stroke a malevolent look, then turned and headed for the house.

"Oh, come on, DeLancey, pack it in," said Number Two. "Not everyone's so frightfully keen on those foul cigars of yours."

"It sticks in my gullet taking orders from that beastly little pipsqueak twerp." DeLancey fumed.

"All coxes are small . . ."

"Bott's no twerp!" Dottie interrupted, flaring up. "He's brainier than the rest of you put together."

"Oh, I say," Cherry protested.

"Well, nearly," his fiancée affirmed, unrepentant. "You've got a good mind, my dear old soul, but his is tip-top."

Cherry looked chagrined.

"Better watch it, Miss Carrick," DeLancey said nastily, "or you'll be an old maid after all."

"Here, I say!" Cherry stepped forward. "You mind your tongue, DeLancey!"

Tish put a hand on his arm. "Don't come unbuttoned, old thing. The best way to make him eat his words is to stay engaged to Dottie."

"I shall!" her cousin snapped, "but I'd like to stuff his rotten words down *his* gullet, all the same."

"This isn't the time for a dust-up. You've got a race to row tomorrow," Tish reminded him.

"Common sense and pretty, too," DeLancey applauded mockingly. "A girl with your looks is wasted on books and lectures. I'd be glad to show you how to have a good time."

Tish turned her back on him.

Number Two, his face red with suppressed fury, said through his teeth, "Didn't I tell you it's your turn to help with the oars, DeLancey?"

"So you did, Captain, so you did." With insolent slowness, DeLancey strolled towards the remaining two oars.

Captain—so Number Two was Tish's Rollo, as Daisy had already surmised. Fists clenched, he stared after DeLancey, then shrugged and turned back to the others.

"I'm so sorry, Daisy," Tish apologised unhappily. "What a welcome!"

Daisy murmured something soothing.

"Oh, didn't introduce Rollo, did I?" The ready blood tinted her cheeks. "Roland Frieth, the crew captain."

"And a pretty sorry specimen of a captain you must think me, Miss Dalrymple," Rollo said ruefully. "Unable to squash dissension in the ranks."

"I thought you squashed it very neatly," Daisy said with a smile."The oars are on their way to the boat-house, aren't they?"

They all glanced at DeLancey's retreating back.

"I ought to have introduced him, too," Tish worried.

Dottie snorted. "He hardly gave you much opportunity."

"One of these days," said Cherry darkly, "he'll go too far and get his teeth shoved down his precious gullet."

Rollo shook his head. "I doubt it. He's a boxing Blue, remember. What I'm afraid of is that one of these days he'll biff Bott."

"Oh, Bott! He can scramble Bott's brains with my goodwill, as long as he waits till after the Regatta."

"But, Cherry, he's twice Bott's size!" Dottie protested.

"I can't see that stopping him," said Rollo. "For all his pater's an earl, the way he goes around insulting ladies proves he's no gentleman, and he's really got his knife into Bott."

"Bott's no gentleman either," Cherry muttered, "even if he is a bloody genius."

"Oh darling!" Standing on tiptoe, Dottie kissed his cheek. "Bott's brains are absolutely the only thing about him I admire. I wouldn't marry him for a million in cash. I mean to say, how could I bear to be called Dottie Bott?"

Laughing, they all moved towards the house.

ABOUT THE AUTHOR

Born and raised in England, Carola Dunn now lives in Eugene, Oregon. Her next Daisy Dalrymple mystery, DEAD IN THE WATER, will be published by Kensington Publishing in July 2002. You can visit her Web site at www.geocities.com/CarolaDunn.

BOOK YOUR PLACE ON OUR WEBSITE AND MAKE THE READING CONNECTION!

We've created a customized website just for our very special readers, where you can get the inside scoop on everything that's going on with Zebra, Pinnacle and Kensington books.

When you come online, you'll have the exciting opportunity to:

- View covers of upcoming books
- Read sample chapters
- Learn about our future publishing schedule (listed by publication month *and author*)
- Find out when your favorite authors will be visiting a city near you
- Search for and order backlist books from our online catalog
- Check out author bios and background information
- Send e-mail to your favorite authors
- Meet the Kensington staff online
- Join us in weekly chats with authors, readers and other guests
- Get writing guidelines
- AND MUCH MORE!

**Visit our website at
http://www.kensingtonbooks.com**

Grab These
Kensington Mysteries

Your Favorite Mystery Authors Are Now Just A Phone Call Away